Deadly Vengeance

by

Joy Brighton

Deadly Vengeance

Cover Art by *Kristian Norris*

The Wild Rose Press, Inc.
PO Box 708
Adams Basin, NY 14410-0708
Visit us at www.thewildrosepress.com

Publishing History
First Crimson Rose Edition, 2017
Print ISBN 978-1-5092-1164-7
Digital ISBN 978-1-5092-1165-4

Published in the United States of America

Liv stretched her neck,
easing the tightly corded muscles, and forced her hands to relax on the steering wheel. Flipping her radio to a classical music station, she drove out of G-Tech's parking lot. Glimmers of a pink and orange sunset hung over the shadowed western hills.

She slowed for a stop sign in the deserted industrial park and glanced at the clock on the dashboard. Damn. She'd be late for dinner if she didn't hurry. She pressed her temples to ease the distant pounding in her skull. The spicy fajita salad she'd eaten for lunch sat in her stomach like an undigested clump of nuclear waste.

But even more painful was the jealousy that ripped at her heart. She missed Mike, but how could she ever trust him again?

This morning, he'd called her, insisting he was ready to consider counseling. She twisted her lips into a wry smile. With Cara at a birthday party tonight, they had the evening to talk. She'd agreed to meet him, although she had zero reason to believe it'd do any good.

She punched the pedal, and the sports car surged toward the freeway entrance. A black monster pickup squeezed into her lane, tailgating her. Five gigantic spotlights on the truck's grill glared into her rearview mirror. Insistent music throbbed through her car. The punishing bass ramped up her pulse rate. Chills stung the back of her neck and crawled down her spine.

A low rider peeled away from the curb, cut in front of her, and hit his brakes. She reacted quickly, but the jacked-up rig behind her slammed into her car. Metal screeched as it rode up her trunk and launched her forward.

Kudos for Joy Brighton

Joy Brighton has won several first-place awards for her series of romantic suspense novels, including the Linda Howard and the Silicon Valley RWA Gotcha!

Dedication

To the Armadillos

Acknowledgments

Countless people have contributed to this book. I'd like to mention a few, without whose help *Deadly Vengeance* would not have been possible.

Most importantly, I'd want to thank my family. My wonderful husband, Dave, who supported and encouraged my writing efforts and believed in me and in my writing career when few others did.

A huge thank you to my fantastic critique group, the Armadillos: Teri Bradburn, Linda Hill, Anne Maragoni, and Janet Periat. The book would never have been finished without your help and support. You are all talented and insightful women. And special friends.

I'd also like to thank the Silicon Valley chapter of the Romance Writers of America. I polished my writing craft through seminars, workshops and the graceful and gentle mentoring of fellow SVRWA members. You're an amazing group of writers, and lots of fun.

My special thanks go to the Los Gatos Monte Sereno Police Department and the Santa Clara County Sheriff's Department for ride-alongs, fly-alongs, and answering what must have seemed to be endless questions. Thank you to she-who-must-not-be-fully-named, FBI Special Agent Julia. Any errors in procedure or weaponry are mine.

Thanks to my web designer and web mistress, Rae Monet. Your designs for the website are amazing.

Thanks to other family and friends who read part or all of various versions of this manuscript, including Dan Baxter, Celeste Dyer, Andy Fischer, Deb McKenzie, Susan Miller, and Deb Mumper. If I forgot anyone, it's not because I didn't value your efforts and input. I owe you lunch.

Chapter One

Liv Gordon's heels tapped a staccato beat as she hurried along the hall toward the employee break room. She had her engineering team working crazy hours even for a Silicon Valley start-up, but it looked like G-Tech just might beat the Department of Homeland Security deadline.

She tugged open the door and stopped short, dodging what looked like a large green bug whirring past her ear.

Alyssa Manchester, her chief technical officer, grinned. "Sorry, Boss. Needed some extra practice with the DR2.0 in small space situations before next week's big test. The company is hiring engineers so fast, there are no free spaces anywhere." Tall, lean, and beyond brilliant, Alyssa brushed back a hank of curly hair.

"Tell me about it. I held a quick review meeting yesterday in the men's bathroom."

Using a hand-held joy stick, Alyssa flew the miniature drone around the break room once more, guiding it under chairs and over the lighting fixtures.

"Looks like you're improving. No more smash-ups?" Liv dug the last slice of pizza from the box on the table. She was starving after a morning in the clean room and had a product analysis meeting in ten

1

minutes.

"Better," Alyssa said. Tongue sticking out of the corner of her mouth, she attempted a soft set down on the top of the fridge, but Dragonfly skidded on entry and knocked over a tall smoothie cup left there. "Damn. Still can't stick the landings."

"You'll manage it. Especially if the engineers ever learn to clean up after themselves." With a grimace Liv stretched to reach the cup and grimaced at the milky scum congealed inside.

When she tipped the contents into the sink, something clunked against the stainless steel. A clump of translucent plastic landed in the drain.

Her heart skittered as she lifted the minute electronic circuitry embedded in the gunk. The tiny hairs on her neck stood on end, and her skin prickled.

Alyssa pushed her glasses up. "What's wrong?"

Liv dropped the filthy thing back into the sink and drew a ragged breath. The oily smell of pepperoni turned her stomach, and her knees threatened to buckle.

"Are you okay?"

Shhh! Out! Liv mouthed and backed away from the sink, motioning Alyssa to grab Dragonfly and head toward the hall. She shut the door and sagged against it with her eyes closed. "Some clever idiot planted a miniature camera on top of the refrigerator."

"A security breach?" Alyssa's eyes widened, and her fair skin went chalky. "The nano team met in there this morning."

"What were you working on?"

"The drone's final product review."

"Shit." Liv tasted bitterness on the back of her tongue and swallowed hard.

Alyssa raked a hand through her corkscrew curls. "But who?"

"Any unscrupulous thug who wants our new drone."

"A competitor?"

"Or a foreign government." A surge of visceral terror ramped Liv's pulse even higher. "Terrorists?"

Behind her glasses, Alyssa's blue eyes blinked rapidly. "Bound to be more inside."

Liv straightened her shoulders. "I'll alert Walsh in security. You gather the team quietly for an all-hands meeting. No phones or announcements." She spoke softly but couldn't control the shakiness in her voice. "Coffee shop down the street, twenty minutes."

"Gotcha, Boss." Drone in hand, Alyssa turned and jogged down the windowless hallway.

Heaving a sigh, Liv flashed her magnetic badge and thumb across the security scanner and wove her way through the cubicle maze. Outside her office, she glanced at her shiny, new nameplate—Olivia Gordon, CEO—and her hands curled into fists.

If that damned device delayed development of their sensor drone, G-Tech would never meet the Pentagon's deadline. Stupid camera. Now everything she'd worked for was in jeopardy. She couldn't let that happen.

****

Later, 6:00 p.m.

Through the glass wall, Liv watched the FBI security team swarm over the engineering lab like dark-suited roaches. She paced, shredding a tissue into thin strips. They had her company paralyzed, and she was powerless to stop them.

She wadded the tissue and flung the sweaty,

wrinkled mess into a garbage can. Glaring through the window, she twisted her long hair onto her head and stabbed a pencil through the thick coil. She dug out her uber phone and checked her calendar. Why had she agreed to teach that Friday afternoon business class?

Alyssa shuffled up and collapsed into a chair. "No other cameras, but they found several listening devices inside the secured area. Now they're concentrating on the lab and clean room."

Liv's shoulders sagged as if she'd hefted a forty-pound kid-pack. "I'll postpone today's testing on the sensor. Scheduled weekend work hours for the team."

Sighing, Alyssa pulled off her glasses and polished them on her plaid shirttail. "Agent Bausch just started interviewing the engineers."

"It's going to be a long night. I'd better find a sitter for Cara. I need to keep this investigation moving."

"Yeah. The feds better finish fast."

Liv glanced at her hands. She'd twisted her fingers together until her knuckles were pale and bloodless. "If we don't make the trials, the venture capitalists will pull our funding."

****

Friday, April 1, 1:00 a.m.

Trees swayed in the breeze, moaning a low, melancholy song. Liv stood on the front steps of her home and stared down the driveway, watching the sitter's taillights disappear around a corner into the darkness.

Alyssa's words echoed in her mind. The national security consequences of never bringing their new drone to market made Liv shudder. She banged the security door shut and set the alarm.

Rubbing her hands over the rough gooseflesh on her arms, she walked past the sunken living room. She loved her home's floor to ceiling windows, but tonight she felt alone and vulnerable.

Exposed.

A faint rustle was followed by a soft whimper. "Mommy?" Her daughter's young voice echoed through the house.

Why was Cara still awake? Liv heaved a sigh and rushed down the hall.

Cara sat up in her canopied bed twirling a blonde curl around one finger. Her lower lip stuck out, and her eyebrows scrunched down, crowding her blue eyes. On top of the comforter, Zoë, their calico cat, snuggled against her legs.

Liv hugged her unhappy seven-year-old and rubbed her warm, flannel-covered back. "You have school tomorrow, sweetheart," she said, careful to keep her voice even.

Cara's chin quivered. "I don't ever want that babysitter again, Mommy. Mrs. Rose is mean and grouchy, and she looks like a troll."

The hurt in her daughter's tone pulled at her heart, but she grinned. "Okay. No more trolls." She'd called six babysitters before she'd found someone she trusted to pick up Cara from day care. Top of the list? Hire a new nanny and replace the flake who'd quit without notice on Tuesday.

"Mommy, Daddy called tonight, but I'm tired of the webcam. I want a real hug."

Liv pulled Cara onto her lap. "When I emailed your Daddy about his next weekend with you, he said he'd be back from Virginia on Saturday. But right now, you need to go to sleep." Tucking in the covers, she kissed Cara's forehead.

She swallowed her own frustration. Her life had suddenly surged out of control. To top it off, her lying-cheating-almost-ex-husband had finished his FBI training and was returning to Sereno.

Liv pinched the bridge of her nose. Her life would be so much smoother once they finalized the settlement and ended their doomed-from-day-one mismatch of a marriage. But until then, Mike was just one more complication she couldn't eliminate.

****

10:00 a.m.

A shadow loomed over Liv's keyboard, and she held up one finger. "I'll be right with you, Agent Bausch." She added two more numbers to her spreadsheet, hit save, and turned toward the silent man.

In the next split second, her brain registered that the man standing before her wasn't the rule-book-up-his-ass agent she'd been dealing with. Her gaze skimmed up the long legs covered in gray pinstripe to a power tie, loosened and askew. She clenched her jaw and rose as gracefully as she could. Before her stood the sexy, charismatic jerk she hadn't seen in the flesh for six months, seventeen days, and—she checked her phone—just over twelve hours.

Her palms moistened. Her heart thudded against her ribs. Damn. She drew a deep, shuddering breath and held it, hoping the pressure would slow her rat-a-tat-tat pulse.

She toed back into her emerald green stilettos and shot him a cool, assessing stare. Looked like the next thing on her calendar would be a face-off. She widened her taut lips into a razor-edged grin. "Mike Gordon. Did you finally sign the divorce settlement?"

The tips of his ears flushed wine red, and his jaw tensed, sending the kissable cleft in his chin into deeper relief. He pulled his spine even straighter. His blue eyes, smoky like a mountain lake after a snowstorm, stared down at her for an eon. She squirmed inside.

His lips twisted. "Nope. Not today. We need to talk first. You avoided me every single time I had a weekend with Cara."

The gravel in his voice sent a quick curl of awareness through every fiber of her body. "Fine. You want to talk. That's great, but this isn't the time or place. Why are you really here?"

"Heard about the breach from a buddy." Mike spiked his fingers through his curly blond hair.

"Is nothing secret? The FBI has my company shut down with only a week before the deadline."

"Liv—"

She crossed her arms. "And now my ex-husband shows up to gloat."

His smile vanished, and he took a step closer. "Husband. Don't jump the gun, Livy."

Ugly memories surfaced. Memories of welcoming him home from an undercover assignment. Memories of opening his duffel bag, only to find a purple silk thong and matching thirty-two A secreted in a side pocket. Memories of watching him stomp out the door and disappear.

Liv glanced down at her own hourglass figure and sighed. She'd been a thirty-two A for about fifteen seconds in the sixth grade. "Will your size four tramp…"

Red mottled his neck.

"...materialize in my living room again?" she asked, her voice narrowed to a rapier point.

"Not likely. She's probably working a case somewhere. I don't keep track." His expression softened.

With pity? Angry heat stole across her face. The last thing she wanted was his pity. Thanks to said owner of the purple undies, FBI Agent Samantha Blackthorn, and her visit one dreadful afternoon, Liv knew in great detail exactly how Mike had cheated on her. It had been the last straw. Fighting for control, Liv took a slow, deep breath.

Mike rubbed a hand across the back of his neck. "I know you're pissed at me, Livy. Maybe you even have cause, but today we don't have time to shovel our horse shit."

Damn cowboy. Give her a wheelbarrow full of horse manure, and she'd dump it on his head. "You're right. There are six more days before the military trials and Agent Bausch..." She swallowed a frustrated growl.

"He has a reputation as a decent agent, but can't see beyond the rules and regs with civilians."

"Exactly."

"I'm not on the case officially. Can't be. But I have clearance, so he might listen to me. What do you need to get G-Tech moving?"

He led her to the sofa, and she slumped onto the cushions. "Why should I trust you?"

One eyebrow hiked. He pulled up an armchair and cocked his head. "Humor me."

"How?"

"Pretend we're on the same team again for a couple days." He shrugged and added in the same low-pitched, even tone, "Maybe we'll both get what we need."

Mike? Compromising? She read honesty, not hostility in his voice. She opened her mouth and shut it again, narrowing her eyes. "And what do you get out of this?"

He hooked one ankle over his knee and met her gaze. "This drone is important to national security. Vital, in fact. That do for now?"

Nodding slowly, she exhaled some of her resentment. If he could actually help, she could put up with him. "I want to catch whoever planted those damn transmitters, but there's no way to track the creep."

****

Midnight

Thomas Morrison clenched the receiver in one hand and leafed through the file spread across his walnut desk. A diamond-studded signet glinted from his pinky.

Even with the phone at arm's length, he could hear his contact rant, although he couldn't make out the words. He rolled his eyes and brought the receiver closer. "Chill, Ahmed," he snarled, layering his voice with venom.

"We need complete schematics for the explosive detection drone."

"Yeah, yeah." Morrison snatched his cigar from the crystal ashtray and waved it. The rich, tangy smoke formed S-curves in the air. He leaned forward, stroking the supple red leather of his chair.

"We must have the plans before they begin manufacturing."

"No problem, but the price doubled while you fucked around."

"What?" Ahmed's voice screeched.

Morrison took a long draw on the Havana. "Hey, if you're not interested, I'll find another buyer easy, once the Army tests that prototype."

Ahmed sputtered, but offered to double the payoff amount. "Take it or leave it."

"I'll take it. I scored pictures, engineering diagrams, plus video of the drone. Report that to your prince." Morrison dumped the phone and chuckled. Stupid foreigner didn't know shit about negotiating.

He glanced around his swanky new office, puffing on his cigar. The faint clatter of quarters and swish of the bill sorter in the next room brought a satisfied grin to his face. He was raking in the bucks. Mostly legit too.

Morrison flipped on the recording system, fast-forwarded past the long blank spaces, and listened while he checked through the file. For once, the bitch had worked in her office. He upped the volume. Sounded like her investors were hammering her.

"No, the FBI hasn't traced them. Both bugs were disabled before they transmitted again."

Good thing he had a backup in place, an almost undetectable transmitter spliced into a timer and enclosed in metal. He leaned back with his hands behind his head. They'd never tie the bugs to him. No more than they'd crack his new identity or spot his new face.

"Yeah, thanks," she said in a smart-ass tone and slammed down the phone, cursing.

He waited, sucking on his stogie. For several

minutes nothing came through except keyboard clicks.

"Mike Gordon?" The name caught Morrison's attention, and cold anger stirred in his gut. About time that son of a bitch surfaced.

Morrison rose and moved closer, his fists clenched. Waving the remote to ramp the volume, he listened to the boy-scout-on-a-mission voice of the man who'd cost him so much. It'd taken years to recover from that disaster Gordon caused.

"But there's no way to track the creep. The bugs are standard issue," the bitch's voice griped through the speakers. He crushed his cigar butt in the ashtray.

Gordon chuckled. "Bausch can't divulge the details, but there are ways. Might take time, but count on it. We'll nail 'em."

Blood pounded in Morrison's head. He paused the recording and rubbed his temples. More dark spots erupted, crowding his vision.

He hurled his ashtray against the wall and stomped across the room for a fresh cigar. But he stumbled and wrenched his bad knee. Pain shot through his leg, twisted his gut into fiery knots.

He deserved justice. He'd taken the blame, but nothing had been his fault. That damn cop had fucked him over, but now was the time for revenge. Morrison crossed his arms and let out a short, satisfied bark.

Chapter Two

Santa Cruz Mountains, Sunday, April 4, 5:45 p.m.

Mike's foot twitched like it had a mind of its own. He sat on the porch swing in front of his cabin with one boot propped on his knee. The swing chains creaked with every jerk.

Through the window behind him he saw Cara sprawled in front of the TV, playing a new video game. Her blonde curls fell forward over her cheeks, and she'd caught her tongue between her front teeth.

He closed his eyes and drew in a lungful of the spicy mountain air, scented by damp earth and evergreens. A blue jay's rasping call echoed across the wooded canyon. Gradually, the peace of the redwood forest seeped into him.

He tugged on his ear and frowned. After six months working his ass off at Quantico, it felt good to be home. Finally, he could square things with Liv. A familiar spasm squeezed his heart. They'd always had the hottest marriage on the planet, but it'd never been smooth. His undercover work had been too unpredictable, kept him away from home too much. She always put her job first too.

Yeah, they'd had their share of blow-ups, what she called communication issues. He kicked his boot against the porch rail and smiled. But making up had always been simple. Hit the sheets half a dozen times, and their problems vanished.

After his last undercover assignment, she'd iced over. Wouldn't talk. Didn't yell. Didn't communicate. She called the lawyer before either of them cooled off, and he stomped off to Virginia, giving up his best chance to straighten out this mess. She'd pissed him off, not trusting him, but he should have postponed liaison training and the new job to work it out.

He rose and paced. The redwood planks of the porch creaked under his boots, and guilt sliced through his belly, eating at his insides.

What a horse's ass he'd made of himself over Sam. Even though they'd hooked up a couple times before he met Liv, he'd ignored all the evidence. To him, Samantha Blackthorn had been just another law enforcement buddy until she'd showed up at Quantico one weekend, expecting to get naked.

Mike heard tires squeal around the corner and tear up the gravel road. His pulse started to jack hammer. Liv's fancy electric Tesla. He pulled one hand through his hair and brushed off his jeans, hungry for another glimpse of his wife.

She stepped out of the car, planting her fists on her hips. Her frown hardened like clay in the sun. "Sorry, I'm late. Where's Cara?"

The strain in her voice dragged his attention away from the hint of cleavage her scrunched up blazer revealed. Away from her tiny waist and curvy hips. Away from the long, dark hair he itched to tangle his fingers through. An electric shiver arced up his body, and he tucked his thumbs into his belt loops to keep from reaching for her.

Hell. One look at Liv, and he was half hard. He scrubbed a hand over his mouth. "Cara's happy playing a game. No need to rush off."

"You probably have things to do. I'll go get her." Maneuvering around him, Liv climbed the porch steps.

He looked closer. Her big, sexy, chocolate eyes were bloodshot, and her shoulders drooped. "You look tired. How'd your weekend go?"

She stood silent for a moment. Then she angled her body toward his and searched his face. "I haven't been home since Friday morning. I'm exhausted."

Should he ask? Stress hit the gas pedal, kicking his heart rate into high gear. His gaze flicked to his boots, but he took a chance. "Why don't you and Cara have dinner with me before you head down the hill?"

"Thanks, but no thanks."

"You hate to cook when you're tired." He grinned. "There's a pot of chili on the stove. Beats cold cereal."

Her eyelids fluttered, and she bit her lip. "A hot dinner would be nice." The deep lines framing her mouth eased, and the first hint of a smile brightened her face.

A fantasy flashed through his brain. A fantasy of throwing her over his shoulder and locking the bedroom door and loving her until she was all soft and yielding and satiated. Anticipation dropped his pulse to his groin.

Cupping her chin, he drew his thumb along her jaw. But she frowned and shoved it away, red flags blazing on her cheekbones.

He dropped his hand, his thumb still tingling from the contact. Right. Nice fantasy. "Fill me in. Maybe I can help."

Frustration and something else flickered in her gaze. She tilted her head to the side and heaved a long sigh, pink tongue darting out to soothe the tooth marks on her lower lip. "Actually, I could use your advice. You know Bausch."

He arched an eyebrow and held the door open, waiting for her to continue.

"He has me stymied, spinning my wheels like a caged hamster."

"No progress, even after I spoke to him?"

"Every single thing I do aggravates that tight-ass. Bausch has forced G-Tech to a standstill, and the venture capitalists are having shit fits. Those damn bugs didn't come to life once this weekend, but he refuses to let the engineers work until he tracks their source."

Mike blew out a breath. "Never happen."

"Logic doesn't matter, he won't budge."

He stuffed his hands in his pockets. "Bausch must be out to prove something. I'll come up with a reason to talk to him again tomorrow."

A wisp of a smile lit her eyes, and she rubbed her chin with the top of her hand. "It did help to know Cara was safe and happy this weekend."

"But?" He slid his arm behind her waist.

She didn't snuggle closer, but she didn't tense. She didn't shrug him off, either, just pushed a wayward strand of silky hair behind her ear. "But I'm afraid we won't have Dragonfly ready for the military on Thursday. Those trials are our one shot."

****

9:00 p.m.

Staring at the still pale skin where her wedding ring had been, Liv sat at Mike's breakfast bar. She pulled her keys from her purse and jingled them in her hand. Maybe she couldn't count on Mike in a tight spot, but he'd agreed to bring Cara home with him after school for the next few days until the agency could find another nanny and slog through the background check.

She could get used to this kind of teamwork. With a quick grimace, she shook her head. No. Not again.

She'd given their turbulent marriage her best effort for over seven miserable years. Ethics? Communication styles? Goals? No, the only things they'd ever had in common were Cara, and baseball, and hot monkey sex. No way she'd pitch her tent twice in the same patch of lying-cheating-swampland.

She sensed Mike standing behind her and swiveled on the stool. Tonight he had on snug jeans, worn soft and faded nearly white across his thighs. Across that tantalizing bulge. She yanked her gaze away from his zipper, but his denim shirt did incendiary, almost illegal things to the breadth of his shoulders.

He leaned his lanky frame against the counter. "Cara's settled in bed."

"Thanks for dinner and for helping with Cara." Liv met his smoky blue eyes. A sweet ache kindled low inside, sending a shiver through her. What a pushover. A bowl of homemade chili, a shoulder to lean on, and her brain fogged with lust.

Mike stalked toward her with a wicked gleam in his eyes. "Kiss me before you leave."

For a moment, her breath deserted her. No matter how wrong he'd been, his diabolical bad boy smile undid her in a moment. Always had.

The painful hollow under her heart yawned, and her good sense screamed danger. No doubt that same smile had seduced Special Agent Samantha Blackthorn. Shaking her head, Liv blocked him with her palms thrust flat against his chest.

A predatory grin flashed across his face. "No harm in a friendly kiss."

Still drawn to him like an ant swarmed onto melted chocolate, Liv sighed and pointed to one cheek. "Fine. Just a kiss."

"Yeah." He pulled her to her feet. His fingers threaded through her hair. "Just a kiss." Cupping the sensitive curve of her neck, he searched her eyes for an endless moment before he angled his mouth and kissed the corner of her lips. Then he gently moved his mouth over hers.

His light, easy caress arrowed through her and heated her to the core. Stunned her. Intoxicated her. Trembling, Liv kissed him back.

Her body remembered his touch, remembered his taste. Dark. Dangerous. Utterly primal.

The insistent craving she'd known since the very first time he kissed her blazed to life. Her breath caught, her skin tingled, and her breasts hungered for his big, warm hands.

She could feel the raw, male heat radiating from his hard body and wanted to snuggle against his chest and soak it all in. She knew she should call a halt, but leaned closer and softened against him anyway.

His tongue traced the boundary of her lower lip, demanding her response. Her lips parted, and the first moist rasp turned her insides molten.

Mike lifted her against him. His tongue stroked, penetrated her mouth with a sensual rhythm.

Her body ached with emptiness. Moist, shattering

need seared her, melted her resolve into mush. She stifled a moan and curled her arms around his neck.

A bare moment later he released her, letting her slide down his aroused body until her feet hit the floor. She drew in a ragged breath.

Shuddering, he rested his forehead against hers and smoothed her hair. "Yeah. Just a kiss."

Liv shoved him away and turned her back, knotting and unknotting her hands. "I will not have sex with you tonight."

"Don't recall asking."

Blinking rapidly, she glanced over her shoulder at him. "Funny."

He held her gaze without flinching, but his lips twisted into a lopsided grin.

Her throat clogged. She wrapped her arms around her waist and turned away. That was exactly how she'd gotten pregnant within forty-eight hours of meeting Mike.

Stupid. Stupid. Stupid.

Chapter Three

Sereno, Monday, April 5, 8:45 a.m.

What if he relocked the mailbox and let the thing rot? Ahmed tugged his bottom lip with thumb and forefinger, staring at the small package in his post office box.

With hands gone clammy, he jerked the parcel free. The scruffy brown paper was addressed clumsily and pasted with stamps from home. But the smeared Arabic postmark was different from the compound where his family was held as guests.

Involuntary guests.

Fear for their safety dried his mouth, parched his throat like a desert sandstorm. Squeezing his eyes shut, he managed to swallow.

No choice. He crammed the package into his backpack and slammed the metal door closed. He flinched at the clang and glanced behind him.

Despite the chilly, overcast morning, dozens of students milled around the open-air postal station, laughing, joking, and flirting. None of them turned to stare, so he let out a sigh.

Yanking his key free, he hurried to his bike and pedaled along the wide path toward the business school. By the time he reached the shadowed sculpture garden, his breath came more easily. He slowed and hopped off.

Leaning the bike against a tall totem pole, he dropped to his knees.

Alone in the forested glen, he brushed one hand over his mouth and tore through the wrapper. Ripping off the tape, he lifted the lid. The sickly smell of baklava escaped. Under the layers of carefully packed pastry, he found a phone and pulled it out. Cold sweat trickled down his spine.

He jammed the incriminating brown paper into his backpack and dumped the box in a garbage can. His footsteps silent on the thick redwood mulch, he surveyed the area. No one nearby. The low fog muffled both sight and sound. He freed the phone from its crinkling bubble wrap, and the trembling in his fingers worsened. Prepaid, with one number listed in the directory.

Ahmed closed his eyes and let the breeze sweep his flushed face. He glanced around again. No one was within earshot. Leaning against the rough bark of a huge redwood tree, he struck a casual pose and waited for the long distance connection.

"Did you close the deal?" a man's voice asked in clipped English.

"Yes. But that greedy American raised the price."

"Regrettable. Will he still deliver on time?"

"Yes. Friday."

The line went dead.

Ahmed flipped the phone from hand to hand for a full minute before hiding it in the pocket of his jeans. He had to keep the foul thing, but the thought of using it again made his skin prickle.

Opening his pack, he ripped the brown paper into tiny pieces. Then he crossed the street and dropped them in a rain gutter. A rush of relief shook him. He would follow orders. He had no choice.

He wheeled his bike toward the building, locked it to a rack, and gave a quick wave to a classmate.

"Does your study group present for Professor Gordon this week?" Miriam Kazan asked in a soft, lilting voice.

Unable to think of anything to say, he nodded.

She followed him into the classroom. When he found his seat, she slipped into the one next to him.

The back of his neck crawled, and his heart thudded in his chest. He froze. She always sat next to him.

Miriam adjusted her hijab and smiled. Her dark eyes met his.

She watched him like a raptor without its hood.

****

10:30 a.m.

Mike stopped short, facing the huge glass wall. G-Tech's clean room was empty. No bunny-suited engineers working today, but next door, the electronics lab teemed with agents. Half a dozen engineers roosted on any available flat surface, watching the show.

Liv and Bausch faced-off in the center of the room. She vibrated with rage, her arms stiff, and her hands curled into fists. An avenging female on four-inch heels. Magnificent.

Bausch leaned over her, his chin thrust forward. His dark, curly hair was mussed like he'd run his hands through it more than once, although his black suit and red power tie were pristine. He wore a go-home-little-girl-and-let-the-real-men-handle-it smirk. Not the most successful strategy with Liv.

Mike sucked in a quick breath. He had his work cut out for him, defusing this confrontation. Any second the two would paw the ground and charge. But he wanted his family back together, and the shortest route to his wife's heart was her company. Time to move in.

Adrenaline pumped into his bloodstream and threw his options into clearer focus. To skate that thin line between potential disasters without any blood spilled, this was why he loved undercover work.

He tapped on the window. Liv and Bausch both turned and glared, like they could melt the glass into slag and then burn him to a smoldering heap of cinders.

Mike grinned and rounded the wall into the lab. "Morning, Liv." He turned toward the agent. "Bausch, is there a secure space you and I could use for briefing?"

Liv sputtered, the angry flush along her cheekbones darkening. "It's my company. Why the— why ask him?"

"Nothing to do with G-Tech," he added smoothly. "Besides, Bausch is in charge."

Six engineers gasped in unison.

"Yee-ikes." Alyssa Manchester cringed and dropped her gaze. "I'll be in my cube. Want to join me, guys?"

Liv wove her arms across her chest, biting her lower lip. Fury sparked in her eyes as she watched her engineering team slink out.

Bausch gave an abrupt cough. "Harold, take charge. Lieutenant Gordon and I can use the clean room airlock."

"I'll be in my office, *Lieu-tenant*." Liv gave him a once over that left his uniform smoking and his staff on high alert.

She pivoted and marched away, her spine ramrod straight. Bausch's lips twitched, but he hooded the triumph in his sharp blue eyes.

Damn good thing, Mike thought. Her teeth-baring smile had promised them both a brutal time unless he could finesse some concessions from Bausch.

The agent led him through the automatic double doors. Gear that looked like it belonged on the space shuttle hung from pegs on both sides. "This case is strictly off limits, Gordon. What the hell are you doing here?"

Pompous jerk. "Relax, FBI. Just delivering a message."

****

10:45 a.m.

The rough spot where Liv bit into her lip no longer screamed with pain. With a sigh, she perched on the edge of her desk and nursed a cappuccino finally cool enough to drink. Containing her temper had left her wrung out and numb.

Mike paused in the doorway. "Got a minute?" At her nod, he closed the door. Twisting his mouth into a rigid line, he frowned slightly, as if considering his words. "You okay? Sorry. No choice but to play Bausch that way."

A spurt of resentment coiled inside her, and the pulse at her temples throbbed. She exhaled slowly and set down her cup, tracing the sharp crease in her slacks with her free hand. "Once I cooled off, I realized what you were doing, but I did need a break. When Bausch pasted that last shit-eating sneer on his face, I almost rearranged his patrician nose."

"Can't recommend it."

"Ya think?"

"Federal offense."

"Hmmmm. What if I just ripped the flag pin off his regulation dark suit?"

One corner of his mouth quirked.

She raised her shoulders. "I have no idea how to handle Bausch. By the time you showed up, I was barely holding myself inside my skin."

Mike's lips bloomed into an electric grin. "I have good news and a suggestion, if you're interested." He moved across the room with easy grace and hitched one hip onto the opposite corner of her desk.

She shifted sideways, away from his magnetic pull, and curled her nails into her palms, digging in until the pain cleared her thoughts.

He might look like a warrior in his midnight-blue uniform. Any closer and he'd send arrows of heat shuddering through her. Arouse emotions she'd buried sixty miles deep.

No. She couldn't risk surrender to this adrenaline-junkie-in-creased-blues. In real life, they were toxic together, like bleach and ammonia.

She rose from her desk and sat in one of two modern club chairs, crossing her legs. "Okay. Good news first."

He followed her and folded his long, athletic frame into the opposite chair. His gaze raked over her before he answered, "The lab and clean room are secured. Alyssa is reorganizing."

Her mouth dropped in shock and the wound-up spring in her belly relaxed. "I'm impressed. So what's your suggestion?"

"You might not like my strategy." He gave a dry chuckle and reached one finger to tilt her chin.

She jerked away. "Try me."

"Take the afternoon off."

She rubbed her aching temples and briefly closed her eyes. "You're not stupid. You know I can't. Or don't you understand how far behind we are?"

"You want Bausch and his gorillas gone? He'll move faster if you're not in his face, and he has free rein." He cleared his throat. "Alyssa doesn't challenge his authority."

She twisted away from him, muttering, "Just like a guy. Stupid macho posturing."

"What did you expect? He's FBI. But I have an idea."

"What?" She filed down the suspicious edge to her voice.

"I'm running a hostage rescue demo for the county bigwigs this afternoon. Come see how my new SWAT team stacks up against the other agencies."

She made a dismissive sound. "Very relaxing, but I can't imagine sitting still."

"Don't have to. The bullets will start to fly and the first percussion grenade will lift you out of your seat."

"Get real. I can't afford the time."

"No, you get real. Hang around G-Tech today, and you'll either rile Bausch until he shuts you out completely..."

"Or go crazy." She sucked thoughtfully through her teeth, chewing over his words. "Maybe."

"I'll make you a deal." He stuck out his hand.

She scowled at his palm like he was trying to sell her the Bay Bridge for fifty bucks. "What deal?"

Joy Brighton

"I have Giants tickets for Sunday afternoon. Give Bausch some space today. If my strategy works and Dragonfly passes the trials, you'll have some breathing room. You can go to the game with me and celebrate."

"Jackson Marino's seats?" She tried to keep her tongue from hanging out.

Mike waggled his eyebrows. "Club level, first base line."

"That new hotshot pitcher's slated for Sunday's game."

"Yep. You know you want to go," he coaxed, drawing out each word.

She tapped her toe, considering the risks. Then she narrowed her eyes and poked a finger at his six-pack. "But remember, we're just a couple baseball fans.

****

Coyote Valley, 3:30 p.m.

Mike rammed a new clip into his MP5 and slipped a weighty Kevlar vest over his head. Adjusting his elbow and kneepads, he surveyed the terrain: rolling hills spattered with twisted, gray-green oaks above grass not yet burned to gold. Warmth grew in his belly and erupted into a grin. Home.

Nate Kapulani clapped him on the back. Although they both cleared six three, the captain outweighed him by fifty pounds of solid, Hawaiian muscle. "Got your new team whipped into shape?"

"Getting there. Still a little rusty on our practice runs, but the guys are psyched for today's competition."

Nate's sharp brown eyes scanned him, his square face suddenly serious. "Nice to see Liv today."

Something inside Mike squirmed, and he searched the metal bleachers. Halfway up the stands, she

26

watched the field, binoculars in place. Good. At least she wasn't on her cell phone again. "Wasn't easy to drag her away from work."

"Had to kidnap her?"

He gave a quick shrug and rolled his eyes. "Nearly."

"The demo might give her some insight into what you do now."

"Hope so. SWAT is a real change from undercover work. A good change." He relaxed his fingers and flexed his hands.

Clearing his throat, Nate punched his bicep. "Bausch was on the horn this morning griping about you butting in on his investigation."

"It's the rule book stuck up his ass."

Nate grinned. "I'll run interference where I can, but be careful. If Bausch swings that rule book at your head, you'll feel the pain."

"No choice. I had to take the risk. My gut's screaming at me. Something dirty is going down at G-Tech, and Bausch doesn't get it. I need to protect Liv."

"Do what you gotta do."

His throat tightened, and he elbowed Nate. "I owe you."

"Ditto."

The small crowd erupted in applause, and Mike glanced at the scoreboard. "Looks like Alameda County took five seconds off their best time. We're next."

Nate pounded his big fist against Mike's shoulder. "Go get 'em, cowboy."

"We can nail this if I can keep Flynn reined in." He tightened the chinstrap on his helmet and hustled across the field to wait for his squad.

Sergeant Jackson Marino jogged up, a grin glinting from his intelligent gray eyes. The guy packed enough strength in his shoulders to bench press a longhorn. "Scorekeeper says anytime. Frost is set, but Flynn's jumpy."

"No surprise. He's green."

"Watch out for him when you go in."

Mike nodded at Marino and gave the officials a thumbs-up. When he signaled, the surveillance helicopter swooped in low, stirring up debris. Dust choked the air.

The judge lowered his hand, and the stopwatch raced in split seconds.

Adrenaline jammed through his system. His heart rate revved. Time slowed to a crawl, sharpening his senses. Energized, he transmitted orders and raised his rifle to cover Marino. "Go."

Body bent close to the ground, Marino maneuvered uphill, leaving a trail in the knee-high grass. He crawled into position and leveled his rifle atop a tree stump.

Head tucked, Mike zigzagged toward the ridge behind him, belly-flopped to the ground, and inched forward between large rocks. "See anything, Marino?"

****

4:05 p.m.

Damn it! Why did Mike have to be right? Liv shook her head slowly. Alyssa's text message reported the progress on Dragonfly. Programming was complete for all but one of the forty explosives. They might meet the deadline yet.

She'd expected to be bored stupid today, but shooting the Glock had been more fun than pouting.

Didn't hurt that she'd unloaded a full magazine

into the center of a paper target while picturing Samantha Blackthorn's flat chest and skinny backside. Liv tapped the perforated target and smiled.

Raising her binoculars, she spotted Flynn and Frost behind a rusty pickup. A helicopter hovered fifty feet above the ground, raising a raucous dust storm. She grabbed a loose strand of hair and tucked it back into the clip. Squinting at the field, she tipped the communicator Mike had loaned her closer to her ear.

"See anything, Marino?" Mike's tense voice crackled through the transmitter, and she stiffened.

Marino crouched over his high-powered scope. "Movement in the south window."

"Cover us from here. Ready?"

"You got it, Boss."

"We're moving," Flynn reported.

Silently, the team closed in on their objective from two directions. Twenty yards of exposed, weed-choked ground fronted the cabin.

Mike ducked behind a faded play structure and disappeared into the underbrush. The timer rounded four minutes.

"Hurry," Liv shouted, bouncing in her seat.

He slithered back into view. She would have raced the last few feet, but he slowed to a stealthy pace, like a cougar on the hunt. Sleek. Controlled. Deadly.

Crossing the weedy ground seemed to take Mike an eternity. She held her breath until he stood, back braced against the cabin wall, gulping air.

"There's a patrol in the yard!" the helicopter pilot's voice boomed through the communicator. "He's moving."

"Opening fire!" Marino hit the pop-up target with a

single shot.

The crack of the rifle exploded through the communicator. Shivers crawled along her spine, raising gooseflesh. Real bullets. Using live ammunition added a whole new, terrifying spin.

Mike signaled, "Go!"

Frost kicked out, splintering the door.

"Police! Freeze!" Mike ordered, hurling a percussion grenade into the cabin.

Liv clapped her hands over her ears, but the discharge rang in her head. She stood, every muscle tense, hands fisted atop her chest. She glanced at the video monitor in time to see three flat targets slide toward an upturned table.

Firing rapidly, Mike hurdled inside and sprinted for cover. He hit his mark with a clean shot.

Frost took down another.

Flynn bolted through the door and hit the remaining target, but he sprayed the hostage dummy and the whole room with real bullets.

The blood dropped from her brain. Cold sweat beaded on her skin, and a metallic taste filled her mouth. Knees shaking, she gasped and sank onto the bench.

Finally, Mike straightened, and relief turned her bones to rubber bands. He tossed the hostage dummy over his shoulder and sprinted toward the finish line.

Liv released a ragged breath, remembering all the ways she'd imagined murdering him these last few months. Slow, painful poison, the biggest gun she could fire, or a very dull knife.

Tough as it was, she had to acknowledge her gut-deep relief that Flynn hadn't killed Mike. She might have new respect for what he did, but his work had helped make their life together miserable. She smiled. Maybe a little torture would be fun.

The Sereno cops jogged across the field, and Liv made her way down the stairs. Thumbscrews? Waterboarding? No, she'd take a bullwhip to his cheating ass.

Mike flopped in the dirt in front of the stands, mangled dummy at his side. He raised his goggles, pulled off his helmet, and beamed at her.

"That was amazing," she said, descending the last two steps.

His grin widened. A warm surge of pleasure washed over her, tugged her under the waves, and flipped her upside down.

"Sorry, Gordon." Flynn collapsed beside Mike, his sandy hair flattened by sweat and a frown wrinkling his baby face. "When Frost busted the door, I could hardly see straight. The bullets just flew."

Shuddering, she grimaced. Didn't that idiot realize the danger?

But Mike punched his shoulder. "Shaved forty seconds off our time and hit every target dead center. If you stop killing hostages, we'll win next time."

He peeled off his Kevlar vest and took her arm. "Come on, Livy. They need someone to play hostage. You're nominated."

She glanced at the bullet-riddled dummy. "Me?"

Chapter Four

Mojave Desert, Thursday, April 8, 12:30 p.m.

Blistering midday heat stole Mike's breath, and relentless wind swirled dust over the parched landscape. He walked beside Liv across the bleak military compound toward an observation tower. Allowing his hand to brush her arm, he guided her past rows of dust-colored camouflaged vehicles.

She was wound tighter than a mousetrap spring. Couldn't blame her. But why was the timeline so tight? He hadn't been able to pry anything out of Bausch.

A Hummer H1-Alpha was parked in the shade of the observation tower, with a pair of large feet sticking out from underneath.

"Hey, Alyssa. All set?" Liv called.

Alyssa Manchester, the beanpole with wild, red hair, scooted out and wiped her hands on a rag. "The transmitter's attached, and the dashboard display is installed. Guidance, good to go. We'll have the sensor array working in a sec, but I need help with the testing."

"Sure." Liv tipped her head and pointed. "Mike. Mind waiting over there?" Before he could answer, she turned toward the vehicle, concentrating on her team.

"No problem." He shrugged and eased into the background, settling in the shade of a California pepper tree a few feet from the blazing-hot asphalt. He shaded his eyes with his hand and scanned the area. Heat waves shimmered above the desert surrounding the isolated base.

When an explosion echoed off sandstone formations, a rush chilled his veins.

She glanced across the dry lakebed at the sooty, black cloud billowing into the air. "Sounds like our competitor's unit found a target the hard way."

He frowned. "What about the driver?"

Her lips curled into a huge grin. "No real danger. Unlike the SWAT competition, these charges are rigged like paint ball. Just lots of noise and smoke, plus a mess on the Hummer."

"We tested the sensor for ammonal. Armstrong's mixture is next," Alyssa called from inside the truck.

"I'm on it." Liv turned back to the vehicle.

Mike dug at a rock with the toe of his boot, unearthing a chunk of flint, and dust drifted onto the black leather. Liv spent more hours working with her engineering team than he could count.

He kicked the rock onto the asphalt. Sometimes his job had absorbed all of his attention too, especially when he was undercover. And this new drone could make a real difference in the world.

They'd agreed the mess they'd made of their marriage could wait, but he wanted to work it through now and move back home where he belonged. He leaned against the tree and sighed. At least they'd have a chance to talk Sunday at the game.

Alyssa shot Liv a thumbs-up. "Field calibrations match specs perfectly. Ready as we'll ever be, Boss."

Liv shielded her eyes and pointed to a paint-spattered H1-Alpha rumbling through the razor-wire-topped gate. "Good. We're next. I'll double-check the readouts in the observation tower."

"I can do it." Alyssa bounded up the steps and disappeared.

Liv grinned at him, and his heart lightened. "Alyssa's been a life saver. I don't know how I'd have managed this week without her."

His smile melted. He'd busted his ass, put his own work priorities on hold to shoulder some of Liv's load. He bent to grab the flint, avoiding her gaze.

She tugged on his sleeve, lowering her sunglasses to meet his gaze. "I appreciate your help too."

Her touch eased the tension in his chest.

****

1:15 p.m.

Fighting her impatience, Liv took a deep breath, but nothing could slow her racing heart. From the observation tower, she scrutinized the video screens displaying the unpaved road their drone would scan for planted explosives. She was aware of Mike's presence, but at least he'd made no move to crowd her.

The transportation sergeant radioed, "All clear. Move out."

On the high-resolution feed, she watched the Hummer edge forward, past rows of dusty camouflage tanks and transports. The gate slid open, and the vehicle moved through. The scanner beeped a slow monotone.

A second monitor showed the drone's view, a hundred feet above the dusty ground.

About a mile out, the beeping accelerated. Two suspicious objects flashed on the screen. She exhaled heavily when the drone documented traces of nitrate explosives.

"Those are the easy ones, even without chemical sensors." Liv's voice wobbled.

Outside, the wind increased, dropping visibility. With Dragonfly's help, the H1-Alpha dodged half a dozen pipe bombs, but her pulse ratcheted higher with each target.

The vehicle turned off the road onto the dry lakebed set up to look like Main Street of any small town. Liv moved closer to the big screen, her chest so tight breathing was almost impossible. "This is the real test."

The Hummer snaked its way across down the tarmac surface. The driver's voice boomed over the intercom, "Scanner shows it's clear, but we're taking it slow. I have this weird itch between my shoulder blades."

Dragonfly sent a long series of ear piercing alerts, and he shouted, "Look out!"

Liv ducked instinctively.

The vehicle skidded.

When they identified and maneuvered around the explosives planted in a garbage can, she released a long sigh.

For the next ten agonizing minutes, she paced the control room. Finally, the Hummer reached its objective, locating in the simulated crowd an additional backpack full of explosives, and a dummy carrying a suicide vest. When they headed back to base, her breath escaped her constricted lungs.

"Dragonfly identified all the threats," Alyssa crowed and headed for the stairs. "This contract's ours."

Mike glanced around the room, and then gave her a

quick thumbs-up.

She met his smoky blue gaze.

****

Sereno, Friday, April 9, 9:00 a.m.

The venture capitalists were ecstatic.

Liv breezed into G-Tech's conference room the next morning wearing her favorite red Prada suit. A general, two colonels, and a quiet dark-suited older man stood. She recognized California's senior senator and shook her hand.

Liv smoothed her fingers across the black lacquer boardroom table and gestured for the assembled brass to be seated. A thrill shimmied up her spine. Smell the power.

General Trevor gave a rumbling throat-clear. "The DR 2.0 sensor-drone performed perfectly on its three test runs."

She hid her smile with her hand. He reminded her of a polar bear, silver-haired and steel-jawed, with huge powerful paws. "In fact," she said. "Out of four competitors, Dragonfly was the only successful prototype at the trials."

Liv dimmed the boardroom's recessed lights, and a 3D video screen emerged. "Our sensor drone's flexible programming accommodates changes in explosives technology seamlessly, like a dog can be taught to recognize new scents. It's almost as sensitive and adaptable as a trained bloodhound. DOD and Homeland Security will be able to adapt our technology for any bomb detection situation. And its miniscule size will perform well in almost any setting."

She kept one eye on her audience as she clicked through the presentation, noting the room full of nodding heads. Adrenaline charged through her and set her pulse pounding.

"Unfortunately, terrorism is part of modern life. Our product can boost security and prevent loss of life in combat zones around the world." She had them where she wanted them now, so she added the kicker, "And at America's most sensitive Homeland targets."

She clicked on the lights. "However, you want more than a video demonstration. Gentlemen, Senator, we have prepared a live field test to demonstrate Dragonfly's impressive potential."

The general sat back in his comfortable chair and crossed his arms. A few minions smiled and looked interested. The senator checked her watch.

"This set of test vials, holding forty specific aromas is a tiny sample of the number of scents Dragonfly can identify, but it safely serves our purpose today." She held out the box and allowed the man in the dark suit to choose a vial.

"Thank you. Now, sir, if you could open the vial carefully, and one at a time, hand it to any three people around the table. Subjects, using the wand, please place a tiny sample of the scent somewhere on your person or around you."

The senator looked skeptical when she was selected.

"These are all harmless to your skin." Liv assured her.

The senator sniffed the scent. "Rose?" she said, and touched the wand to her ear. The other two subjects followed suit.

"Let's invite our latest sensor drone into the setting." She opened the conference room door.

Alyssa entered and placed the bug-sized drone on the table. Several people leaned forward to examine the drone. It sat on six metal legs, its body eerily like that of an oversized dragonfly. Yeah, but this bug was packed with nano-technology and the latest in micro-communication equipment.

Alyssa had insisted the drone be painted metallic green, and Liv had to agree. It lent an air of drama to their invention. Even its antennae tail looked realistic.

Liv swallowed hard before she spoke again. They'd walked through this demonstration at least a dozen times, but her heart-rate ramped. Even usually confident Alyssa wore a wide-eyed, worried expression on her face.

"Ms. Manchester will navigate Dragonfly around the room to demonstrate the precise handling we have achieved."

The drone's iridescent wings spread, and a soft whirring sound emitted from the bug. It rose a few inches off the table on tiny helicopter-like blades positioned over the main fuselage. "Its optical sensor is now scanning the space for obstacles," Liv said.

Alyssa moved the joy stick forward, and Dragonfly zoomed to the end of the table, did a loop-de-loop over the chandelier and dodged the gentlemen, weaving between their shoulders with ease.

Palm up, Liv held out her hand, and Alyssa coordinated a perfect landing. A few chuckles and a light round of applause came from the onlookers.

Liv held the vial and introduced the scent to the drone. It emitted a rapid series of low level beeps. "The drone is processing the chemical components of the test scent. Now we'll order the drone into automatic find. It will no longer depend on the navigation system but will seek out the recognized scent automatically."

Dragonfly rose to almost ceiling level and hovered for a few seconds, turning in four directions. Then it flew to the closest test subject, the colonel who had placed the chemical on the palm of his hand. The drone hovered over the man's hand and gave a beeping alert.

"Could you turn you palm upright, sir."

When he started to move, an ear splitting warning filled the room.

"Once the scent is identified," Liv continued. "The drone will return to its preprogrammed high point and recalibrate for the next find."

The second subject was a few seats down and across the table. Dragonfly slowly circled the room, but then focused on the underside of the man's chair.

Laughter and applause erupted after a second set of beeps signaled the scent was underneath the chair where the man was sitting.

"One more to go." Liv crossed her fingers behind her back.

The drone circled the room once, then again. Liv licked her dry lips.

"Is it having a problem?" asked General Polar Bear.

The drone flew closer and closer circles around the woman in the blue suit until it faced the senator and drew within inches of her nose. It hovered but didn't signal. "Maybe it smells my perfume," the senator offered.

"It's differentiating between two similar scents," Alyssa explained. "Give it a sec. It's filtering through its database of chemicals."

Without warning the drone landed on the woman's shoulder and placed its sensor on her neck. The noise was loud, the applause louder.

The drone flew across the room and landed on the top of Alyssa's curly head. Liv could swear they were both taking a bow.

After Liv closed the door behind the departing duo and returned to the conference table, the three military men and the senator were huddled together, whispering.

General Polar Bear nodded sharply, rose and offered his hand. "Thank you, Ms. Gordon. When will your company be prepared for a second round of field testing?"

Her feet wanted to dance a rumba on the spot, but she replied calmly, "Immediately. We have several beta devices on hand."

"What would it take to secure ten devices this month?"

"Three weeks?" Liv gulped. Back to work twenty-four, seven. "Let's go ask my CTO, but we'll need a sizeable advance."

The senator rose and cleared her throat. "One more thing, Ms. Gordon. We all know this project's classified. The DOD and my committee have concerns, given your recent security breach."

Liv's pulse raced, but she met the woman's stern expression. "Agent Bausch assures me G-Tech now exceeds top security protocol. Nothing will stop Dragonfly."

Chapter Five

San Francisco, Sunday, April 11, 3:30 p.m.

"Top of the seventh, one on and one out. Think they'll salvage the shut-out?" Mike grinned at the huge fielder's glove sculpture on the highest tier of Giants' Stadium.

"You bet." Liv gave him a sidelong glance, her cheeks dimpled. Her ponytail, threaded through the back of her baseball cap, made her look younger, more carefree.

The pitcher released the ball, and Mike's fist slammed into his palm. "Strike two!" He nudged her with his shoulder.

She bolted upright, focused on the field. "Watch out! He's going to steal!"

The pitcher pivoted and smoked the ball to first.

"Got him." Liv whooped, her eyes shining, like the fun, impulsive woman he'd fallen in love with.

Warmth glowed in his chest. He reached for the garlic fries, gaze returning to the field. His hand bumped hers, and the glow heated.

She pulled back, and he snagged a fry, lifting it to her lips.

Her eyes met his while she nibbled the fry, but bright red stained her cheeks. She laughed and licked the garlic off her lips.

41

Tingles started at his fingertips and spread in sizzling ripples through his body. His lungs took a vacation, his mouth dry as dust.

He wrapped his arm around her shoulders and slowly drew her closer, tangling a hand in the thick silk of her hair. Tipping her black and orange cap with one finger, he lowered his mouth to hers for a quick kiss. Her lips felt smooth, soft, yielding.

He couldn't resist. His tongue flicked over the seam between her lips. He tasted the spicy, salty garlic. He tasted Liv. His Liv.

She broke the kiss, nudging him with her elbow, and shrugging off his arm. "Pay attention. With one more strike, he'll retire the side."

His blood pulsed heavy and urgent, but he drew back a hair's breadth and turned toward the action, grinning. He'd pushed her hard enough. Any more and she'd bolt. Damn, all of a sudden, his whole world seemed to have flipped right side up.

The batter hit a long fly toward triples alley, and Mike held his breath until the center fielder caught the ball just short of the warning track.

The fans roared.

"Seventh inning stretch. I'll go inside and get us a couple beers." Scooting into the club lounge ahead of the crowd, he grabbed two brews and a bag of peanuts, galloped down the cement steps, and slid back into his seat.

He set everything in the holders and brushed his hand over her long ponytail. "I've missed you, Livy. Being here together feels…" Words failed him. He shifted in his seat, rubbing his knuckles over his thighs.

She fixed her gaze on her glass, but her expression

telegraphed her feelings. She punched his shoulder playfully. "None of that. Remember? I'm just one of the guys today."

He took a long, slow drink, swallowing the stinging rejection along with the beer. Silently, he grabbed a peanut and snapped the shell in two.

Her tongue darted out and moistened her lips. "I've enjoyed the game, Mike. Thanks."

He gazed beyond the field to the choppy waters of the bay. "My pleasure. We should get an extra ticket and bring Cara next time."

"I needed a break, but I don't know when I'll get away again. I'm not sure how to pull it off on the Pentagon's timetable. We'll have to ramp production in a big hurry."

A slow smile spread across his face. "You'll let me know if I can help."

She opened her lips and closed them again, shaking her head gently. A mischievous glint lit her eyes, and his pulse jumped.

He inched closer and tilted her chin with his thumb. "What?"

"It's been a long time since we did something fun together," she whispered.

Mike cupped her cheeks with his hands and slowly leaned down for another kiss. The crowd milling around them faded, and his focus narrowed to her beautiful face. He put his arms around her, pulled her close, and kissed her thoroughly, loving the taste of her, loving the texture of her lips, loving her scent, her soft skin, her warmth.

She shivered, and he sucked her lower lip into his mouth. His heart pounded, but no blood made it to his brain. He thrust his tongue into her sweet mouth, needing to move her, needing to make her feel a small part of the aching loneliness he'd endured.

Her lids eased open, revealing eyes gone huge and glassy.

Tenderness washed over him. He rose and pulled her to her feet.

Trembling, she blinked but didn't move away. Instead, she snaked an arm around his waist and turned to snuggle against his hard chest. The rhythm of her racing pulse matched his.

In an agony of need, he stroked her back. At that moment, he wanted her more than his next breath, craving more than sex, although God only knew how bad he wanted her naked.

Liv tipped her head to meet his gaze. He slanted his mouth, stroking her swollen lips with his tongue and sealing them.

Her hands splayed on his shoulders. She moaned and pressed against him, imprinting him with the touch of her soft breasts, tipped by pebbled nipples. The yielding, feminine hollow of her belly sharpened his need.

He hungered to claim her here and now. To hell with the ballpark full of fans. He growled and crushed his hips against her, letting her feel his arousal.

He lowered his mouth again, but a finger poked his arm, slamming him back to reality.

"Mister? Excuse me, mister. Can I get by?" A boy wearing a bright orange sweatshirt that matched his freckles, glared at him. A woman with a hint of a smile tugging at her lips followed the kid.

"Sorry." Mike and Liv separated and leaned to let

them pass.

"No problem. You were busy." The woman chuckled. "Newlyweds?"

Mike peeked at Liv. She'd buried her face against his shoulder and scrunched her eyes shut. He grinned sheepishly, looked straight at the woman, and lied, "Caught us."

Liv withdrew, her blush slowly fading. She sank into her seat, avoiding his gaze. "Liar."

The sarcastic edge to her voice grated on his nerves. "Livy, we need to talk. I never slept with Samantha."

"Bullshit." She snatched a peanut and twisted the shell between her fingers until the shell cracked. "You spent a month undercover in her bed posing as her husband."

Vague guilt nagged at him. "Not in her bed. I never made love to Sam. We had to pose as a couple desperate to buy a baby for the sting." He rubbed his hand over his hair. "I didn't tell you the set-up so you wouldn't worry. I didn't think you'd ever find out."

"Drop it."

"Damn it, Liv, we did important work. Think about how you'd feel if we lost Cara. Sam and I exposed the kidnapping ring and recovered six kids."

She shook her head, staring off into right field as she demolished another shell and crunched the nut between her teeth.

"If you won't listen, how can we ever fix anything?" He reached for her hand, but she jerked it away.

"Damn it! I said drop it." Anger whiplashed through her voice, and tense white lines bracketed her mouth.

Mike crushed the pile of empty peanut shells littering the concrete with his boot. He took another sip of beer and popped his knuckles.

She drew in a fragmented breath and lifted her chin, her red-rimmed eyes glittering. "You claim you want to reconcile. I don't believe we'll ever be able to live together and get along. But you've worked hard to help me with Cara and make my life easier, so I'll make you a deal."

He crossed his arms. "I'm ready."

"I'll bet you can't sit through marriage counseling while we work on our differences."

"You want us to see a shrink?"

"We had problems, Mike, long before Sam. Big problems. It's the only possible—"

He laid a hand on her knee, cutting her off. "If we can't talk one on one, airing our gripes in front of a stranger won't help."

She narrowed her eyes. "Dare you."

****

Sereno, Tuesday, April 13, 9:30 a.m.

Payback had been a long time coming. Chewing on a torpedo-shaped Cuban cigar, Morrison flipped through the set of black and white prints piled on his desk. He squinted, trying to make sense of the diagrams, then shrugged. He'd get the rest of what he needed and let those rag heads figure out the details.

He'd found his target and would turn a nice profit too. Chuckling softly, he pulled a color photo from his bottom drawer—a cop holding a little blonde girl with his other arm around a dark-haired woman.

Hatred burned in his gut. He rasped a hand across

the stubble on his jaw, remembering the day he first vowed revenge. He deserved justice. "I owe Gordon, big time," he muttered. "That asshole deserves to suffer."

From his perch on the walnut desk, Sidney Sylvester, Esq. cleared his throat. "Who's Gordon?"

Morrison glanced at the legal eagle the bosses back east had sent in to spy on him. The veins in his temples throbbed, but he kept his expression blank. Barely five eight, with close clipped brown hair and not much flesh on his bones or face, Sid looked sharp, from his sharkskin Armani to his Italian loafers. Too sharp for a real man. Maybe he'd dig around, just in case he ever needed some dirt on the shrimp.

Leaning back in his chair, he took another puff of his cigar and blew a long stream of smoke. "Gordon's the cop that fucked me over eight years ago."

Sid's eyebrow arched, and his mouth formed a thin half-smile. "They never pinned anything on you?"

"Nope. Got away clean, but the new identity cost me a bundle."

"Heard your uncle saved your ass."

He hooded his eyes and thought about rearranging the jerk-wad's face. No, not yet. He let his teeth show and steepled his fingers. "No shit."

Yanking on his ear lobe, Sid shifted his weight off the edge of the desk and retreated a step. "So how do you plan to get Gordon?"

Now the cop was back in the picture, Morrison needed help to pull off this operation. He drew on his cigar and pointed to the dark-haired woman. "I already targeted his wife. She's CEO of the company where I lifted these."

"Cool."

"She's a ball buster, drives everyone nuts, but I've got the stuck-up bitch buffaloed." The muscles at the back of his skull tensed. This smart-ass lawyer was quick, but could he be trusted? "While you set up the hit for tonight, I put a watch on Gordon's kid, just in case. Even paid their nanny to take off."

Sid's face paled.

Morrison ground the burning tip of his cigar into the photograph. "I'll give them all what they deserve." Smiling, he watched flames curl the faces to ash.

****

6:45 p.m.

What wouldn't she give to string that fed up by his power tie and invite Cara's tee ball team to play pin-the-tail-on-the-agent? Another three-hour session with Special Agent Bausch obsessing about security had almost pushed her to violence.

Liv stretched her neck, easing the tightly corded muscles, and forced her hands to relax on the steering wheel. Flipping her radio to a classical music station, she drove out of G-Tech's parking lot. Glimmers of a pink and orange sunset hung over the shadowed western hills.

She slowed for a stop sign in the deserted industrial park and glanced at the clock on the dashboard. Damn. She'd be late for dinner if she didn't hurry. She pressed her temples to ease the distant pounding in her skull. The spicy fajita salad she'd eaten for lunch sat in her stomach like an undigested clump of nuclear waste.

But even more painful was the jealousy that ripped at her heart. She missed Mike, but how could she ever trust him again?

This morning, he'd called her, insisting he was ready to consider counseling. She twisted her lips into a wry smile. With Cara at a birthday party tonight, they had the evening to talk. She'd agreed to meet him, although she had zero reason to believe it'd do any good.

She punched the pedal, and the sports car surged toward the freeway entrance. A black monster pickup squeezed into her lane, tailgating her. Five gigantic spotlights on the truck's grill glared into her rearview mirror. Insistent music throbbed through her car. The punishing bass ramped up her pulse rate. Chills stung the back of her neck and crawled down her spine.

A low rider peeled away from the curb, cut in front of her, and hit his brakes. She reacted quickly, but the jacked-up rig behind her slammed into her car. Metal screeched as it rode up her trunk and launched her forward.

Her already tense muscles hardened like tempered steel. "Idiot. I don't have time for this." She slammed her fist against the wheel.

Movement drew her attention, and she glanced at her mirror. The silhouettes of two large men appeared in front of the spotlights, advancing toward her car. She squinted to see their faces. A cold, twisting spasm started in her stomach and filled her with dread. "Shit." They were wearing stocking masks.

One man cocked a tire iron for a swing. The other grabbed her door handle, brandishing a switchblade. She shrieked, cranked the wheel, and stomped on the accelerator.

The car surged, and the switchblade thug leaped backward, but her rear window shattered with a deafening crack. Pebbled glass shards flew.

She jammed the pedal to the floor, smashed the bumper of the low rider, and jumped the curb, scraping the undercarriage.

Heartbeat echoing in her ears, she ripped through a flowerbed, made a hard left, and ran a red light. Dodging a UPS van, she squealed across three lanes of traffic onto the main drag. Horns blared.

Ahead, the railroad crossing lights began to flash. Eyes wide, knuckles white, she craned her neck and spotted the truck six cars back. "No, no, no." They were following her. She'd be caught between the glaring spotlights and the train.

Her pulse pounded in her throat. She ignored the clanging alarms and roared between the falling barrier arms. The train's horn boomed, but she bounced across the tracks and skidded back onto the road.

She glanced over her shoulder and sucked in a long breath. A huge black metal tire iron had stabbed through Cara's booster seat.

When her cell phone chimed, she jumped in her seat. Heart hammering, she groped for her purse and dragged it up by the handle, but the contents scattered on the floor. The phone continued to ring from somewhere beneath the passenger seat. She fumbled for it, but it stopped.

Even with jangled nerves, she could think again. Chewing her lip, she weighed her options and accelerated onto the freeway.

Finally, Liv pulled into the restaurant parking lot and scanned the area. Shadows lurked behind every car. She gulped, pulled off her heels, and sprinted for the entry.

****

7:05 p.m.

Where the hell was Liv? Mike checked his watch again and paced the courtyard fronting the Italian restaurant.

They'd made a connection at the SWAT competition, and she'd been a good sport playing hostage, although the image of Liv with that dummy gun pressed against her head still made his skin crawl.

He'd thought they were making more progress at the baseball game. Then she'd gone stiff and distant and insisted on counseling.

Sam's little stunt had done a number on Liv, and he had to admit his stupidity in the whole mess. Once tangled in the web, he'd tried to bluster his way out. Idiot. But he'd never seen it coming, never expected Sam to confront Liv and spin a web of barefaced lies. No wonder Liv didn't trust him.

He kicked mulch back into a flowerbed, feeling like a rat stuck in a booby-trapped maze. Taking the liaison training and giving up undercover work hadn't made any difference to Liv. So how could he convince her? There'd been no one else since he'd first caught a glimpse of her at Nate's wedding. There would never be anyone else.

He sank onto a tiled bench with his chin propped on his hand and gaze glued to the parking lot. Did she miss him as much as he missed her? No. She'd stood firm. Kept him locked out of her life unless he caved and saw a freaking shrink.

Mike checked his phone for messages. Nothing. Then he dialed her number. No response. Weird. Liv usually kept her phone close.

Unable to squelch a peculiar sense something was wrong, he rose to pace again. He walked into the crowded restaurant and edged his way to the hostess desk to check for a message. No luck.

The door banged opened, and Liv staggered inside. "Mike."

His heart galloped, fast and hard. She stood barefoot, with her hose in tatters. A thread of dried blood trailed down one cheek, but the panic in her face launched him to action. He opened his arms, reaching for her. "What happened?"

"S-someone carjacked me," she stammered, as if she could barely squeeze out the words.

His guts turned to molten metal, but he controlled the rage. "You're in shock." Mike helped her to a quiet alcove. When he checked her for injuries, he came up empty handed. "You okay?"

She took a deep, ragged breath against his shoulder. "I'm fine now, just shaken."

"Did you report it?" He smoothed her tangled hair back from her face.

Liv shook her head, her hands trembling in her lap. "They followed me. I was afraid to stop."

****

9:45 p.m.

Mike surveyed the damage to Liv's poor car. Probably totaled. She'd been damn lucky she could drive it and escape.

Thank God Cara wasn't in her car seat. He signaled the tow truck operator, and the rig eased out of the restaurant parking lot onto the street, its emergency lights flashing.

Liv had been right about one thing. They'd never

track her attackers from the information she gave. She hadn't seen their faces. Didn't even get a plate.

Anger stirred in his gut. Tonight had shown him exactly how much he'd give to keep her safe. Exactly how things would shake out.

He slid into his truck and lowered the window, inhaling the cool evening air. "After we pick up Cara, you're coming to the cabin with me."

"Mike—"

"No arguments. I'll sleep on the couch, but I refuse to leave you and Cara alone tonight."

"You don't have to." She chafed her palms along her arms. "I'll sleep in Cara's extra bed."

He scowled at the windshield. Cara's room? Aw, hell.

"Anyway, I was probably a random target. They wanted my car or maybe my purse," Liv insisted. She didn't sound convinced.

"I contacted Nate. He'll organize protection starting tomorrow. Until we know for sure, we have to assume you were their target." He glanced at her, his jaw clenched. "Still are their target."

She scratched at a tiny sliver of glass embedded in her wool skirt. Her face looked drawn, pale in the dim light. She pulled shaky fingers through the knots in her hair and drew bare feet underneath her.

His gut kinked like he'd been sucker punched. He'd failed her and needed to make it right. "Livy, I'm sorry. I'm sorry I didn't tell you the truth about the sting set-up."

Searching his face, she remained silent.

"All I want now is to keep you safe."

"Trust is important."

"You're right."

At least she was listening. He rubbed a sweaty palm against his thigh. Might as well try. He took her hand, and her fingers curved and clung to his, heating his blood.

She squeezed tighter.

His pulse raced. Mike glanced at her face and saw her eyes glimmer. "Why didn't you talk to me, Livy? Try to work it out? When I saw the divorce papers I felt abandoned."

She dropped her gaze, but when he reached for her, she scooted over next to him and sighed. "Will you agree to counseling? We need to face our problems, not pretend they don't exist. We need help to really talk them through."

He hesitated for a long moment. The very thought of exposing his weaknesses to a stranger made him want to puke.

Chapter Six

Santa Cruz Mountains, Tuesday, 11:00 p.m.

"And they lived happily ever after." With a brief frown, Liv snapped the storybook closed. Too bad her own Prince Charming had rusty armor.

She glanced down. Cara's golden eyelashes brushed against her sleep-flushed cheeks. Zoë the cat curled up on the pink gingham quilt. She leaned over and kissed her baby, taking a mental snapshot, but her hands shook as she tucked in the frilly covers and turned off the princess lamp.

Too close. Much too close. She shivered and went cold inside. Thank God her daughter hadn't been in the car. What would those lowlife thugs have done if they'd disabled her car, and she couldn't escape? *No. Don't think that way. Get a grip.*

Sucking in a deep breath, she gritted her teeth until her jaw ached. But true crime horrors slithered through her imagination, triggering a rolling dizziness like her first Ferris wheel ride.

She tiptoed into the hall and closed the door, leaning against the wall until the vertigo passed. Then she headed toward the living room.

Mike knelt before the brick hearth, stoking the fire with a poker. Sparks whirled above the crackling flames like fireflies.

The pungent spice of burning evergreens drew her, promising warmth. Struggling for a believable smile, she banded her hands around her upper arms to control the shakes.

He smiled over his shoulder, stood, and walked toward her. "Cara out for the count?"

"She never makes it to the end of the st-story."

His expression hardened. Frown lines formed on the sides of his mouth and between his brows. He touched the bandage on her cheek and folded her into his arms. "You're trembling."

Her stomach lurched again. "I can't stop seeing Cara's booster seat covered in glass. And that horrible tire iron. What if—"

Steel glinted in his eyes. "No more what ifs. You did the right thing."

"But—"

"What have I always told you to do if you're attacked?"

"Run. Then get help," she repeated what she'd heard a thousand times.

Mike nodded at her. His lips quirked upward again.

She squeezed her eyes shut for a second. "There's not much left of the Tesla."

"Doesn't matter. A car can be replaced. You can't." He reached for a pair of tumblers on the mantelpiece.

She gave him a questioning look. "Scotch?"

"Medicine. You're still in shock."

The expensive single malt stung her mouth and throat, but warmed her from the inside out. She wiped the corners of her eyes and chuckled. "Wow! Powerful."

He tossed back a mouthful. "You'll have a guard round the clock until we catch these guys."

"I'll hate it, but okay." She took another sip. The warmth spread from her belly to her frosty limbs. She turned the crystal in her hand and stared into the warm glow of the treacherous amber liquor. Scotch always meant sex, had always been one of their signals to each other, like perfume at bedtime or shaving after dinner.

Remembering other nights in front of this fireplace, she bit her lip and replaced her glass on the tray. "Thanks for the drink. I have to work tomorrow so I better get some sleep." She dodged his outstretched hands and turned toward Cara's bedroom.

Mike followed, caught her in the hall, and turned her toward him.

Her heart kicked into a sprint, but she kept her gaze focused on his chin.

He drew one hand across her cheek and through her hair, curling the other around her waist. "Livy. You and Cara. You're more important to me than anything, anyone. Do you believe me?" he demanded. His rumbling tone stirred her to the depths of her soul.

She was quiet for a couple of beats, and then exhaled noisily. "Yes." Liv stared at her bare feet. She should think about anything but the lingering flavor of peat. She'd be lost if she looked at him.

His thumb gently stroked her chin and raised her gaze to meet his. "I love you, Liv."

Damn. Lost. Lost in his bottomless blue eyes.

His mouth whispered over hers, and the tip of his tongue swiped her lips. Liquid heat shot through her.

She should push him away, should stay focused on

that damned purple thong.

But his next kiss was hotter, more demanding.

She opened her lips to him, and electric current sizzled over her skin. Moaning, she snaked her arms around his neck and pressed closer.

"Liv," he growled, mouth fierce and hungry on hers as he caressed her breasts. Her nipples pebbled under his touch, and ferocious pleasure blazed through her.

He squeezed her hard against him, smiling into her face. Her heart, already racing, skittered at his intense expression.

Using his body, he parted her legs and eased her back against the wall. He pulled her sweater over her head and tongued her nipple through the lace of her bra, used his teeth to tease it gently into a stiff, aching peak.

When he reached down and released her bra clasp, she threaded her fingers through his hair and held his head closer. He suckled hard and pulled her nipple deep into his tight, wet mouth.

She gasped. Her belly clenched in delicious anticipation, and her core dampened and pulsed.

He looked up and met her gaze. His pupils were large and dark, with scorching depths she could drown in. "You're so soft, so full, so beautiful, Livy," he murmured, rolling her peaked nipples between his fingers.

"Touch me."

With his gaze never leaving hers, he maneuvered his hand, lifting the hem of her skirt and bunching it at her waist. Then he cupped her moist, needy center.

"Yes," she hissed and arched against the pressure. With her eyes wide open, she slid one hand lower and measured his erection through his jeans. A quick thrill raced through her. She scraped her fingernails along the rough denim shielding his length.

His lids drooped for a second, and his hand stilled, pressed against her.

"That's good. But it's been too long. You first." Slipping his fingers beneath the fragile silk of her panties, Mike circled her sensitive nub with the broad tip of his thumb.

Her heart thundered in her ears. She whimpered, rubbing hard against him.

He flicked his thumb, and her body exploded with rhythmic pulses. She bowed, instinctively trying to draw him inside, but he covered her lips with his and held her close until the throbs quieted.

Her breath came in shallow pants. The release wasn't enough, and she ached for him. Liv gazed up with her lips parted, hoping he'd understand her desperation. Hoping he'd understand the hot emptiness inside her demanding to be filled.

"I need the words, Livy. I need to know you want me."

She remained mute, blinking, unable to voice how her naked bottom felt vulnerable and exposed against the wall, or how the cool air gusting over her wet nipples made them pebble harder, ravenous for his warm mouth and rough tongue again.

He pressed a hard kiss against her lips. "Livy, if you want me, unzip me."

That she could manage. She undid his jeans and his erection jutted heavily into her hand. Steel within hot silk. She bent over and licked the drop of moisture glistening on the tip.

He gave a deep groan of pleasure and lifted her off her feet.

Wrapping her legs around his waist, she pressed against him. Even moist and swollen from her orgasm, she was too tight for him to enter easily, but the head of him strained at her, warm and full.

He supported her with his big, strong hands as if she were weightless and wedged her against the wall.

He slowly ran one hand over her breast and belly, touched her jutting hipbone, stroked her thigh. "You're my fantasy, Livy."

A hot, urgent ache pulsed low in her body. She kissed the cleft in his chin, drawing her tongue in a tiny circle.

He shuddered and thrust inside.

Nothing but desire existed. She linked her fingers behind his neck and drew him closer.

"I've never loved anyone else. Not since the day I met you." He kissed her again and again, hungry searing kisses, mouth closing fast over hers.

Her nails dug into his shoulders as he penetrated deeper, inch by inch. She gasped for breath, for sanity.

She cinched her legs around his hips. Her mouth opened wide, suckling his neck. She inhaled his hot male scent and tasted him. Mike. Blood rioted in her veins.

He braced and drove into her again, pounding her against the wall. Her world shattered in multicolored, ecstatic shards, and he swallowed her scream.

****

11:55 p.m.

In the twin bed across from her sleeping daughter, Liv couldn't close her eyes. Her thoroughly pleasured body tingled with satisfaction. After facing danger, even death, she'd needed to reaffirm life in the most basic way. Yes. Sex tonight was the result of a mega-dose of adrenaline. Mike was there and familiar and willing.

Her breath broke in shudders. But why had she let her traitorous body take over? She'd come apart for him, and if she hadn't remembered Cara they'd have spent the night practicing every position in the Kama Sutra.

Twice.

Mike had said he loved only her. She snorted, punching her pillow in frustration. What the hell did that mean, when he'd cheated?

She remembered the obscene package of ribbed condoms she'd found in his bag. Turning in the narrow bed, she curled into a ball.

No, she wouldn't forget. How could she ever forgive his lying, cheating ass? She couldn't live with Mike, couldn't trust him with her heart or her daughter or her life.

Chapter Seven

Kings Mountain, Tuesday, April 13, 11:55 p.m.

The massive wrought-iron gate clanged shut. Morrison slammed his car door and limped up the long, gravel path. A sharp chill knifed through to his bones.

Tall pines hid the ten-foot rock wall fencing the property. Security lights blinked on as he approached, casting long, watery shadows, but thick, swirling fog hid the path ahead.

Sid had found the perfect place to stash a hostage. Morrison rubbed his hands together, imagining the thrill he'd have squeezing info from the bitch.

A Rottweiler surged toward him, and his pulse hammered. He froze, then yelled, "Hey, call off your stupid dog."

Sid opened the front door, flipped on the porch lights, and shouted a command. The dog dropped to the ground, but growled deep in its belly, white teeth visible in its snarl.

Morrison stood his ground while Sid locked the brute into the kennel with three others. "You let that sucker run loose?"

Sid snickered. "Discourages visitors."

"Run through the commands with me later." Morrison followed him onto the porch steps, wheezing from the trudge up the hill, but anticipation gave him an edge. "Where is she?"

"Well…"

Anger chewed his insides, but Morrison closed his eyes and clamped down on his temper so he didn't grab the asshole by the throat. "What happened?"

"I, uh, had to use a different crew."

"And they botched the job." His hands gripped the railing, but he kept his voice low and level while Sid filled in the blanks. "What kind of screw-ups did you hire?"

Sid ducked his chin and blabbered, "I don't have the same quality of contacts I do on the East Coast. They came highly recommended, but…"

Glaring, he hissed a breath, and the weasel closed his whining trap. Smart. "You had her followed for days. If three guys wasn't enough, you shoulda been on the job yourself."

"I'm an attorney." Sid crossed his arms and set his pathetic jaw. "I don't do grunt work."

"Enough," Morrison yelled, unleashing the edge of his temper. He got in Sid's face with one hand curled around the little creep's neck. "Don't. Make. Me. Hurt. You." He squeezed, and the asshole turned an ugly red. "Grunt work or not, you do it right, you stupid fuck."

Morrison released the punk with a shove, and he stumbled backwards, mouth gaping, fighting for breath. "You've blown everything wide open. The feds will be crawling all over her, and the guys you hired could squeal."

"No way. Cops won't find them," Sid croaked.

"Better hope they don't, asshole." He poked a finger at Sid's chest. "Cause you'd go down alone."

Sid flattened against the kitchen door and stumbled

inside.

He gritted his teeth and followed Sid into the house. Gut roiling, jaw clenched, Morrison remembered eight years back. Remembered returning to the East Coast in disgrace. Remembered the disaster that fucking cop had caused.

"You stupid creep." Louie Souza cuffed him across the face. "You really screwed up this time. That jailhouse hit cost me a bundle."

His cheek stung, and he reached up to staunch the flow of blood. "But Uncle Louie, how was I supposed to know those pricks followed me? I had 'em suckered into believing I was their stoolie."

Louie Souza radiated rage, his eyes glittering, his face twisted. "Idiot! You shot a cop. They don't forget. Ever. Wanna explain why I shouldn't cut my losses and snuff you now?"

He sat silent and cowed before his uncle. Humiliation ground through him, turned his bones to slush, and painted his spine yellow.

"Good thing you brought the money. Otherwise you'da ended up dumped in the river in an old Coke machine. Now get out of my sight, you sack of shit."

Yeah, he deserved justice, Morrison thought. That meant he still needed this weasel. "I don't get why you ordered the carjacking. You have the diagrams. Aren't they enough?"

"I was listening to the bug in her office. The drone's not all of it. There's some sensor gadget we gotta get too. These buyers ain't gonna walk away with half a load and leave your head attached."

Sid's Adam's apple bobbled.

"And I want that bastard, Gordon, in a world of

hurt." He smacked his fist against the rough wall of the cabin. The pain cleared the spots fogging his sight.

"I could arrange another hit on Frau Gordon."

"No. I got a plan, and this time you're gonna run the job yourself, jerk wad." His lips twitched. "We'll make Gordon bleed."

****

Santa Cruz Mountains, Wednesday, April 14, 8:10 a.m.

Liv glanced at the hearthrug and hissed. Heat flared across her cheeks. She grabbed the scrap of her bright pink thong and stuffed it in her pocket.

Peeking around the corner into the kitchen, she frowned at the early morning light slanting through the cabin's soaring windows. The smell of coffee almost drove her wild, but she was an hour late for work and didn't want to face Mike. She chewed on her fingernail. He hadn't noticed her yet. Could she sneak through the garage?

Damn. No car.

Maybe the best thing to do was pretend nothing had happened last night. Taking a deep breath to cool her pulse, she waltzed into the room, hoping her blush didn't give her away. She wouldn't really die of embarrassment. Only felt like it. "You shut off my alarm. What a dirty trick."

Mike turned and handed her a travel mug with black coffee brewed strong, exactly the way she liked it. Although the corners of his lips twitched, he remained silent.

So far, so good, but she didn't dare meet his gaze. "Don't try to look innocent. I know you did it. I was due in a meeting ten minutes ago." She blew on the cup, sipped, and forged on in her breeziest tone, "The commute takes forever when I leave this late."

With his palms on the counter, he eased his long legs into a relaxed stance and gave her a knowing, self-satisfied grin.

Warmth flared on her neck and cheeks. She closed her eyes and tucked her hair behind her ears. Stay strong. Remember what he did. Remember the constant hell of living together, not what happened last night on the floor by the fireplace.

"You needed the rest," he drawled. His tone ignited a rush of heat that raced straight to her soft spot. "You should take the day off, but I bet I'd have to handcuff you to the bed."

Temptation licked at her core. She glanced at him. The humor in his blue eyes tickled her, but she hid her smile and hitched her purse onto her shoulder. "Fat chance, cowboy. You know you'd die a slow death when you finally let me go."

"Might be worth it." He plunked a bowl of fresh strawberries in front of her, his eyes twinkling. "Five minutes to take care of yourself. I already called G-Tech and warned Alyssa you'd be late."

Struggling to maintain more than a micron of anger, Liv breathed a brief sigh of surrender. She sat on a stool and let her purse drop onto the counter.

Mike looked too good this morning, moving around the kitchen with sexy, loose-limbed confidence. His worn jeans were snug in all the right places, and the navy polo made his eyes look like bottomless mountain lakes.

She popped a berry into her mouth, savoring the ripe, tart flavor. "Luscious. I guess an energy surge couldn't hurt."

He laid a stack of waffles on the breakfast bar and refilled her cup. The muscles in his arms bunched under tanned skin dusted with golden hair. "I'll keep Cara this morning, let her sleep in. It's an in-service day at school, and we have shopping to do. I can drop her at day care when I go in to the station."

She started to interrupt, but he raised his hand. "I got it covered, Livy. We'll stop by G-Tech at lunch."

Mischief glinted in his eyes, and her brows shot up. "What are you planning?"

"Trust me."

"Right."

"Look, if I'm off base, you have veto power."

She shrugged and concentrated on buttering the crisp waffle.

He nodded, silently watching her annihilate the meal.

"Your ride will be here in five."

"Long as I'm not cuffed and shoved into the back seat."

He snorted at her attempted joke.

Her pulse hammering in her ears, she stared at the floor. Coward. Just say it. She took in a long, steadying breath and glanced at him from under her lashes. "Mike, about last night."

The tiny lines at the corners of his eyes creased. "Last night was incredible, Livy. But I wanted to wake up with you in my arms."

She blushed so hard the roots of her hair felt singed. "But we haven't solved anything yet. We have to protect Cara, so she doesn't get her hopes up."

Barefoot, he padded around the island, and she gripped the granite for support.

"You don't want this divorce any more than I do." He leaned over and kissed her, smoothing her hair.

Her throat blocked. "Yes I do, Mike. Living together drove me crazy."

"If you want counseling, I'm willing. Anything to be a family again," he whispered, his lips so close she inhaled his breath.

She shivered and withdrew, wrapping both hands around the red metal mug. Silence hung in the air while her heart did a two-step. It was a huge concession for him, one she'd honestly never thought he'd make. She had to keep her word.

"Okay. I'll find a counselor."

"Sounds like your ride's here." Without further comment, he escorted her outside and down the steps to a waiting black and white. His warm hand at the back of her waist made her feel safe and cherished.

She turned to give him a brief smile.

He winked and opened the passenger door. "Morning, Linden."

Liv peered at one of her favorite cops. "Hi, Kathy. I'm glad you're driving me."

The petite blonde grinned, her blue eyes shining with fun. She looked more like a perky cheerleader than a seasoned police officer. "Are you kidding? I volunteered. We'll have a blast."

"Fine, but keep her safe." Mike closed the squad car door and stepped back.

Liv drew a finger along the edge of the window, watching him while the car rolled down the driveway. Maybe he was redeemable after all, but he had a long way to go to prove it to her.

****

Sereno, Friday, April 16, 6:15 p.m.

"Trust you?" Liv glared at Mike across a low table in the counseling office. "After Samantha's sultry voicemail about playing patty-cake undercover? That woman could make a bundle giving phone sex." She hitched in a breath and worked hard to restrain the fury driving her pulse.

Their therapist, Dr. Bridget Holden, sat impassively, taking notes from a green leather wingback chair. She studied Liv through thick glasses, her fluffy gray hair curling softly around her face.

Liv flashed him a pissed-off glare.

Mike met her gaze briefly and then glanced away, his hands clenched on his knees. "I didn't tell you about going undercover with Sam because I figured you'd be upset."

"And then you lied again after I found her underwear. Didn't you, slick?" She could see him struggle, but he had to admit what he'd done, or she'd never trust anything he promised.

In the corner, a small copper fountain gurgled in a nest of twisted bamboo. She drew her lower lip between her teeth, focusing on the water splashing.

"There are reasons I don't tell you everything, Liv. Things about my job I don't ever want to say out loud." He shook his head. "I didn't tell you about the little girl Sam and I couldn't save, and I won't now. You don't want that picture stuck in your brain."

Glancing down at her lap, Liv tried to tamp down her overactive imagination.

"How many times do I have to tell you? I lied about being undercover with Sam, but I didn't cheat."

She swallowed the lump of hurt in her throat. It

collected frost on the way down, hitting her stomach like a rain of party ice. "You admit you lied. Admit you slept in the same room with that badge-carrying cockroach, but expect me to believe you didn't screw her? Mr. Twice-a-night went a month without sex?"

Mike frowned, his jaw locked, the cords in his neck bulging like steel cables. "It's not the same. Sam isn't you."

Talons of pain ripped through her chest, squeezed her heart to the size of a walnut. He could look her straight in the eye and tell her the biggest whopper in history. She'd been a fool to even try this. "Give me a break. That woman stood in my living room and told me every titillating detail."

Mike looked ready to explode, but dropped his gaze. He intently picked a speck of lint off his trousers and flung it away. "She lied. Sam did a number on you, and you fell for it."

"Aw. Your little fuck-buddy lied too?" Liv drew out the last word. Face hot with anger, nerves bruised and battered, she widened her eyes, hand covering her open mouth. "Wait. I think I see a pattern."

He rose and faced her squarely, shoulders back, chin level and jutting out to battle the world. "Why rehash this anyway? I'm not lying now, but even if I had screwed around, it'd be old news. Nothing I can change." He held his hands wide. "After we made love the other night, I hoped you'd finally listen."

Confronted by his vulnerability, she could only blink.

"I want to fix what's wrong between us so I can come home where I belong."

Bridget Holden tapped her pencil on her notepad.

"When a couple confronts infidelity—"

Mike growled deep in his chest and flashed the therapist a lethal glare.

Dr. Holden met his gaze."—suspected infidelity, the roots of the problem often lie elsewhere. Let's table this discussion while you help me understand your marriage and families."

He thumped back into his chair and swiped his hand across his face.

Turning toward Liv, the doctor asked, "How did you handle former significant others during your courtship?"

Liv met Mike's swift glance. Her mouth opened, but she couldn't think how to explain, so she snapped it shut again.

"Did you date for long?" Dr. Holden focused on each of them in turn, her expression growing puzzled. "How long did you know each other before you married?"

Her cheekbones warmed. Liv shifted in her seat, smoothing her hands down her thighs. "Three months."

He cleared his throat. "Two months, and Liv was working in South America for most of it. She met Sam a week before our wedding."

"So you didn't have much chance to explore your differences before marriage." The counselor tapped her pencil and waited.

Liv twined her ankles together and tucked them beneath the chair. "No. Actually, Father Walsh waived counseling because I was expecting Cara. We'd met at our friends' wedding and we, um, we…" Her words trailed off into a whisper.

Mike eased a finger under his collar. "We couldn't

keep our hands off each other. We ditched the reception."

Waves of heat seared her neck and engulfed her face. She flashed him a dirty look.

"I understand." Bridget Holden eased back in her chair. "How would you describe the family dynamics you grew up with? Mike?"

"Basic." He chuckled. "Picture five guys on a working ranch. My mother took off when I was ten. My youngest brother was in kindergarten. We've only heard from her a half dozen times."

"That forced you to mature quickly," Dr. Holden said.

"Yeah. I—"

Liv interrupted, "What your mother did was wrong, but I couldn't live on that bleak, lonely ranch with your crabby father—"

"Pop stuck it out when she left. We had food on the table and clothes on our backs. He's an angry old man, but I owe him."

Her foot tapped a cadence on the floor, and her hands curled into fists. She'd heard it all before, but Mike never listened to her side. "Your father targets me with his red neck attitude. I grew up with Papa's Latin macho garbage. I'm sick of mule-headed males who won't admit their mistakes."

His blue eyes frosted. "You're the smartest person I know, but you don't get it, do you?"

"I don't get it? Then explain it to me, Mike." She let sarcasm drip from every word.

He drew himself to his full height and glared at her. Raging hurt and icy control played tag across his face. "Why do you think I'm here, letting you rip my heart out in front of a stranger?"

She stared at him. He really did hate this.

"I'm here because I don't want to turn into my father. Alone. Pissed off at the world. But unless we talk about things we can change, I won't come back."

Chapter Eight

San Jose, Monday, April 19, 11:50 a.m.

Dan Bausch was up to his *cojones* in a bubbling bath of bureaucratic bullshit. He couldn't let the threat of a terrorist attack materialize. Somehow G-Tech's sensors had to be in place before May first.

He sat at his desk, staring at the case file. He had a report due yesterday, but had zero solid leads, and no inspiration.

He grimaced. The special agent in charge was on his ass, big time, wanting something, anything, sent upstairs. Couldn't blame the SAC since Washington had *his* balls in a vise.

His phone buzzed across his desk. He rolled his eyes and groaned. Damn it! Not another interruption. He snatched the phone. "FBI." Pulling the growl out, he added, "Special Agent Bausch."

"Gotta call you might want to take," Dan recognized the southern drawl of the main phone operator.

"Connect me."

The phone was silent, then a male voice said, "I got some information." The caller's deep voice sounded raspy and nervous over background traffic. Heavy New Jersey accent.

"What info?"

"My boss is meeting with terrorists. Stuff about drones."

Dan's pulse rate notched higher. Drones? He ran his hand through his short, wavy hair. "Who am I talking to, sir?"

"Shit! Never mind. This was a stupid idea."

"Okay, okay. Why don't you tell me about the terrorists and let me decide?" His mouth went dry, but his palms started to sweat. Had they finally gotten a break?

"Look, I know you're recording this. I want to meet somewhere. I ain't no freak. This is for real."

Dan tapped his finger on the blotter. Last thing he wanted was to spook the guy. "You don't sound like a kook. Bet you don't wear an aluminum foil hat to keep aliens from reading your brainwaves."

A snort traveled through the phone. "Thanks a heap, jerk-off."

He stretched his legs out, crossed his ankles, and asked, "Where do you want to meet?"

"Burger Joint. Downtown on Santa Elena and Tenth. Make it noon in the kiddy lot."

His eyebrows shot up. "That's less than ten minutes."

"No time to set a trap."

Maybe this dude wasn't a total idiot. "How about 12:30? Look for a yellow tie."

"Show up alone or forget it."

****

12:25 p.m.

Dan surveyed the empty play lot and cleared his throat. "Can you hear me?"

"Loud and clear," the voice in his ear responded.

"An unmarked white van parked a block away. Driver could be your contact. Six-three, two-fifty, Raiders T-shirt."

"Roger." Tucking his mirrored, wrap-around shades into his pocket, Dan scanned the restaurant and flipped his tie outside his jacket. He bought an iced tea, loaded it with lemon, and strolled out to wait on a child-sized bench.

A good old boy with a military crew cut and a Kiddy Meal pushed through the door. Dan snickered silently, watching him clomp past the play structure before settling on the bench.

While he sucked on the iced tea, Dan memorized the guy's broad facial features and Marine Corps tattoo.

"You Bausch?" the man asked. His gaze twitched around the space.

"Kind of public if you're worried about someone recognizing you."

"My boss don't eat this shit." The informant glared and dumped the box in the trash. "Look, I don't want no big deal. If I was to give you a name, what could you do?"

"Check databases. Maybe put a tail on him. I'd need more to go deeper."

The jarhead screwed up one corner of his mouth. "Guess I wasted my time."

Dan shrugged long and slow and swirled the ice in his cup. "Give me his name and address, maybe his business. I'll poke around. Depending on what I find, we could meet again in a few days."

Silent deliberation clouded the stoolie's eyes. "Maybe."

"I don't need your name. We can arrange a

meeting now or you can call me when you're ready."

"That did the trick, now reel him in," the voice in Dan's ear said. He handed the informant a card. "My direct number, no operator."

"He's Morrison, Thomas Morrison. Owns Atlantic Partners," the big guy blurted.

Dan's heart raced, but he focused on his hands. "You work for him?"

"Yeah. Morrison met with some foreign dude. I overheard 'em when I came in early from a delivery." The guy leaned closer. "They talked about getting specs for a drone. Then the foreigner went off about some stupid bug he wanted. It don't smell right, you know?"

Prickles rolled along his arms. "Bug?"

"Yeah. Go figure." The jarhead shrugged.

"Holy shit. Do you think he means Dragonfly?" the voice screeched, battering his eardrums. "There's the connection."

Dan inclined his head. "Why tell me?"

"What the hell you mean, why? I'm an American. I got no truck with fucking terrorists." The informant shoved a porky finger in Dan's face. "Look. I ain't no angel. I don't talk about nothing but the foreigner."

Jaw rigid, Dan glared at the finger two inches from his nose. "Fine by me."

The guy backed off and squirmed on the narrow bench, eyes shifting from side to side in his ruddy face. "In fact, I get immunity or this don't go no further."

Dan squeaked his straw around in his paper cup. Did the snitch have trouble with the law? Made sense to check.

Worried his source would wriggle off the hook, he leaned back to telegraph reassuring calm. "The FBI isn't interested in small time stuff. You know the foreigner's name?"

"Morrison didn't say, not when I was around." The goober pulled a red bandana from his pocket and mopped sweat from his brow.

"Can you find out? Get a photo?"

"Maybe."

Two screeching rug rats raced through the door, heading for the slide.

The guy jumped in his seat. "Time to split."

"Look. Call me in a couple days. I'll nose around in the meantime." Dan walked away, leaving the snitch to depart on his own terms. He'd return later and fish the Kiddy Meal from the trash. Nice set of prints.

****

Sereno, 12:45 p.m.

Mike leaned forward, every muscle tense. "You say you don't need me. You want the divorce. So go to your damn shindig alone."

Dr. Holden watched from her wingback chair, silent for the moment.

"You're still my husband." Liv sat on the low-backed leather sofa with her spine ramrod straight. "We aced the military trials, and the investors want to celebrate. Why can't you just come schmooze with me?"

His hands fisted on his thighs. Husband? Since when? Her words hit a raw spot like Tabasco sauce on a canker sore. "Forget it. Those patronizing snobs all sneer at your blue-collar boy toy. A bunch of trust fund babies who've never held an honest job."

"Yeah, a few of them can be arrogant jerks, but nobody laughs."

"Bullshit. Hang a tux on me and I turn into the invisible man." He snapped his fingers.

"I know you don't enjoy formal dinners—"

"No, I hate being dolled up in a gorilla suit with a tie choking me and making nice."

"But there's so much at stake, Mike. My company is on the line, or I wouldn't ask. This is Cara's future too." She stared at the floor. "Having you with me is important."

Seeing her vulnerable made him soften his tone. Marriage was about give and take, right? "That's the only reason I'd ever go, Livy." He touched her knee. Reaching each other had always been simple before, his lips on the back of her neck. Her fingertip on his chin. He missed that intimacy.

She blinked, a slow smile blooming across her face. "Please, come with me?"

Mike stared at her mouth and took a deep breath before meeting her gaze. "Fair's fair, I guess. You came to the SWAT competition."

"I enjoyed it. You and your guys were fantastic. I sure wish I'd had an AK-47 when those thugs attacked my car. I'd have blasted those damn spotlights."

"Give a woman a big gun and watch where her fantasies go." His mind jumped back to the cabin hearthrug. He stared at her smile again, remembering what her lush lips and tongue could do.

Dr. Holden shifted in her chair. "Integrating your individual career demands has been challenging."

"Sometimes it's a huge problem." Liv touched one side of her face. "Mike, can we talk about your job?"

He frowned. Here we go again. "Liv, my job came with the package." He pointed to the badge on his uniform.

She grimaced, but kept her mouth shut.

"I was a cop when you married me, but you weren't a CEO. We got along fine until you started at Nova Stream."

"But I was still in school. Why do you think I got my MBA? To stay home with Cara?"

"Woulda been fine with me. I never needed six thousand square feet on two acres. I wanted a bungalow full of kids."

"I love Cara, but I'd be absolutely stark raving nuts without my job."

"Figured that out a long time ago. Doesn't mean I liked it."

"Well I hated the weeks without you. I never knew where you were or if you were still alive. I hated having you undercover."

Mike rose, stretched his legs, and faced the window. The tense set of his shoulders probably telegraphed his unhappiness at being attacked. Again. "But undercover work was…" How could he explain the high from riding the edge? The satisfaction? "I loved putting one over on crooks and knowing what I did made a difference."

"I understand. It's the same for me. My people depend on me. Our country is depending on me. But you're still playing cops and robbers."

His ears burned, and he blew a big raspberry. "Some people swear I'm a hero. Like the parents who got their kids back when Sam and I busted that kidnapping ring."

She glanced down, biting her lip.

"You wanted me home more, so I trained for

liaison and SWAT. Gave up undercover. It's done. Why bring it up now?"

"Because I used to lie awake, wondering if you were alive. Now I'd imagine you and Samantha—" Liv broke off, her hands rigid, and her fingers splayed.

His pulse drummed in his ears, and he felt like the air had been sucked from the room. "Trust me. Sam's not part of the equation."

"Why would I ever trust your word about that bitch?"

He thumped the wall with his fist, feeling like he was staked out, naked and covered with honey, in a field of fire ants. Female fire ants. "I'm fed up with this...this torment."

"Mike, you two are trying to find compromises you can both live with. It can be difficult." Dr. Holden's voice remained calm.

Condescending.

Incendiary.

His nostrils flared. "Thanks for reminding me. You know, I feel like I'm doing everything Liv wants, but never scoring any points."

Dr. Holden's gaze didn't waver. "I understand you're uncomfortable."

He threw up his hands and muttered dismissively, "Both of you are happy talking about feelings and relationships and stuff that's over and done. Waste of time. If something's broken, we should fix it, not sit around yakking until my *cojones* fall off."

Dr. Holden covered a smile with her hand. Liv sniggered.

Mike shot the therapist a defiant glance before turning to Liv. "I'd give half the national debt if you'd spend an hour in my skin. Then you'd see what makes me tick." The pulse point at his temples twitched. He tipped his chin. "I'm a cop. The badge means more than just a job. Being a cop is who I am."

"You make it sound like I want to change you into someone you're not," Liv said in a low voice, chafing her wrists fitfully.

"No? Feels like it from here." His gaze honed in on her. "If you wanted a tame investment banker to play dress up with, you shouldn't have married a cop."

"I just wish—"

"Be careful what you wish for, babe. No straight-laced banker boy could keep up with you in bed. Assuming he'd even survive hearing what turns you on." He gave a low chuckle

Blushing crimson, she hissed through her teeth, "I don't want to talk about sex."

"Fair enough, Livy, but I'm doing what you want. I'm here today. I'm even going to your stupid party. It's time for me to get some of what I want too."

"Yeah? And what do you want?"

"Counseling's hard. Why can't we live together while we work on stuff? I..." He shifted in his seat, palms rubbing his thighs.

Liv's gaze moved to her glass, but a brief glimpse at her expression answered him before she opened her mouth. "I'm afraid we'd fall into old habits. Not all our needs can be met in bed."

"I agree, but it's sure a place to start."

She shook her head. "That's always been your answer. Whenever we have a problem, you think sex is the solution." Grinning, she waved her hand in the air and chanted, "Abracadabra, open sesame. A roll in the hay to the rescue."

He chuckled, unable to resist temptation. "Only one? How about starting with three or four—this afternoon?"

Liv buried her bright red face in her hands. "Mike!"

He tilted her chin up until she met his gaze. "Seriously, Livy, it's like we're two halves of the same soul. When we reconnect, the good stuff spills way past our bedroom. Everything is better. I want that again."

Liv peeked at him, her expression unreadable, and flipped her hair over her shoulder.

His throat seized. He remembered the way he used to lift the thick dark fall and kiss her nape while she fixed dinner. He longed to feel her shiver and press back against him again.

Her brow puckered, and she hesitated. "But great sex doesn't solve our problems."

His tongue swiped his dry lower lip. "Okay. Say we stick with counseling. What more do I have to do?"

She looked away, staring at that ridiculous little fountain. The freaking water gurgled relentlessly, wearing at his nerves.

Dr. Holden tapped a pencil on her notebook. "Liv, Mike asked you a question. What would it take for you to be comfortable living together while you continue counseling?"

"I'd need to be sure I can trust him." Liv fixed him with her bittersweet chocolate gaze, looking serious and vulnerable. "Before we even start dating I need to know what happened with Samantha. Tell me the truth."

"I have." He heaved a long, weighty exhale. "Fine. One more time, but don't ever ask me again."

She nodded.

He touched her icy hand and felt her pulse race. "I've been faithful to you since the day we met. I haven't had sex, any kind of sex, with Sam or with anyone but you."

"All the things she said—"

"Pure manure." He brushed his knuckles across his mouth. Spit it out Gordon. Go for it, balls out, full tilt. "Didn't tell you this before, but one weekend about a month after I got to Quantico, I discovered the hard way your instincts about Sam were on target."

"What do you mean?"

"Sam orchestrated that undercover assignment to rope me in." He cranked his arms to stretch his shoulder blades. "She showed up in my room one night, naked and ready to rumble. Had the crazy idea I'd dump you 'cause she'd always been my soul mate."

Chapter Nine

Sereno, Monday, April 19, 6:30 p.m.

Liv flattened against the wall of her front entryway. Her pulse beat wildly in her throat, but her heart had been galloping even before she heard Mike's truck. Through the sidelight framing the door, she could see him amble along the brick driveway toward the house carrying a grocery bag.

She massaged the tight muscles in her neck. Had she made the right choice this afternoon? He'd been willing to stick with counseling even though he hated it, and that had earned him big points. Although she didn't believe his story completely, she'd caved and agreed they could date openly.

Then he'd caught her off guard and offered to bring over dinner tonight so he could see Cara. She'd figured it'd be a quick and simple, low-pressure first date. Plus she had to admit she'd wanted less temptation than if they were out alone at an elegant restaurant.

She stared at the floor. Chalk up another huge strategic screw-up. Now that she'd thought it through, a family dinner at home was far more intimate, far more dangerous than any meal in public.

Too late. She had to keep her word. Had to smile and let him inside. She blew out a quick breath. Had to suck it up while keeping a steel fist around her feelings and her libido.

Mike pushed the buzzer.

She took a step forward just as Cara wiggled up behind her. "Mommy, Daddy's here! Let him in!"

Liv clicked the deadbolt, but her clammy hands trembled, making it tough to turn the knob. When she unlocked the door, Cara bounded past her, crying, "Daddy!"

He set down the groceries and gathered their daughter into his arms, grinning like a maniac. "How's my baby girl?" he asked. His voice sounded choked up.

"I missed you." Cara kissed his cheek and hugged him fiercely, burrowing her face into the curve of his neck.

He smoothed a hand over their daughter's head and tweaked her chin with one finger. "I saw you this morning. You helped me pick out Mommy's new car."

"Yeah. I 'membered that Mommy likes red. But you know what I mean, Daddy."

A scatter of emotions played across his face. "Yeah, I missed my girls too."

Liv swallowed with difficulty and watched him kiss Cara's forehead.

"I'm so happy you're home. Come see my new computer." Cara squirmed out of his arms and bolted toward her room shouting, "Come on, Daddy."

"Don't go anywhere, Livy. I'll be right back."

She smiled and picked up the groceries. Mike's big black truck clicked with heat under the olive tree. He'd had the sensitivity to park in the driveway instead of in the garage next to the shiny new monster SUV he'd bought her today.

She relocked the door and watched Mike and Cara

disappear down the hall, hand in hand. Glancing around the vaulted living room, she shivered. She'd avoided the space since the day Sam had taunted her here.

Samantha Blackthorn sneered through Liv's memory: blonde where Liv was a brunette, a head taller and lean, a cross between a distance runner and a runway model.

Sam drew one perfect nail down her flawless, pale peach cheek to her pouty lips and cooed, "I have to say, you've trained Mike well. He's got more tricks under his zipper now than when we were together before."

Liv had blinked, frowning open-mouthed at the blonde.

"Oh my God, that man has talent. And stamina. What a lover. After celebrating last night—" Sam broke off with a blissful moan accompanied by an ecstatic shimmy. "He was so hot, so hard, so insistent all night long. God, I could hardly walk this morning."

A cold numbness engulfed Liv, and her mind blanked. Sam's smirk and half-closed eyes ripped through her heart like no knife could.

"Mike feels a little guilty. He wanted to break the news himself. But I'm surprised he stuck with you this long. You know how he hates…" Sam oozed forward a few steps and snickered. "…soft, chunky women."

Pulsing with hurt and rage, Liv wrapped her arms around the bag of groceries, clutching it against her middle.

When Mike laid a hand on her shoulder, she jumped. He turned her toward him, scanning her expression, and his eyes blazed. "Forget Sam. She lied."

For a split second Liv let herself lean back against

his chest while she subdued the ghost of self-conscious doubt that shrieked in her head. She pressed her lips together and stepped away. Her vaulted living room glowed with evening light, no longer cold and empty. The floor to ceiling windows and natural rock filled her with warmth. Home.

He laid his arm across her shoulders. "I'm glad we're working out our problems, Livy. It's amazing what I've missed."

His heat spread through the silk of her red blouse. Her skin flushed. Tremors radiated out and raced up her spine. She looked down at the bulging canvas bag in her hands. "I need to put this stuff away."

"Sure. Let me take that." Mike released her, followed her into the kitchen, and started unpacking groceries. "You doing okay, Livy? Past week's been rough."

She managed a cheeky smile. "Work is still frantic with the production ramp-up, but at least the domestic agency is investigating a couple of possible nannies."

"Great. But I'll miss the excuse to pick up Cara." He pulled a pricey Napa cabernet from the bag. "We should celebrate. Want a glass of wine while I fix dinner?"

At her nod, he uncorked the bottle, poured, and handed her a glass. He raised his glass for a toast with a devilish glint in his eyes. Garnet red sparkled through crystal. "To second chances."

She kept her glass at waist height and fought off the frown. "We've made a start, but we have a long way to go."

"You were right about one thing. I hate it, but counseling has helped us talk."

"We still need to take this slow. I refuse to raise Cara's hopes until we figure out how we can live together and not want to kill each other twice a week."

"Okay, but until then, come out on the deck while I light the grill." He kissed her hand and drew her toward the patio door. "I found some prime New York steaks."

She arched one eyebrow. "Shopping? That's new. I figured you'd bring take-out."

"Sort of." He shrugged. "The market you like had some grilled vegetables and twice-baked potatoes. Just need to pop 'em in the oven."

She couldn't keep the grin from leaking out. "I'm impressed."

"Better get used to it."

Sipping her wine, she followed him onto the deck and watched him go through the familiar motions. Something scraped, flames rose, and the faint tang of propane wafted toward her.

Liv wandered to the edge of the patio. Deep blue flag irises swayed in the light breeze. Her pulse rate still tracked around one ten, but the tension in her shoulders uncoiled. She'd missed quiet evenings spent grilling on the patio.

Mike moved to her side, meeting her gaze with his smoky blue eyes. He entwined his fingers with hers and lowered his head for a brief kiss. The cabernet on his lips tasted rich and dark. Sinful. Overlaid with his own heady flavor. He took her glass and set it on the wrought iron table. Holding a hand behind her head, he kissed her again.

Liv opened her mouth to the rasp of his tongue. Lightning bolts ignited low in her body. Shit, that felt good. Too good. But she leaned into his kiss just for a minute.

He eased his hand into the vee of her blouse. Drawing one finger along her collarbone, he slid the silk sideways, and his lips left hers to trail along her cheek.

Tilting her head, she allowed him access to the arch of her neck. His lips traced the curve, not exactly nipping her sensitive flesh, but letting her know he had teeth. Electric quivers raced through her. She closed her eyes and hissed. He knew that spot drove her wild.

He slid his hand lower and smoothed her breast through her lacy bra.

The friction tore a low purr from her throat and arrowed straight to her core. Damn! She'd missed the feel of his big hands on her, but she couldn't let him touch her this casually.

She pushed him away. "Mike, we need to stop now. Cara will be back soon. We can't upset her."

He shifted her blouse up onto her shoulder, but grabbed her hand, his thumb idly caressing her fingers. "We're safe. I left her chatting with Avery. They can spend hours on the phone."

She shuddered. Her heart beat hard and fast, and her skin tingled where his fingers rubbed. Safe? She didn't feel safe; she felt like a teenager sneaking out to meet her boyfriend. She felt wicked and sexy and aroused.

She drew her nails up his arm. Goose bumps rose on his skin, matching hers.

His gaze, clear, intense, and intimate, never wavered. It sent a delicious sizzle through her body that jump-started the ache at her core. She slowly leaned toward him, her tongue moistening her lips.

The screen door scraped open. "Mama, I'm hungry."

Liv dropped back into the moment with a thud and pulled her hand out of his. Thank goodness for little girls. "Your father just started the grill. Grab some string cheese from the fridge."

The refrigerator slammed, and Cara's feet pounded back toward them. Nibbling a strip of white cheese, she shoved the sliding door open, stopped, and studied them closely. Then her face crumpled.

"What's wrong, sweetheart?" Mike sat and drew Cara onto his lap.

Her blue eyes, so like his, filled with tears. "I don't want to be divorced anymore. I want Daddy home all the time."

Liv's chest felt so tight, she couldn't draw a breath. Damn it! Exactly what she'd wanted to avoid.

"I hate being divorced. Please, please, Mommy, let him stay." The child hiccupped through her words.

Liv bent and cupped her daughter's chin. "Your Daddy and I like being together too, but marriage is more than happily ever after."

Mike caressed Cara's cheek. "Sometimes grown-ups need to talk, work out their problems. You hated it when we fought all the time."

Cara sniffed and nodded.

Liv took her hand. "We both love you, Cara. We always will."

****

10:15 p.m.

Liv's stomach danced a tango. She looked up at her reflection in the wide bathroom mirror. Her cheeks were flushed, her eyes were huge with dilated pupils.

She could see the stiff peaks of her nipples beneath her red blouse and bra, and there was a warm, moist emptiness between her thighs.

Her body knew what she needed. Sex.

Hot, hard, mindless sex.

Sex with Mike.

Her heart did a flip-flop, and her legs squeezed together. She closed her eyes and bit her lip. Yeah, just like at the cabin, her body wouldn't have any trouble making the choice, but her mind wasn't as comfortable with the tantalizing idea. This time it would mean something.

Sure they'd started working through their problems, but hadn't resolved that much. Her almost ex-husband still seemed like a stranger, one she wasn't sure she could trust in her life. He had changed, agreed to counseling, even started his new job. But face it. Who knew if the changes would stick?

When she clasped her hands together, her palms felt greasy. She looked at her glistening skin and chuckled. She'd just smoothed on lotion for the third time. Shaking her head, she wiped her fingers on a plush towel.

A delicate crystal bottle sat on the green veined granite countertop. She opened the perfume and inhaled the musky scent, awakening eight years of sensual memories. On their honeymoon, Mike had this unique perfume made especially for her. He'd told her the fragrance captured her essence: beautiful, fresh, and spicy. For a big, tough cop, he showed a surprising romantic streak sometimes.

Liv replaced the stopper and gently returned the bottle to the counter. She closed her eyes. Her breasts, her whole body ached with need, but could she take the chance? Cara was fast asleep and had been long before Mike finished reading to her. Their daughter probably wouldn't wake until morning.

Should they risk it?

What if they got caught?

Invisible knifepoints stabbed at her core, turned the moist ache low inside her into a raging throb, and sharpened the arousal pulsing through her. She bit her lip and resisted the temptation to touch herself.

No, she wanted his hands on her. Wanted him. But could she take her pleasure and walk away? Remember that sex was just sex, not making love? Mike was like chocolate—delectable, but dangerous.

Addictive.

Enough questions. Liv sucked in a determined breath and dabbed scent at the pulse points of her throat and wrists. Perfume at bedtime always meant sex. No way Mike would miss her signal tonight.

But just in case, she slipped off her bra, tossed it into the hamper, and re-buttoned her blouse. After a quick glance in the mirror to smooth her hair, she checked on Cara and closed her daughter's bedroom door completely.

Liv opened the slider and looked out over the darkened patio. He stood at the edge of the deck with his hands in his pockets. His shoulders looked broader than ever in silhouette, but his neck was bent, like he was looking at his feet and thinking.

The stream below the house glimmered, reflecting the twinkling solar garden lights. Frogs sang to their mates in the damp grove, lush with ferns and rhododendrons under the evergreens. The evening breeze blew through the screen and caressed her skin, tickling her nerve endings. Under the thin blouse, the skin around her nipples puckered.

Nature was staging a giant mating dance tonight and dragging her along for the orgy. She listened to the sensual night sounds, smelled the fresh, cool air. Gradually, her jagged nerves calmed. She moved to his side and murmured his name.

He glanced at her upturned face and grinned. Shifting behind her, he lifted the heavy fall of her hair to one side and kissed her nape. His mouth was open and moist and warm on her neck.

She shuddered, and his arms came around her and linked in front of her waist. His warmth seeped through her clothes. Heat pulsed from his skin, his hands, his hard, muscular chest.

"I've missed holding you." He rested his chin on the top of her head, toying with her hair. Shivers trailed across her back. Nestling against him, she felt the slow, steady beat of his heart.

Mike buried his nose against the curve of her neck and drew a deep breath. He shuddered against her. "Perfume, Livy. You mean it?" he asked, his voice deep and gravely against her skin.

She turned and met his gaze, ignoring the heat searing her face. "This afternoon you said you thought sex could help us solve our problems."

His eyes lit, and his grin blossomed. "Not a bad place to start."

"Were you serious? Can you think of sex as a beginning, something for tonight?" Her words came out in a rush.

He drew a finger down her blazing cheek.

She slowly flipped open the buttons of her blouse. The cool night air hit her skin, and she hissed. She met his lips, moving his hands to cover her bare breasts.

His mouth was warm and firm and deliberate on hers while his hot fingers tugged on her nipples, rolled them into firm points. He cupped her breasts, kneading the soft, sensitive flesh while he sucked her earlobe into his mouth and bit gently.

Pleasure speared through her. She rubbed against him, felt his arousal jut against her belly. "I want you inside me, Mike. Now. No one will see us out here. I want you hot and fast and hard."

He made a deep, rumbling noise that sounded like a no, scooped her up and carried her inside. "This isn't a quick fuck, Liv. When I make love to you, it means something. Everything. I want to take my time tonight."

Her arms closed around his neck. She stretched up and nuzzled his ear. How could a big, tough man have such baby-soft places to caress?

"That feels good." Mike shivered and set her on their bed. Standing over her, he kicked off his shoes and unbuttoned his shirt. His powerful shoulders flexed and the well-defined muscles of his abdomen rippled. A long arrow of pale, curly hair grew between his pecs, circled his navel, and disappeared below his jeans.

Her gaze swept back up his body to his face, drew over his strong, cleft chin and past the flush cresting his chiseled cheekbones to his luscious blue eyes surrounded by thick, dark lashes. She almost drowned in the liquid heat smoldering in those depths.

"I want you, Livy. Take off your clothes for me." His voice was urgent with desire.

She stifled a groan and dragged her gaze away. A

shiver quaked through her body and more dampness formed between her legs. Her gaze locked on his, she undid the last two buttons and slipped off her blouse. When her hand brushed over her sensitive nipple, she drew a harsh breath.

Reaching behind her waist, she unzipped her skirt, squiggling it off and out from under her. She hooked her thumbs under her black thong and pulled it off, leaving only her thigh highs and heels.

Mike tunneled a hand through his hair. "You're so beautiful." He released his belt and shrugged off his pants and boxers. His penis stood hard and huge and ready.

"Very nice." She moistened her lips and reached her arms toward him. She raised her knees and spread them, gazing up at him. "Come here."

"In a minute." Mike took her shoes off one by one, massaging her toes and the curve of her arch. Pleasure and pain surged through her as he worked the cramped muscles. He drew down her hose slowly, inch by inch, until she closed her eyes and groaned.

When he lay down beside her on the bed and drew her close, she snuggled against him, nestling her head in the hollow of his shoulder. He framed her face with his long fingers and kissed each eyelid and the tip of her nose before moving to her lips.

He slid one finger down the side of her face. The back of his hand brushed her jaw and collarbone. He covered her breast and flicked his thumb over one sensitive nipple.

She swallowed hard. Her skin tingled. Heated. That hungry, wet ache blossomed low in her body. She smoothed her palms across his shoulders and down his arms, explored the line of curly hairs on his chest, circling his flat male nipples until they hardened like hers.

"I want you, Livy," he said in a voice deep with passion, and ran his hands over her, balancing his weight on his side and one elbow. His fingers grazed her ribs and shaped her waist, combed through the curls between her legs.

Gasping from the exquisite pressure, she spread her legs wider for him.

He hooked her knee over his hip, and his hand danced over her sensitive nub. When he slipped one finger inside, her hips began to rock ever so slightly against his knowing touch.

Heat and moisture and delicious tension coiled inside her. Through half-closed eyes she gazed at him, revealing the dampness of her core and the way her heart fluttered.

He slid a second finger inside her, stretched her. Pleasure seared through her.

Her head fell to the side, her breathing came in short, shallow gasps. She couldn't stand one more minute and circled the head of his erection, spreading the tiny drop of moisture over the tip with her thumb.

He rewarded her with a swift, harsh moan and slipped his fingers from her. Pressing open her thighs with the palms of his hands. Slowly, he pushed his length deep inside her with one delicious stroke and began to pump.

She might melt from the fierce, mind-numbing pleasure. Her inner muscles clenched. Hot colors burst behind her eyelids, and she screamed his name.

****

11:35 p.m.

Ahmed's mind felt full of sludge. The meager meal he had choked down earlier had congealed into cold, undigested lumps. The words all melted together on the screen. English had turned to gibberish and made his head fog. On his spreadsheet, all the numbers ignored formerly unbreakable rules.

He yawned and ran a nervous hand over his mat of curly black hair. He'd neither eaten nor slept well since he had come to his government's attention. He'd been naïve enough to accept their sponsorship despite all the obligations it entailed.

Tonight he was unable to concentrate on his studies, unable to contact his family and reassure himself of their safety. Unable to sleep, knowing he would commit a heinous crime tomorrow.

A great shudder shook him, left him trembling. His gaze darted around the apartment, but nothing was out of place. The suitcase full of cash still peeped from behind the door.

With sudden resolve, he shut down the laptop and pushed away from his desk. He dug in the bottom drawer, coming up with the prepaid cell phone.

His heart beat painfully. The matte black surface of the phone looked clean, innocent, but he knew better. He opened the device and flicked it on anyway. He drew a deep, gasping breath and poked the speed dial.

"Yes?" his contact answered, voice gruff.

"Let me talk to my father."

"Impossible."

Sweat trickled down his temple. He swiped a hand across his brow. "Then I will not take the risk tomorrow. I will not pick up the—"

"Watch what you say."

"I will not pick up the schematics unless I can speak with him. I need to be assured my family is safe." Ahmed squeezed his eyes shut, waiting for a response.

"Risk? You realize the punishment you risk with your insolence?"

"Yes," Ahmed replied, hoping his voice didn't betray the tremors running through him.

A moment later, his mother asked, "Ahmed? Is that really you?" She spoke to him in the dialect of their clan.

His heart steadied, and his breathing eased. "Yes. Are you well? How is Father?"

"Ahmed, they took him away. They said he went to the hospital. I'm so frightened—" she broke off. A muffled grunt came through the earpiece, and the sound of a scuffle.

Blood pounded behind his eyes and panic ripped through him like a pack of hyenas disemboweling a gazelle.

His contact came back on the line, tone low and laced with threat. "Fulfill your duty. Your father needs surgery. But it's expensive…and risky."

****

Tuesday, April 20, 5:45 a.m.

Through half-closed lids Liv saw that faint light filled the high-ceilinged bedroom. Outside the window, the treetops glowed with the dawn.

Mike's hard body spooned behind hers. He breathed heavily into the tangle of her hair with one arm beneath her, the other around her waist. His fingers stroked the tender sides of her breasts and then gently toyed with her nipples.

Liv relaxed back against him. With each breath, the warm musky scents of Mike and sex filled her senses. Still muzzy from sleep, she stretched gently and felt twinges of soreness and pleasure.

The hard ridge of his morning erection nestled between the cheeks of her bottom. He pushed against her and pressed the blunt tip inside.

Sighing, she burrowed back, arching her hips to draw him deeper.

He plucked her nipples and teased them to life. Ripples of heat stirred deep within her, and her breath quickened. He pressed his wet, open mouth against her nape and bit gently.

Liv shuddered her pleasure. The flame inside caught and stoked the liquid fire low in her body. Still half asleep, she squirmed against him, making lazy, sexy noises.

His deep laugh rumbled against her back and set up a delicious quiver. He grasped her hips and thrust again, slow but deep, while he drew damp circles around her nub without touching it. Teasing, tantalizing circles. Trembling from the exquisite torture, she moaned.

"I'd almost forgotten how magical it is to wake up in the morning and make love." He brushed her nubbin once with his thumb.

A hot coil of sensation had her gasping and pulsing around his hardness. She whimpered, her hips shifting restlessly. But something wasn't right. She shook her head to clear the sensual fog. "What do you mean?"

He plunged into her again, withdrawing and returning with slow, shallow thrusts. "It was a long six months, love. I missed you, missed making love to you in the morning. It's good to be home."

"Morning?" Her eyes popped open. "Oh shit! It's morning! Stop, Mike. You weren't supposed to sleep here. Cara will catch us."

She tried to twist away, but he pressed into her hard and held her hips pressed against him with one arm. His stiff thickness stretched her. "I'll stop if you want, but we won't wake Cara if you're quiet." He delved between her damp folds and caught the tiny bundle of nerve endings between his fingers.

Her breath caught. She moaned, "Don't stop."

Rocking with fast, shallow thrusts, Mike throbbed inside her.

Waves of pleasure slammed through her. She bit her lip to smother the sound, but a high-pitched cry escaped her throat, and she roared over a dizzying crest.

He bowed back and stroked hard once more. A low groan exploded from his lips.

Chapter Ten

Sereno, Tuesday, April 20, 11:50 a.m.

Liv's body hummed a loose-limbed, satisfied song with each swaying step. Grinning, she followed the hostess and scooted into a corner booth decorated with a spiny fishhook cactus in a terra cotta pot.

She inhaled. The aromas in the tiny Mexican restaurant had her mouth watering. Hot oil and grilled onions layered like a taco with the tang of jalapeños and fresh cilantro.

Sipping on a frosty, salt-rimmed margarita, Liv traced the colorful blue and yellow tiles on the table with her fingernail. Sex with Mike was definitely worth all the crazy subterfuge. After this morning, she almost understood the jolt he got from undercover work.

The pulses of her last orgasm had barely faded when she'd hustled down the hall wearing a smile, her bathrobe, and the scent of Mike and sex on her skin. She'd hugged Cara good morning, and sat on the bed listening to her daughter chatter about having Daddy home for dinner.

Cara didn't have a clue. She'd kept her daughter occupied and away from the window while Mike dressed and sneaked out the back door like the mailman in a bad soap opera. She'd dodged questions about the beard burn on her face and neck and patiently withstood

Cara's incessant why-can't-he-come-again-tonight, maybe-forever pleas.

But she couldn't let him. Yet. New job or not, Liv knew Mike. Give him half an excuse and he'd disappear back undercover and incommunicado for nobody-knew-how-long, dumping all the responsibility for their family on her.

But sex on the sly was amazing. She wiggled her shoulders and smiled to herself. Maybe Mike wasn't the only adrenaline junkie in their family.

Liv heard someone say her name and looked up to see Jana Kapulani hurry in. She had shed her lab coat, but still wore blue surgical scrubs. Her copper hair was brushed back in a layered cut above wide hazel eyes, but her freckled face looked pale.

"Hey, girlfriend. I ordered tamales," Liv said brightly.

Jana gave her a hug, pressing a cold cheek against hers. "The carjacking scared me. Are you okay?"

Liv's stomach jittered, but she managed a smile. "I'm fine. I was shaken up for a day or two."

Frowning, Jana sank into the booth and closed both clammy hands over hers. "I'm worried you're still in danger."

Something nasty wiggled at the base of her brain. Her friend had uncanny intuition, but Liv couldn't cope with anything negative right now. She shrugged. "The carjacking was bad luck, that's all. I'm fine."

From behind her, the waitress cleared her throat. She looked like Lucy Ricardo forty pounds and forty years later with the same engaging smile.

"Hold on a sec. Here's lunch," Liv said in what she hoped was a breezy, cheerful tone.

Shoulders hunched, Jana closed her eyes and took a deep breath. "Smells heavenly."

"Believe me, I wouldn't want to go through the carjacking again, but no harm done except to my beautiful car." She scanned the platter in front of her. "Let's relax and eat."

Jana opened her lips to speak, but sighed and loaded a tortilla chip with salsa.

Liv felt a wide, kid-with-a-mouthful-of-chocolate grin escape. "Mike and I had a date last night. He brought over dinner, grilled for Cara and me."

"What? What about Samantha?" Jana asked, eyebrows arching.

"He swears nothing happened."

"And you believe him after the way that witch acted?"

"I know she played me and manipulated Mike."

"That's all she did?"

Liv waved her fork in the air. "Who knows? He's such a freaking guy. Sam must have had some reason to believe what she said, but whatever happened didn't mean anything to him."

Deeper lines appeared in Jana's brow. "And that's good enough for you?"

"For now." Liv leaned in close and a defensive edge sharpened her words, "But don't let me anywhere near her with an AK-47."

Jana snorted, and one corner of her mouth quirked. "I'll bring a spare magazine. Or maybe Nate's Glock."

Liv leaned against the booth and brushed her hair from her face. "Good thing they can't arrest us for our fantasies."

"You know, Sam tried hard to snare Mike for over

a year." Jana took another bite of tamale. "Remember your engagement party?"

"Ugh. I was two months pregnant and the smell of beer made me sick. When I came back from the restroom, there she was kissing him." Liv flashed on the icy sweep of insecurity that kiss had brought on.

"She timed it. Just before you stepped into the room, she jumped in his lap."

"Mike swears they were never an item, never more than friends with benefits."

"At the time, she claimed he had a ring in his pocket."

Jealousy smoldered in the pit of Liv's stomach. "I didn't know."

"I think when he married you, she fled to the FBI academy because she was caught by her own lies." Jana scowled and shook her head.

"Hard to believe she's carried a torch for Mike that long. Even harder to believe she had the gall to make another play for him."

Jana squeezed her hand. "Seriously, protect yourself and Cara."

"Hopefully, we'll never see Samantha again." Liv toyed with her glass, scraping salt off the rim of her drink with a nail.

"How's Cara doing with her daddy home?"

"She was so happy last night she beamed. And we did have a nice evening. He was on his best behavior."

"And after Cara went to bed? Did you tear up the sheets, girlfriend?" Jana gave a sly grin. "I know you two."

Liv closed her eyes and sighed. "Yum."

Jana laughed aloud.

Liv joined in. "I had to sneak him out the back door this morning."

Jana's phone vibrated. Still smiling, she checked the caller ID. "It's my service." She asked several terse questions while gathering her things. After she finished the call, she riffled through her purse. "Sorry. A patient's in trouble. I have to go."

"Lunch is my treat." Liv stood and hugged her friend. "Don't forget, the hospital benefit's Saturday."

"Wouldn't miss it. Getting Nate in his gorilla suit is such a kick." Jana dashed toward the door.

Liv sat and nibbled another chip piled with guacamole. Jana had honed in on all her own niggling doubts. But counseling would help. In another week or two, her life would settle down. The benefit would be over, she'd have a new nanny, and the initial production drones would be on their way to Homeland Security. Then she'd decide if she'd ever be willing to live with Mike again.

A stocky, dark-haired man with a toothy smile approached her table. He had his hand outstretched, a signet ring sparkling on his hairy pinkie. "Liv. I thought it was you."

"Tom. What a nice surprise."

He grasped her hand in both of his. "You look great today. Life must be agreeing with you."

Heat crept up her neck. The guy always seemed to get too close. She withdrew her hand, but grinned harder and patted the arm of his leather jacket. "Can't complain."

Tom's eyebrows flickered upward. "Good. Did you get my donations for the benefit?"

"Yes. You outdid yourself."

"Always a pleasure to do my part. Plus, it's easy when I'm working with good people." Closing the distance between them again, he beamed at her.

The skin on her nape squirmed, but she locked her knees and stood her ground. Since she had his attention, she'd try another tactful reminder. "Sorry to be a stickler, but I need the paperwork soon, and you'll want the documentation come tax season."

"No problem. I'll send it over with one of my guys." A beguiling, sheepish grin crept across his face. "Guess clean-up isn't my forte. I'm at my best in the thick of the action."

****

1:30 p.m.

Muscles pumped from shifting pallets, Les Hamlin pulled the bandana from his pocket and mopped his forehead, looking over the Silicon Valley Vending warehouse with gut-level satisfaction.

He liked order. That had been the best part of triple hitch in the Marines. He had always known where he should be, what he should do, and just how he should do his job.

He wiped sweaty palms on his shirt, feeling edgy about facing the boss. No, damn it, he was scared shitless. Did he do the right thing, squealing to the FBI?

A sick sense of dread twisted in his gut. Hell, that kiddy meal might cost him his life. Would the boss smell a snitch?

The thought of Morrison bent on revenge— revenge against him, made him shiver. Morrison would see right through his lies, and he'd wind up without kneecaps.

A strong hand clamped on his shoulder.

Les jerked around and met Morrison's sharp brown eyes. "Boss!"

"About time you finished. Didn't you start your routes at four a.m.?"

"Three thirty."

"Quitting time, but get your ass in my office, first," Morrison ordered.

With his heart thumping double-time, Les followed. "Want me to go over and work on them machines at the skate park on my way home? One's jammed again. I ain't found a repair guy to replace Sancho, yet." He brushed twitchy fingers through his regulation crew cut and licked his dry lips.

"Not now. Shit." Morrison snapped a pencil and hurled the pieces to the floor of his office. "Chandler bitch stole another account."

"You're kidding. Which one?" Les hesitated in the doorway, wishing he could steer clear of the boss's foul mood.

"She cheated me out of another car dealership. Who'd she screw to get that account?" Morrison stalked behind his desk and plopped in his leather chair. "Get in here and sit. I gotta think how I'm gonna teach her a lesson."

"Sure, Boss." He perched on a small chair facing the desk, trying not to fidget. A good five inches lower than Morrison, he was trapped in the hot seat. A bead of sweat trickled down his neck.

"She doesn't belong in a man's business anyway."

"Yeah, takes strength to heave them pallets around."

"Dames can screw a man senseless. Make money on their backs," Morrison ranted. His jaw muscles twitched on one side.

"No shit." Les nodded in agreement, sitting at attention. His breath came quickly. Too quickly. The boss was acting freaky today. Any minute, he'd start slobbering.

"The damned benefit is Saturday. The Gordon bitch keeps bugging me. Drop this by G-Tech when you do their delivery." Morrison shoved a manila envelope into his hands and glowered over him like a turkey vulture eyeing road kill.

Les gulped, trying not to look like dinner. "Pushy broad."

"Left me five messages about this fucking paperwork. Then I ran into her in the Mexican joint at lunch, and she had the gall to nag me. She has the fucking donation, so why's she griping?"

Les kept nodding like a bobble-head, stood, and edged toward the door. "So, want me to take care of the jammed machine, Boss?"

"Sure, sure."

"Anything else? Maybe mess up something of Chandler's? I got a new steel cutter. I can rip off a couple bill stackers."

"Maybe." The phone rang, and Morrison answered, pointing at the floor.

Recognizing the signal to wait, Les shifted from foot to foot. Shit.

"Yeah? What is it, Judy? Crap. He's early. Stall him a minute." Morrison hung up the receiver. He cracked his knuckles and a sneaky grin twitched across his lips. "If everything goes okay today, I'm gonna collect a bundle."

Les did his best to look clueless. His fucking neck

depended on it. But sweat had soaked the back of his T-shirt and puddled under his arms. "What's up, Boss?"

"I'll let you in on a secret. I got a big deal in the works. You take care of your end, help me, and you'll get your share."

"Sure. Sure, Boss. Sounds great." Terrified he'd give something away, he stared at his spit-shined boots.

He followed Morrison, but stalled outside the counting room, where the coin machines clattered, counting and rolling quarters from the morning runs. "I-I'll get right on the jammed machine. Let me know if I should tackle any of them special projects."

"Hold off for now." Morrison opened the door into the reception area, a broad, welcoming smile on his face. "Hey, how ya doing? Good to see you. Come on back to my office."

Heart pounding wildly against his ribs, Les ducked into the warehouse, fumbling for his cell phone. This time he'd snap a shot of that damned foreigner.

****

6:05 p.m.

How could she keep Ahmed alive? Miriam Kazan hurried through the oak trees that dotted the beautiful campus. She dumped her notebook from Professor Gordon's class on a picnic table. Scanning the area, she pulled out her cell phone. Daylight was fading fast, but she had to find privacy before her contact rang.

As if on cue, the phone vibrated on the wooden surface. She checked the caller ID and answered, "Kazan."

"Report."

"The student made the exchange with a courier as anticipated, but—"

An exasperated huff traveled through the phone. "If you observed the transaction, why didn't you take them both down? You're authorized."

How could she explain her reluctance to harm Ahmed? She hushed her tone. "Too many civilians in the student union. I couldn't isolate the courier." Miriam gritted her teeth, remembering the tall, solemn man who glided into the hall, exchanged backpacks with Ahmed, and vanished before she could trail him.

"What about the student? Arrest him. If he resists, eliminate him," her contact ordered.

A couple strolled along the gravel path edging the park, hands swinging between them, talking and laughing.

Her pulse rate spiked. Probably not headed this way, but to be safe, she adjusted her scarf lower on her forehead and turned sideways, shading the phone from view. "I searched his room and found the plans. The miniature drone means nothing because he still doesn't have the sensor technology."

After the couple continued past with no indication they noticed her presence, she released a pent up breath.

"His actions demonstrate guilt. Interpol wants him out of play," he insisted, speech clipped and impatient.

Her heart beat faster. An execution? No. But she kept her voice cool and detached. "The student is a small, frightened player in this affair. He flinches at shadows."

The man on the line made an impatient noise.

"He's not strong enough to have masterminded this theft. He's being used."

"And?"

"And if we let the scenario play out, let Ahmed

continue to muddle through alone, my instincts say the prince will have to send in a clean-up team."

"Hmmm. Has possibilities."

With a broad grin, she added, "Capture the rescuer and we'll finally implicate the palace and free Krzystan. I'll stake my life on it."

"Precisely."

Chapter Eleven

Sereno, Wednesday, April 21, 9:35 a.m.

Jana's arms ached with weariness from hours of pre-dawn surgery. Her eyes felt gritty and each foot seemed to weigh more than her two-year-old, Molly.

White coat slung over her arm, Jana hurried through the private entrance to her office. The receptionist looked up, ruffling her short, spiky black hair. A smile lit her round face. "I phoned your first four patients and rescheduled them with no problems. One guy came in around half past eight and decided to wait." She cleared her throat. "FBI."

"What?" Jana's eyebrows twitched with surprise. "Send him in. I'll see what he wants." She went into her consulting room and waited beside the desk.

A tall man with dark, curly hair and bright blue eyes entered and surveyed the room, businesslike and confident in a dark suit and red patterned tie. One glance and something screamed Fed. Maybe it was his polished-to-a-glare wingtips.

"Dan Bausch." He offered his badge. "Thanks for seeing me, Dr. Kapulani."

She indicated a chair and settled across from him. "What can I do for you?"

"This meeting is confidential." Adjusting his coat, he folded his identification back into his pocket. "I'm overseeing security at G-Tech. Olivia Gordon's your friend."

"Are you here about the carjacking?" She focused on his eyes, trying to read his enigmatic expression.

"What can you tell me about Ms. Gordon?"

She shifted in her seat. The agent had ignored her question, but she wasn't willing to push the point yet. "Liv works hard. I don't know much about her current project. I wouldn't. The details are secret."

"Not surprising. You work in very different fields. Spend much time together?" he asked, his posture casual and tone conversational.

Her lips flattened into a straight line. "I have patients waiting, Agent Bausch. Exactly why are you here?"

"A few more questions, and I'll let you go."

Let her? Thanks a heap. Jana bit back the sarcastic comment, but intuition hummed in the corner of her mind, and a sense of unease rippled through her like a fish through cold water.

"Ms. Gordon has a lot of money for a woman early in her career."

A quick flash of heat clenched her jaw. Bausch left his sly implications unsaid, but she wanted to grab him by the throat and shake the faint sneer off his face.

Frustrated impatience bubbled, vying with curiosity. Curiosity won, and Jana showed him her teeth. She'd play the game, but she let her rising annoyance sharpen her words, "She was fortunate to find her job with Nova Stream Robotics right after her MBA. Fortunate their IPO skyrocketed. Fortunate they spun off G-Tech and made her CEO."

"I see."

"I've known Liv since we were roommates in college, and her ethics are impeccable."

The agent's expression remained cool, his hands still. He was good, even though he had the personality of a rock.

Agent Bausch reached for his briefcase and pulled out an enlarged photograph. "Do you know this man?"

She scrutinized the grainy action shot of a well-dressed, middle-aged man exiting a car. Her intuition twitched again. A ghostly finger traced her vertebrae one by one, and she stiffened. "There's something about him. Can you tell me his name?"

"Thomas Morrison."

"The name sounds familiar." Tipping her head to one side, she studied the older man in the photograph again. "His eyes are in shadow, and he's looking downward. People's eyes are my primary recognition point. Is he local?"

"Only recently. He hails from the East Coast."

A creepy sensation triggered a new crop of goose bumps, but she passed the picture back. "Sorry."

He stood and offered his hand. "Good to meet you, Dr. Kapulani. I have no more questions now, but I might be in touch."

"May I discuss this with my husband?"

"Yes, but otherwise keep our conversation confidential."

She debated, drumming her fingers on the desk and frowning at him. "What is this really about? My cop radar is beeping like crazy."

Two shallow furrows formed on his brow. "Interesting name for…intuition."

She grinned. A reaction. Finally, she had him ever

so slightly off balance. "Once upon a time, I considered studying medical forensics so I did a six-month internship with Sereno PD. Obviously, I decided otherwise, but my training had an impact."

"Good to know. If you think of anything about Mr. Morrison, please call my number." He handed her a business card.

"Sure."

The office door thumped closed behind him. He had sidestepped all her questions. She'd call Nate when she took a break and see what he knew. Radar was radar, and she'd learned from experience to listen to her hunches.

****

12:35 p.m.

Nothing moved. Glancing through the peephole, Ahmed scanned the shaded courtyard once more. He double-checked the lock on his student apartment, closed his eyes, and rested his forehead against the door.

He had completed the assignment. Would he be released from service today? Ahmed mouthed a quick prayer for his parents and brother. No matter how it was expressed, they were held hostage.

With shaky fingers, he powered up the cell phone and sat at the table. Staring at the display, finger poised, he took a quick breath, and pressed a key.

Seconds later, a familiar voice said in Arabic, "You failed."

His heart faltered. Despair curdled his stomach, and he shifted backward in his chair. "I-I don't understand. I sent the plans."

"You fool. We can purchase a drone off the

Internet. The market is flooded. We need the explosive detection technology."

"But what—"

"G-Tech's chemical sensing unit threatens to make our bomb making technology obsolete."

His throat clogged with fear. "I will inform our contact of the error."

"The xerogel device can expose us." The speaker's voice became louder, more resolute. "The timing is rigid. Our targets must be vulnerable at the appointed hour."

"I understand, sir," he said fervently, wiping the sweat from his lip. His family. How could he protect his family now?

"Time is of the essence. Because of your failure, the prince has ordered me to board a plane. Until I arrive, use all leverage at your disposal to acquire the technology." The connection broke.

Head spinning, he rose and stumbled toward the window to peer through the blinds. "The prince's cousin, coming here?"

A dark certainty grew. He must correct his mistake, or his life and the lives of his family would be forfeit. But first, he needed a secure meeting place. He had gone to Morrison's business too often.

A knock sounded on the door, and the blood drained from his face. He froze in place.

"Ahmed? Are you ready?" Miriam knocked again. "Ahmed? Did you forget our lunch?" He smoothed damp palms down his trousers and opened the door.

Her gaze raked him from head to toe. "Everything okay?"

"I need a favor."

****

12:45 p.m.

Fucking useless. Mike slammed the folder onto his desk and ground his teeth. The preliminary carjacking report had nothing. No ID on the perps. No tags. No fingerprints. Not a single fucking lead.

He rubbed his eyes and leaned back, stretching the crick between his shoulder blades. Maybe he'd take a quick break, get his blood circulating again. As he stomped through the bullpen, uniforms scattered, and patrol officers hugged the walls to let him pass. His foul mood cleared the way.

"Gordon!" Nate called from his office.

He poked his head inside, and his jaw clenched at the damn regulation dark suit sitting in one of Nate's chairs.

Scowling, Agent Bausch stood and offered a hand. "Time you got something straight, Gordon."

"Hold on a sec." Nate closed the door and perched on the corner of his desk.

Hands on his hips, Mike stayed on his feet. "The carjacking investigation's stalled. Dead ends all around."

"That's not why I'm here." The agent unbuttoned his jacket, taking a small pad from his pocket.

Mike studied his serious expression and an itch rippled across his neck. "Then what?"

"You're hovering around G-Tech too much."

Widening his stance, Mike nodded. "Matter of opinion. Liv's my wife."

"You can meet your wife for lunch every day, Gordon, for all I give a damn, but you have a conflict of interest. A big conflict of interest." Bausch crossed his

118

long arms and a deep frown creased his forehead. "When you pimped investigation details from my agents, you crossed the line."

Nate flashed him an I-warned-you-he'd-swing-the-freaking-rule-book shrug, but Mike just lifted a shoulder and angled his head. "So I took Harold out for a beer."

"Back. Off." Bausch's face went unreadable, but his voice hit forty below. "Stay the fuck out my investigation and away from my agents."

Sudden tension gripped him. That was too powerful a reaction for a first warning. He straightened to his full height, a hand taller than Bausch's bare six feet. "But that's not the reason you're here," he said in a slow, careful tone.

Bausch glared at him for a long moment, his eyebrows drawn into a sharp vee. Then he pointed to the extra chair and sank back into his own.

Mike sat, but needles of anxiety poked at his spine and triggered sharp, slinking chills.

"This briefing is need-to-know."

"Understood."

"An informan—"

"Liv didn't mention an informant."

Bausch cleared his throat, his blue eyes glacial. "She hasn't been apprised."

"First the breach at G-Tech. Then the carjacking. Now a CI?" Mike tallied them on his fingers. Then he slumped back against the chair. "There's more."

"The bureau is coordinating an international, multi-agency task force that has G-Tech under scrutiny."

His gut clenched like a steer had walloped him. He narrowed his eyes to slits. "Their drone is top priority, but your crew has a handle on that. How much danger's Liv in?"

"We haven't verified a threat to her."

"What about the jacking?"

The agent shrugged. "No connection that we can find."

"Yet."

Still pokerfaced, the agent handed him a photograph.

Nate shifted and looked over Mike's shoulder. "And this is?"

"Do you recognize him? Either of you?"

In the grainy photo, a middle-aged man wearing an expensive suit exited a black limo. Mercedes, blonde bimbo, silk square in his breast pocket. This scumbag oozed dirty money. But something about the set of his jaw niggled at Mike's memory. "He's familiar. Name?"

"Thomas Morrison. Probably an alias."

Eyebrows raised, Mike rubbed the back of his neck and passed the photo to Nate. "Priors?"

"No record. On the surface, he looks legit." Bausch spread out a file.

"Can't ID him." Nate dumped the photo on his desk. "But I agree with Gordon. He's familiar."

"Let me know if you place him." The agent offered a grim smile. "Our informant alleges Morrison has links to a terrorist cell."

"Alleges?"

"He could just be a goober with a grudge." Bausch rose to his feet and tunneled his fingers into his hair. "But we can't rule anything out at this point."

Mike's hackles lifted, and his pulse jumped. The agent had sounded nonchalant, but the pitch of his voice and stiffness in his stance rang false. He drew a slow, deep breath and zeroed in. "What's Morrison's connection to Liv?"

"So far, nothing concrete." Bausch rubbed his clean-shaven jaw. "But I have a team going through his business dealings. Atlantic Partners. It's a roof rat's nest of interlocking shell corporations."

His heart rate kicked into a dead run. "Gotta be a connection. With G-Tech secured, Morrison went after Liv in hopes of extorting her invention."

"Agent?" Nate prompted.

"Given the scope of the investigation and the targets we believe to be in jeopardy, we're taking the informant seriously."

Mike's gut churned like the sawdust under a bronc's hooves. "So get off your ass. Haul the creep in for questioning."

"We can't risk alerting Morrison."

"Why the hell not?"

Bausch's tone dropped another twenty degrees. "G-Tech is not your case, Lieutenant."

"But we could—"

The Agent glared at him as if he was something a dog had dropped.

Rubbing his fingers across his creased forehead, Nate said, "Morrison hasn't hit our radar, but we could watch him."

Every sense on high alert, Mike stood and paced the office. Protecting Liv was his first priority. "Need somebody to stake out Morrison? No official ties to Liv means no conflict of interest."

"Now wait a minute, Gordon." Nate argued. "The FBI can place an agent."

"That'd take time. Plus they'd need a warrant from a federal judge. We could at least fill in until that happened."

FBI looked interested.

"As Sereno PD, I'd be covered by a local warrant." Brushing his hand across his nape again, he gave Bausch a crooked grin and jabbed a finger at him. "Uh huh. That's it. You didn't come in here to slap my wrist, did you Bausch?"

FBI grimaced and shoved his hands in his pockets. Then he cocked one eyebrow. "Assuming you'll obey orders, even my stuffy SAC couldn't object to surveillance by the locals."

Nate sucked in a breath, his expression dark. Then he stood. "Covert surveillance only. No undercover for Gordon."

Bausch agreed with a sharp nod. "Our timetable's short. So far, Morrison's the only chink in the bad guys' armor. Could blow the whole thing wide open."

The bronc in his gut dumped him on his ass, knocking the wind out of him. He stared at the stone cold, calculating bastard-in-a-dark-suit. "Shit. You want Liv as bait."

FBI assessed him with a sparse smile that never reached his eyes. "Wouldn't put it quite that way."

Mike moved in, nose to nose with the asshole. "But another attempt on her would clarify the situation, maybe reveal the players, right?"

Bausch leveled his gaze. "And you can help assess the threat."

"That's callous." The tension in Mike's shoulders ratcheted up another notch. If it wasn't a federal offense, he'd clip that jerk on the jaw and knock him on his rulebook.

He turned and stared out the window, rubbing his hands over his face. He wanted to be on the next plane to South America with Liv and Cara, but he'd never be able to yank her away from G-Tech right now.

Mike brushed his knuckles across his mouth and leaned a shoulder into the wall. Sitting in the bullpen picking his nose would drive him nuts. Better play nice, or Bausch would lock him out. No choice. He'd go along with the plan. For now.

"Thanks for your cooperation, Captain Kapulani." Bausch angled toward Mike, face rigid. "I need surveillance in place at Atlantic Partners immediately."

"Yes, sir." But first, he'd get on the phone and warn Liv.

Bausch paused by the door, giving him the fish eye. "Nothing, absolutely nothing about Morrison, the CI, or the scope of the investigation goes beyond this office."

Another surge of anger narrowed his vision. "You're leaving Liv exposed, but don't plan to warn her?"

Nate stepped between them. "You should brief her now."

"We will, soon."

"Tomorrow?"

"Look, she's well protected. Any change in her behavior might tip off the suspects. Could put her in added danger."

Fists clenched, he moved forward. "If you think—"

The Agent's gaze remained frigid. Cold son of a jackass didn't even blink. "This is priority one, Gordon, but I can't fill you in on the whole picture, even with your clearance. G-Tech and her invention are our best shot at preventing a 9/11 repeat but on an even bigger scale."

Nate shook his head. "Huge mistake to leave her in the dark. Dangerous."

Menace in his tone, Bausch cut in, "We have to shut these guys down fast. Follow orders. Keep your mouth zipped." He turned on his heel and let himself out.

"The set-up stinks." Mike grimaced, face aching with tension.

Nate clapped him on the shoulder. "Sticks in my craw, but remember, we don't have the full story."

Chewing on the inside of his lip, Mike grabbed a pen. Click. When he tried to swallow away the toxic metallic taste, his tongue stuck to his teeth.

Click. Click. He stared out the door into the bustle of the bullpen, mind racing through scenario after scenario, none of them good.

Click. Click. Click.

Chapter Twelve

Sereno, Wednesday, April 21, 4:50 p.m.

Stiff from sitting on cold concrete, Mike tugged on the sleeve of a ratty plaid shirt. No help. Still four inches too short. He pulled off his filthy, taped-together glasses. Much better.

He'd followed Morrison from Atlantic Partner's posh uptown offices to an East Sereno warehouse in a seen-better-days industrial park. Silicon Valley Vending was a small brick-and-mortar wedged between a funky auto repair shop and a specialty machine shop. Morrison had spent the entire afternoon inside.

Why? Mike had no clue.

He itched to pull out his phone and research the company while he waited, but that didn't quite fit his undercover persona as a homeless dude. Instead he took another sip of strong tea from a booze bottle masked by a crumpled paper bag.

Across the street, the glass double doors opened. Despite the distance, he got a better look at the suspect. Over fifty, clean-shaven, bulky like he worked out. Morrison was taller than he had imagined from the grainy FBI photo. Judging by his appearance, criminal activity probably wasn't a big stretch, but traitor? Mike gritted his teeth. If this creep had Liv in his sights, he'd nail him.

Sipping from a paper coffee cup, Morrison ambled over to a dark blue BMW and eased behind the wheel, hitching one leg in. Bum knee? The sedan pulled onto the side street.

Mike sprinted toward his truck, feeling a surge of excitement. He eased into traffic with one eye on the BMW, keeping several cars between them. No overt moves or sudden changes of direction. Morrison hadn't spotted him.

The BMW approached the I-880 interchange, but Morrison drove past the freeway entrance and turned left into the light rail lot. Mike whipped in after him and searched for parking, while keeping an eye on the suspect's movements.

Morrison pulled into a handicapped space, hung his blue placard, and bought a ticket. When the light rail train hissed into the station, he boarded through the front doors.

Heart pumping, Mike vaulted into the next train car. Through the window in the connecting door, he spotted Morrison and grabbed a pole, rather than taking a seat.

Two stops later, a woman entered with a backpack slung over one arm. Small stature, a hundred pounds at most, pretty face, and long, dark hair. She wore a colorful blouse, jeans, and sneakers.

Although there were vacant seats further back, she stood near Morrison and nodded the barest greeting. Mike pulled his cell phone from his pocket and snapped a quick shot of her.

The train screeched to a halt. She took off and the doors clanked shut behind her. Seconds later, the train jerked back into motion.

Baffled, he grimaced and peered through the window at Morrison. What was that all about? Then Mike checked the floor. She'd abandoned her backpack! But Morrison sat, unmoving, apparently ignoring it.

When the train pulled into the downtown stop, he jumped up and exited, the backpack dangling from one beefy fist. But he left his coffee cup behind. The tautness around Mike's mouth eased. His grin started small and then exploded.

He wormed his way through the crowd of passengers jostling to exit at the main station. Grabbing the empty cup by the lid, he shoved it inside his shirt and hurried toward the parking lot. He searched for his mark, but Morrison had vanished.

****

6:15 p.m.

Where was Mike? Liv's fingers clamped around her purse. Butterflies turned cartwheels in her stomach. Had she made a huge mistake and pissed him off by hustling him out the door this morning? Would he eventually show up? Or blow off their counseling appointment today?

"Liv." Dr. Holden stepped through her office doorway into the waiting room. "Mike called. He's stuck in traffic, but he'll be here shortly. Come on in."

"I don't know how much we can accomplish without him. Should we reschedule?" Stuck in traffic? Hah! Liv stomped into the office and flounced onto the couch. Typical Mike. Always angling for control.

Dr. Holden closed the door behind them and settled in her chair. "Can you set aside your irritation?"

"Certainly." Liv worked harder to mask her

127

emotions. Without Mike to draw the counselor's focus, she felt like a specimen on a microscope slide.

"You seem to have recovered from the carjacking. No lingering trauma?"

"I'm fine. Mike's still freaked."

"Can you empathize with his feelings?"

"I suppose he feels scared, protective. He insisted I have a bodyguard. I like Kathy, the police officer, but it's a pain having someone chauffer me all the time." She brushed her hand over the nape of her neck.

Dr. Holden laced her fingers and laid them in her lap. "Yet you compromised."

Liv arched an eyebrow. "I guess so."

"Since it's just the two of us, we have an opportunity to discuss your feelings about the progress you and Mike are making."

"Feelings? Actually, things have improved since we started counseling. He even admitted it last night at dinner." Struggling to appear relaxed, she leaned back on the sofa and drew a fringed pillow across her lap.

Dr. Holden's gaze followed her motions.

Heat crept up her neck and scalded her cheeks. Damn it. The counselor had noticed her defensive gesture.

"How do you feel about the decisions you made last session?"

Liv shrugged and stared out the window. How did she feel? Scared, but she couldn't say so. Embarrassed that last night she'd had sex with him more times than spiders have legs? She sure couldn't admit that. Guilty she'd treated him like someone she was ashamed to be with? Hell. Mike wanted to spend the night openly after the G-Tech party tomorrow night, but she'd been skittish and put him off. Wrong.

Soft creases bracketed the doctor's smile, but she remained silent.

Liv sighed, determined to spin her response and distract Dr. Holden. "I'm afraid I gave in too quickly. Afraid the progress we've made will all fall apart because Mike won't keep his end of the bargain. Afraid my daughter will be hurt."

"Do you trust him to continue marriage counseling?"

"Not if he has a choice."

"Establishing change in a marriage is difficult."

"It'd be easier for me to stay at work."

"What makes you feel safe at work?" Dr. Holden prodded in an even, calm tone.

"I'm in my element. I know how to form a team and accomplish goals. I'm in charge," she admitted flatly. "I grew up feeling my world was out of control."

"Families differ. What was yours like?"

"I took care of things at home while Mama and Papa worked. There was never much money and every month brought a new crisis. Papa had come as a kid from Puerto Rico, never finished high school. Mama was an authentic California girl."

The doctor looked puzzled.

Liv flashed a peace sign. "Love beads, long hair, organic food." That got a grin. She crossed her arms over the pillow, fingers digging into her elbows. After all she'd achieved, why did the way she was raised still embarrass her? "They both worked crazy hours in the store. I can't remember a time I didn't care for all six younger brothers."

"You had a lot of responsibility."

Her lips curled in a crooked smile. The urge to scream it wasn't fair bubbled through her. "I watched the kids, cooked dinner. In high school, my next oldest brother filled in sometimes, if I twisted his arm. Bottom line? I still shouldered the responsibility."

"So being in control is what you know. Is it what you enjoy?"

Oh! Zinger! This was why they paid her big bucks. She forced her fingers to loosen their grip, studying Dr. Holden's intelligent face. "That's a different question."

"Can you imagine sharing part of your burden with Mike? Trying team work?"

"I tried every day for eight years. His job was unpredictable, and it always came first. Every time I thought I could count on him for something, he'd disappear without warning and leave me scrambling, with work and home and Cara to juggle."

"But his situation is different now, isn't it?"

"He hasn't proved that to me yet. Unfortunately, today looks like more of the same."

"What about the impact your own job has on your family? Do you expect Mike to flex and accommodate emergencies or crunch times?"

The impact of her job? Liv hugged the pillow tighter, but before she could answer, she heard a knock, and a roughly dressed man wearing a matted gray beard peeked into the room. She recognized him instantly and smiled at the look of shock on the doctor's face. "Hey, Mike. You made it."

"Lieutenant Gordon?"

"Sorry I'm late." He peeled off a scruffy plaid shirt and drew a hand over his false beard. "Pile-up on 880."

Liv sat forward. "Why are you in disguise?"

"I'm on a case. Short term assignment." He sat next to her, taking her hand. Good thing he didn't smell as dirty as he looked.

She warmed at his touch, but the butterflies in her belly still fluttered like crazy. "You said your new job didn't include any undercover work. What happened?"

"Manpower shortage. Needed someone to stake out a suspect. Mostly I just sat on a cold curb and looked drunk today." He rested his hand on her shoulder and kissed her brow, but wouldn't meet her gaze. "Marino's subbing in for a couple hours. Have to go back when we're done here."

Her heart bumped. "But you're not going to disappear undercover?"

"Promise."

****

11:30 p.m.

The curtains were closed, but shadows moved across the wide expanse of window. Mike topped up his coffee from the heavy, turquoise Thermos, stretched his legs, and slumped low in the seat of his truck. He blew on the cup and took a drink.

His phone buzzed.

"Where are you?" Nate asked.

"Down the street from Morrison's place. Got a clear view. You know if I hadn't seen that drop today, I'd believe Bausch was full of hot air."

"Listen." Nate cleared his throat in that I-gotta-break-some-news-you're-gonna-hate-way.

A cold tickle crept across his neck.

"I've had three guys on our new upgraded databases since Bausch gave us the connection between Morrison and the vending business."

"They find anything?"

"Yeah. He bought the company last fall. Services mostly new start-ups. Including G-Tech."

The ice clawed down his spine. "Shit. That's the connection." He leaned his head back and closed his eyes.

"Flynn's on his way to relieve you. Come in to the station now. We need to brief Bausch. He can score a warrant and collar Morrison first thing tomorrow."

"Sounds like a plan." Mike jerked up in his seat. "Hold on a second. The garage door opened. He's backing out the BMW."

"Gordon?"

The front gate slid open on the upscale home, and Mike ducked below his window. Headlights swept past him as he heard the car accelerate.

His pulse rate kicked up another notch. "Yep, there he goes. Call Bausch. I'll check in later." Not waiting for a response, he clicked the phone off and eased his truck from the curb. Where are you headed this late, Mr. Thomas Morrison?

Mike swung around the cul-de-sac and followed the BMW south. They drove along a main thoroughfare past darkened, glitzy shops and restaurants closed for the evening. Slowing, he let a white Suburban pull in ahead of him from a side street. Good cover.

Morrison's high beams left the boulevard and flashed up a hill to the south. Dousing the truck's lights, Mike tailed him along the steep, curving road to Hakone Gardens.

Good spot for a late night rendezvous. Over the years, he and Nate had used the formal Japanese garden for more than one clandestine meeting. He continued a hundred yards beyond the parking area and hoofed it back along the trail.

Nestled into a patch of bamboo, he raised his binoculars and scanned the scene. Two cars. Two men. Arms crossed, Morrison looked annoyed, even from here. The new suspect had his back to Mike. He was almost a head shorter than Morrison, slim build, and wore a baseball cap.

The conversation was muffled by distance. Could he move nearer without rustling the bamboo? He inched closer. Obviously they thought this was a secure site. If he advanced another ten feet, he could hear the heated discussion better.

Mike tested the ground underfoot. The damp leaves would muffle his steps. No moon tonight, so his dark clothes blended into the foliage. Holding his breath, he crept within earshot.

"You did not provide what we require," Shorty declared in a clipped accent.

"Uncovering high value information's always dicey. But since they've upped their security, it'll cost you more," Morrison replied.

Shorty jerked his arms over his head.

Mike scooted closer, unable to hear, and Morrison turned, peering into the darkness.

Mike froze.

"We paid you, and the information is useless," Shorty shrieked.

"That's your problem. You got what you ordered." Morrison scanned the bamboo again, and then refocused on Shorty. "You want more, you pay more."

"We're out of time," Shorty yelled.

"I'm on it. Top priority," Morrison insisted.

"Can't you use the camera again?"

"Nah, I had to pull 'em, but I've got other options," Morrison said.

Mike's breath stopped. He silently swore into the darkness.

What options? He couldn't hear the reply. Mike grimaced, but didn't dare edge closer. Morrison was jumpy, and the single security light in the parking lot beamed directly ahead. Any further movement would give away his position.

"You don't need to know my business," Morrison shouted.

"Mumble, mumble, mumble."

Shaking his fist, Morrison interrupted, "No, God damn it! I'm gonna get her."

Her? Mike's gut gripped with dread. A spurt of alarm raced down his spine. Did Morrison mean Liv? Were they planning another carjacking?

Urgency laced Shorty's reply, but Mike couldn't make out distinct words. Hoping for a better look at the suspect, he adjusted his binoculars.

The two men turned toward the parking lot, and Mike caught a glimpse of Shorty's profile. Turned up collar, sharp chin, prominent nose.

The cars' engines revved within seconds. Mike crouched deep in the bamboo and prayed the headlights wouldn't expose him. He'd never reach his truck in time to trail them.

He dragged out his phone, rooting through old memories. Where he had seen Morrison? Tommy, Tom, T. Morrison.

Leaning on his heels, he rehashed what he'd heard. What a cluster fuck.

Chapter Thirteen

Sereno, Thursday, April 22, 1:05 p.m.

Dan paced the waiting room of the small business with his hands jammed into his pockets. Those damn cops had uncovered the connection between Morrison and G-Tech that his team of federal flunkies had missed.

Miserable Silicon Valley techies could always outstrip his federal research dinosaurs. And that late night pow-wow Gordon witnessed put Morrison right in the middle of this circus.

Dan gritted his teeth. Guess he should be grateful somebody's brain was on duty, but he'd do a year's worth of phone detail before he said thank you to that jackass, Gordon.

A young woman entered the room. Five two, dark hair and eyes, excellent figure. It took him a moment to refocus on her face, but she waited patiently.

"FBI. Daniel Bausch." He flashed his ID and pushed forward to shake the young woman's hand. A warm tingle punched up his arm, but he shook it off.

"Barb Chandler." She led him into her sparse, but efficient office, and sat facing him. The clean lines and retro style suited her. "I'm curious. What do you think I can do for the FBI?"

"I need to know how a legitimate vending business

operates for a case I'm investigating."

Her full lips arched in a faint curve. "Thus the tour and ride along."

"If you don't mind. I also need to know about unsavory industry practices." Need to know how a crook like Morrison exploited the business for espionage, Dan added silently. He pulled a small notebook from his coat pocket.

She shot him a wide, shrewd smile. "Okay. Most of us are clean, but we deal in cash, so there are lots of ways to cheat."

"Underreporting receipts?"

"You got it. I know one of my competitors cheats on his accounting."

"How did you find that out?"

"By accident. I had talked to the customer, gotten to know him. My competitor gives lousy service, so—"

"Right place, right time, and you moved in?"

"Exactly." Her dark eyes sparkled, and her face shifted from pretty to gorgeous.

An uncomfortable awareness kindled within him.

"But when I saw the guy a couple weeks ago, he accused me of getting the account the easy way. On my back." She flushed. "As if."

An X-rated picture flashed behind his eyes. No way, Bausch. Not while you're on a case. "Who was he?"

Her cheek muscles tensed, and her lips thinned to a laser line. "Thomas Morrison. The slimy, macho sleaze took over Silicon Valley Vending last year."

"Interesting." He bounced his eraser against the pad, frowning. Had Morrison moved in intending to target G-Tech? Dan glanced up at the scrappy young woman.

"Ready?" she asked, ponytail swinging as she turned. Her slacks hugged her tiny waist and curved over her very nice ass.

Focus on the job, Bausch. He flipped his notepad shut and stood.

"My truck's out back." She led him into a two-story warehouse filled with pallets of beverages and snacks. A dozen modern vending machines lined one wall.

He whistled appreciatively. "It looks like Aladdin's cave in here, only the goodies are better organized."

"Thanks!" She shot him a perfect grin. "I need to replace one soda machine, so I'll load that first. A former employee broke in with a steel cutter and stole the money, bill stacker and all. I lost five hundred bucks."

"Ouch."

She shrugged. "I caught it on the camera, and the police already nabbed the guy."

"Surveillance?"

"Oh, yeah. We all have systems."

Another domino snapped into place. "Give me a demo?"

****

4:45 p.m.

Wincing at the sharp bottom-of-the-pot bitterness, Mike let the hot coffee trickle down his throat. He leaned back in his scarred, wooden chair.

Nate knocked on the doorframe. "Hey, partner."

"Pull up a chair."

Nate sat and stretched his long legs in front of him, setting his coffee cup on the beat-up oak desk. "Jana wanted me to remind you about the hospital benefit Saturday."

Mike let out a long, painful sounding moan. "Two in one week. There's another command performance tonight, celebrating Dragonfly with the VCs. Hell of a way to spend my time."

"Frost is watching Morrison. Relax and enjoy a night off with your wife."

"Gonna try. And thanks for keeping Cara overnight. Makes tomorrow morning, uh…"

"More fun?"

"Something like that." Grinning, Mike spiked his fingers through his hair. "But I just don't see why Liv gets such a charge from dressing me in a monkey suit?"

"It isn't only Liv. Jana loves to see me all spiffed up too." Nate gulped his coffee.

"Get this. The last time I griped about the tie, Liv offered to wear one anytime I'd wear hose and heels."

Nate choked on his java and jumped to his feet, shaking the splatters off his fingers. "You in drag?"

"You never know," he said, batting his eyelashes.

Nate lost it, doubled over with laughter, and gasped for breath.

Mike thumped him on the back. "I need to get a move on. Have to pick up a little surprise I ordered for Liv. Something sparkly."

"Always a good plan." Sinking into his chair, Nate studied his expression. "You know, it sticks in my craw not to brief Liv."

"She grilled me on the phone this morning. I figure she'll tear a strip off Bausch when she discovers his no info policy." Mike clicked his pen. "Any matches on Morrison's prints?"

"No, damn it," Nate groused. "Record's absolutely clean."

A cold sensation gripped his nerves. He twirled the pen between his fingers. "Did Bausch give you a timeline for when he's going to move on the scumbag?"

"Not yet."

"Morrison makes my skin crawl."

****

9:20 p.m.

No apparent threat. Trying to be subtle, Mike watched Liv across the open-air patio in the century-old hotel. She stood by the buffet talking to one of her engineers. Kathy Linden, dressed in sequins, heels, and a thigh holster, hovered three paces away.

Tonight was one more hurdle Liv wanted him to clear. Mike's black bow tie choked him, so he inserted a finger under his collar to loosen it. He didn't really mind the rest of the get-up too much. Last year she had lassoed him into buying his own tux. She'd been right. The pants were actually long enough, and the custom-tailored jacket fit perfectly with extra room under the arm for his weapon.

The patio blazed with lights. Tall metal space heaters pumped islands of warmth into the chilly air. He leaned one shoulder against a stucco arch and scanned the room for interesting faces.

Mike spied the angry scowl of a small, heavy-set man. Five-eight, maybe. One-ninety. But what was with the pink polka-dot tie? The man stroked his salt-and-pepper goatee with three fingers, shifting his weight from foot to foot while speaking in strident whispers to his companion.

He watched the pair. Yep, the other guy was

pissed. Clean-shaven, taller, and very wiry, his angry voice carried. Mike tuned in when he heard Liv's name.

"She won't make the deadline," Mr. Wiry practically shouted. "The partners at my firm are considering withdrawing our investment."

Mike frowned.

Mr. Goatee held up his hands. "But G-Tech has the contract. The beta tests are surpassing specs. Can't you reassure—"

"I can't reassure anyone about a company's management when I have doubts. I talked to my contact at the Bureau." Wiry looked around and lowered his voice, "They're freaked out. Even the Pentagon is goosey."

Pulse buzzing, Mike strained to hear the response. He wandered closer, grateful this once, for his invisibility in a tux.

Wiry had the floor. "My protégée is an ex-SEAL with an MBA. The security leaks would vanish if he was G-Tech's CEO."

Mike's stomach pitched.

"Liv can pull this off," Goatee argued. "The FBI has been all over her like a case of shingles, and she's still early and under budget. Did you hear about the demo the other day? Even the senator is on board now."

"Fine, but if there's even another hint—"

Goatee pointed his finger at Wiry's potbelly. "If your firm wants out, I'll hold the door. I know several investors who wish they'd jumped in early, but they won't get a second chance. I'll snap up the equity myself. They don't call Liv a wonder kid for nothing."

Mike exhaled and drew a needed breath. Wonder kid. Yep. Time to check on her.

He located Liv on the far edge of the dance floor, deep in conversation with one of the venture capital principals.

The music ended, and she shook the guy's hand flashing him a brilliant smile before moving smoothly through the crowd.

Man, look at her body. He whistled under his breath. The slinky red dress clung to her flat tummy and sleekly rounded hips. It shimmered across her high, perfect breasts, revealing just enough to tantalize and send his libido spinning blindly.

He smiled and knocked back the last sip of his tonic water. Tomorrow morning he'd confess to eavesdropping and warn her of the potential threat to her job.

Intent on moving in for the kill, he handed his empty glass to a passing waiter, but when he turned, he found Alyssa Manchester in front of him and gave her a startled grin.

"Great party."

She had tamed her hair and worn a little makeup. "You look nice tonight, Alyssa."

"Yeah, well, I'm not crawling out from under a super-heated Hummer." She chuckled and modeled her little black dress. "Tonight's a big deal for us."

"You put in the hours. I know what it took to get G-Tech moving. Liv said she had to twist your arm to steal you from NASA."

"With my stock options? Not much twisting." Alyssa beamed. "Besides, I'd rather work for Liv."

****

9:30 p.m.

"You bet we'll deliver on time. Would you excuse

me for a moment?" Liv shook hands with the investor and scanned the room for Mike.

She spotted him standing by one of the big space heaters talking to Alyssa. And hello? He had a genuine smile on his face.

Liv skirted the floor, hoping she could fit in a dance with him before another financial type cornered her.

As she approached, Mike looked up, smile widening into a dazzling grin. His dark blue eyes sparkled like sunlight on deep water. Their seductive pull lit a curl of desire low in her body.

A fleeting frown creased his brow, and he dipped his head toward Alyssa. "Sorry, didn't catch that. A certain vision in red distracted me."

Alyssa faced her with a grin. "Turns out he's not a bad guy."

"You doing okay?" Liv asked her.

"Great, but I'm about ready to call it a night." Alyssa yawned and checked her watch. "I'll wait until after your speech, but I have to be in the lab by five a.m. When are you going to get it over with?"

"Give me ten minutes. I want a dance with this guy first." Her gaze flashed to Mike, and her mind hazed at the look of naked desire on his face.

"I've been waiting to get my arms around you all night, Madame CEO." Radiating warmth and strength, Mike slipped a hand behind her waist and swung her onto the dance floor.

The band began a quick tango, and Liv smiled.

"You're gorgeous this evening, Olivia. Want to come home with me?"

Her fingers smoothed the shiny lapel of his tux as

she matched his smile. "What kind of a girl do you take me for?"

His eyebrows rose. Something hot and primal flashed in his eyes. "The only one I'll ever want."

Her focus narrowed, and the dancers near them blurred. The truth sideswiped her like a text message from the universe, weakened her knees and parched her mouth. He'd meant it. He'd never touched Samantha. Damn. The woman had been delusional. Liv snaked her arms around his neck, melting against her husband.

"You smell like heaven." He nuzzled her and trailed moist kisses where her neck and shoulder met. Need built, electricity jumped between them like a magneto and zapped her from head to heels, hitting all the good spots in between.

Her skirt swept around his legs, and he slid his fingers underneath her gown to caress her bare back. Her nipples formed tight buds.

"I like you in red, Livy."

"Why do you think I wore this?" She ran a hand through the lock of hair trailing onto his forehead.

He brushed his lips against her ear and whispered, "I'd like you even better in nothing."

The dampness between her thighs pulsed with the exotic tango beat throbbing in the background.

Mike circled her, concentrating fiercely, gaze never leaving hers. As he passed, one finger traced the line of her jaw.

Under his scrutiny, she retreated, her steps matching the beat of the music.

Step for step, he stalked her like a graceful, muscular panther with his prey in sight.

Her pulse raced, pounding in her ears, but she

couldn't wrench her gaze away from his.

He was almost upon her, leaning forward. Intense. Intent. He shifted direction, and her head snapped around, drawn by his enraptured expression.

A quick side step and his foot thrust between her legs.

She rubbed one arched instep along his calf.

A smile nudged one corner of his mouth, and his blue eyes smoldered, pupils dilated. He supported her weight as she submitted to his lead.

Held safe in his arms, need blazed. She trembled. Each breath came in a heart pounding, raspy little gasp. She needed him naked and inside her, filling her aching emptiness. Her tongue darted out to moisten her open lips.

The music reached a crescendo, and his fingers tightened convulsively around her waist. Bending her backward, he leaned over her and kissed her. "I want you, Livy," he said in a low, fierce voice.

She dragged a nail across his bottom lip. "Even if I've been a naughty girl tonight?"

****

11:50 p.m.

A tingle of anticipation fizzed in Mike's bloodstream. He followed Liv up their front steps with his hand on her warm, smooth back. He traced the shallow valley of her spine.

Goose bumps rose on her skin, and she hummed a few bars of the tango they had danced to.

He grinned. Good thing Nate and Jana had taken Cara for the whole night. They had the place to themselves, and he had a couple surprises planned.

She dropped her silver bag on the entry table and

slipped off her shoes with a groan. "I've wanted to do that for hours."

"You should have. You're the boss."

"That's exactly why I couldn't." She walked across the tile and into the kitchen.

"Is pain the price of success?"

She hesitated and turned toward him. "Didn't you have a good time?"

"A great time. Loved the steak." Damn, she knew him too well. He rummaged in the side-by-side, hiding his expression. "I just don't know everyone like you do."

"You were patient tonight. Thanks. You even charmed Alyssa." She slipped her arms around his waist from behind.

His blood surged, heavy and hot. He pulled a bottle of chilled French champagne and a small turquoise jewelry box from the vegetable drawer where he'd stashed them when he came to pick Liv up. He turned in her arms and handed her the box, hoping she saw his lecherous grin. "Do I get a reward?"

"Maybe." She took the present. "When did you get this?"

"I have my secrets." He set the champagne on the counter, grabbed two crystal flutes, and popped the cork. While she tackled the wrapping, he poured.

Her mouth opened with a gasp as she held up a ruby and diamond bracelet that matched her necklace. "It's beautiful. Thank you."

His eyebrows did a Groucho impression as he fastened it around her wrist. He kissed her lightly on the pulse point at the base of her palm, handing her a glass and lifting his own. "To my beautiful wife."

A flare of arousal lit her eyes, and she took a sip. "Clever boy. Time for the real party." Smiling, she turned and prowled across the kitchen.

She flicked the light switch, and the room softened to shimmering moonlight.

He could see her, with her dress muted to dark maroon, her full breasts luscious against the silk. Her expression reminded him of a bobcat he'd cornered in a tree when he was a kid. Only now, she had him cornered. Man, this was fun.

She sipped the pale amber liquid, eyeing him hungrily over the bubbles. Then she snagged his glass and set them both on the island. "I've been thinking about sex all evening."

His brain fuzzed. He kissed her hard and turned toward the stairs.

Shaking a finger at him, she slipped one hand into the waistband of his trousers and purred, "Here."

He hardened in a blink, his mouth dry with need.

Reaching up, she kissed him languidly. Her fingers walked a trail down his chest, and she traced him through his trousers with one long, red nail. "Have I ever told you how much I love your body?"

"Um, yeah," was all he could croak.

She sank to her knees and lowered his zipper. Slowly. Tooth by tooth.

He sucked in air.

Her small hands freed his erection from his boxers and slid down to cup his balls while she licked from base to tip like a kid with an ice cream cone. A cone where the ice cream was melting all over the place, and the kid wanted to capture every delicious drop.

He grunted something incoherent and strained

toward her luscious mouth.

Licking her lips, she said, "Um. Very nice."

Mesmerized by her lush, red lips, he quivered in her hands. "Olivia," his voice rumbled and then cracked.

She drew him inside a little at a time, and he held still. Her warm, wet tongue rasped, varying the pace and the pressure until he was achingly, painfully hard.

Spots danced before his eyes. He gasped, realizing he hadn't taken a breath in over a minute. Was it the picture she made? Or the magic she worked?

She tilted her head and did an incredible half-swallowing move, drawing him in deep, making every nerve ending in his body pulse.

He drew back and hung on to the counter. Torrents of sensation cascaded through his body like a fast moving avalanche as her mouth and throat caressed his whole length. Afraid he'd explode, he smoothed his shaky hands over her hair and slid out.

He reached for her, but she dodged. She rose gracefully and stepped backwards. Her sultry laugh echoed through the room. Slipping her fingers under the straps of her dress, she let it fall in a pool of silk at her feet.

His chin dropped. Brilliant sparks seared through him with scalding intensity. His pulse raced, but no oxygen made the trip north.

Oh, man. He reveled in the sight of her, drinking her in. She was nearly naked, wearing only thigh high stockings, and the rubies and diamonds at her throat and wrist. Look at all that soft, creamy skin.

He closed his mouth and grinned. "Naughty little CEO." His voice had dropped an octave.

"You love it when I'm bad." She grinned back. "I almost told you on the dance floor, but I figured you'd throw me over your shoulder and head for the door."

"Got that right."

She shifted her weight, right knee forward, hips off-center. Silver moonlight danced over her beautiful body.

He took one more sip of champagne and moved to her side, planning to carry her to bed, but she had other ideas. She rose on tiptoes and scooted backwards onto the center island. Better plan.

Her move brought them eye-to-eye and everything else matched too. He had already shed his coat and she worked her way down his dress shirt, releasing the studs.

"Your hair is so beautiful." He removed the crystal clasp, and the waves unraveled, dark and silky, down her naked back.

Her scent thrilled his senses. She moved closer and spread her warm palms on his chest. Closer. Blood pounded through his groin in pulsing waves.

Cupping her nape, he kissed her mouth, cheeks, nose, and eyelids.

Her neck arched against his caresses.

His lips moved to her ear, hands sliding over her smooth skin.

She sighed, and her nipples tightened under his palms.

Running his hands up her stocking-clad thighs, he shifted her legs apart and moved her closer to the edge of the island. He probed her moist warm folds. She was so ready for him.

She tensed and drew in a swift breath. "Now,

Mike, please. I've wanted you all evening."

He closed his eyes, focusing, holding on to the last of his sanity. "Nope. This is way too good to rush."

Leaning forward, he caressed her neck and collarbones with tongue and lips. His open mouth slid over her breast, and he suckled them in turn, teasing her nipples to stiff, rosy peaks.

Moaning, she shifted restlessly and drew her nails along his arms while he trailed kisses across her belly.

He blew on the damp flesh between her legs, hands shaping her hips, and she whimpered. He plied gentle pressure between her folds and tasted her, loving her scent, loving her texture. Loving the way she responded to him, all moist and swollen and ready.

He drew her nub between his lips, and Liv made small, mewling gasps as her fingers speared through his hair. Then he straightened, lifted her forward, sheathing himself in her slick, scalding velvet.

Arching to meet him, she wrapped her legs around his waist, her hands grasping his shoulders for leverage.

Mike was bathed in sweat. He shook and gasped for breath with each thrust. His heartbeat hammered in his ears.

She tightened around him and screamed his name. Her shudders sent him reeling over the edge in great, pulsing waves of pleasure.

Chapter Fourteen

Sereno, Friday, April 23, 2:35 p.m.

Dan Bausch drummed his fingers on his knee and stared at the two onyx-faced cops. Background noise from dispatch sifted through Kapulani's closed door into the office. "My undercover coordinator came up blank. With that attack near those generating plants taking so much man power, there's no one else I can tap. I need Gordon now."

Lieutenant Gordon vibrated with anxiety, his angry face scowling. Not a happy copper. "Give me a minute and let me think." He rose and stared out the window, hands fisted on his hips.

From the seat behind his desk, the captain watched with a stony expression and hooded eyes.

Alternatively stretching and tensing his shoulder muscles, Dan sifted the limited options through his mind, but nothing new popped. Gordon was a grenade-with-the-pin-pulled rolling across the floor.

He wanted a different scenario with an operative he could control, but he couldn't make that happen in time. "If you don't think you can handle it," he prodded.

Gordon turned, his features livid. "That's not the problem!"

Dan faced him, palms up. "Look, you were the one who insisted the perps are poised to act. There's no time to snag a federal warrant, bring in a specialist, and get him briefed. If we blow this, we can write an obit for a vital defense secret."

"Not to mention my wife," Gordon snapped, slamming his fist against the wall. "Damn it, Nate. Did we get anything on the tags at Hakone?"

Kapulani folded his hands in front of him. "Stolen from a couple of female profs on sabbatical in Costa Rica."

Dan glanced at the floor to cover his blatant lie. "Nothing on the woman with the backpack, either." No way could he disclose Miriam Kazan's real employer.

Kapulani hoisted an eyebrow and leaned back in his chair, but remained silent.

Dan met the cop's angry black stare without flinching.

Thumbs hooked in his front pockets, Gordon crossed the room and loomed over Dan. "I don't like the set-up."

"What would convince you?"

Kapulani tipped forward, and his chair made a long, grating squeak. "Hold on a minute, Bausch. Granted, we're racing a stopwatch, but your scenario goes against all the regs. Thought you were the rules and more fucking rules guy?"

"I'm not thrilled about it either, but since Gordon was already involved investigating Morrison, the SAC documented his conflict of interest and cleared him for the assignment. You got a better option?" Dan demanded.

The captain turned to Gordon. "Both Underwood and Santana are up to their asses in gangbangers. Can't yank either of them or we'd jeopardize that sting. Even pulled a couple guys from Alameda County to investigate those eastside murders."

"Marino has a full calendar too." Gordon cracked his knuckles. "But damn it! She'll never understand. I flat out promised Liv no undercover. Besides, I need to stay home to protect her and Cara."

Kapulani blew out a slow breath that verged on a growl. "Nobody else in the department can handle the assignment."

"Wouldn't matter anyway. None of them have my clearance," the lieutenant muttered. He grabbed a pen and started clicking the freaking thing.

Pulse thudding, Dan spread another layer of flypaper. "If Gordon's personal connection makes him too involved…"

Eyes unblinking, face red and stiff, Gordon stared at him. The pen snapped in two. "Damn straight, I'm involved. Liv is an innocent civilian. I need to be by her side, not stuck undercover hauling fucking candy bars."

Dan fought the urge to loosen his collar. The snarl on the lieutenant's face would have had most guys beating a retreat, but he stood, straightened his tie, and returned the glare. "Unfortunately, you're my only option, at least for the next couple days."

The captain pinched the bridge of his nose. "Mike, if it makes you feel better, I'll personally supervise the guards around Liv until you're back."

"If I agree. Liv comes first."

"Mike's the best, and we know why he's even considering this assignment, but I won't order him to go." Square jaw jutting, Kapulani added, "His decision."

Dan counted three seconds of silence, his tension

melting with each tick. "He reports to me."

"One condition." Gordon held up a hand. "Before I go under, I brief Liv."

"Impossible. We need her focused on the drone."

"She needs to know."

"Do it and I'll lock your ass up so tight—" Dan broke off and sucked in a breath. "You have no idea what's at stake. Absolutely no conditions."

"Then fuck off. My wife and my marriage come first. We're taking the next plane to Buenos Aires," Gordon said in a laser-edged voice.

Dan jerked, but let his forehead wrinkle and brows cramp together. Shit. He hadn't anticipated that response. He crossed his arms and spoke in a low, emotionless tone, "So, you're willing to have twenty or thirty thousand civilian casualties, maybe more, on your conscience?"

The cop didn't reply, just stared at his hands. But his pale, stiff face spoke volumes.

Dan softened his expression and his voice, but not much. "Gordon, the best chance we have of keeping your wife alive is to keep her in the dark a few more days. No briefing. No fucking conditions."

Both cops scowled at him. "Huge mistake," Kapulani muttered.

"Another two days, max. Then you can spill your guts to her."

Gordon grunted his distaste, but nodded. "Forty-eight hours."

Ignoring them, Dan buttoned his coat and straightened his lapels, savoring the satisfying buzz of triumph. "My informant's expecting you at four thirty. What name do you want to use?"

****

4:25 p.m.

Swirling an iced tea that looked like whiskey, Mike hunched over a tall corner table in the microbrewery.

He pitched his voice higher than normal and colored his speech with the hint of a twang, "Been on the wagon five years. Need to impress this guy. Don't want him to know I used to drink."

"Got it, honey." The short, bleached-blonde waitress smiled, a gap visible between her two front teeth. "I'll make sure you only get tea. Don't you worry 'bout a thing."

"You're a doll." He slipped her a couple twenties and shoved his metal-rimmed, aviator-style glasses back onto the bridge of his nose.

Mike sat facing the door and pretended to watch the giant TV screen. The baseball game and conversation from the happy hour crowd merged into a droning roar. He stretched out the crick in his back and scanned the crowd, waiting for Bausch's contact to show.

For the tenth time, Mike fingered his hair, cut short and darkened to match brown contacts. He had applied a droopy moustache one tiny hair at a time, added streaks of gray at his temples, and waxed his forehead, making his hairline recede. Dye tinted the stubble on his face and putty disguised the cleft in his chin.

An itchy layer of padding around his belly, stooped shoulders, and a pronounced slouch gave him the depressed, ineffective look he was going for and shaved inches off his height. A wide belt with his dad's calf-roping buckle suspended worn jeans above down-at-the-heel cowboy boots. He inspected the grease under his fingernails and rolled the frayed cuffs of his blue work shirt. This disguise could fool even Liv for a few seconds.

Bausch's snitch pushed through the double doors of the bar. Over six-two, Les Hamlin had a buzz cut and massive arms and shoulders. According to Bausch's intelligence, the guy didn't have a record, but Morrison used him for muscle.

The familiar hormone-hit raced in his blood, and he drew a deep breath through his nose. If it weren't for Liv, he'd enjoy the rush of clarity.

His guts twisted into fiery knots as he remembered the promise he'd made yesterday. This had to be an exception. Liv was in grave danger. He'd gone undercover to protect her, but he hadn't spoken to her or explained, only left the message that he couldn't pick up Cara.

He glared at his drink and took control, calming his heart rate and breathing. When the guy paused in front of him, Mike made eye contact. "You Hamlin?"

"Yeah, Les Hamlin. Mickey O'Neal?"

Mike noticed the anchor tattoo on the informant's left forearm, remembering the Popeye cartoons he'd watched as a kid. He inclined his head toward the empty chair across the table. "Sit? Want a drink?"

Hamlin perched on a stool. Checking the room's dark corners, his eyes were never still. He leaned in close. "I'm pretty sure the boss don't suspect nothing."

Mike stared at him, but didn't reply.

"He, uh, he ain't a guy you want mad at you. Got a long memory when he's looking for revenge."

"Got it."

"What's the deal? You don't look like one of

Bausch's suits."

"Temporary."

Deep lines creased Hamlin's forehead.

Mike passed his newly minted FBI ID under the table.

Hamlin scrutinized the picture, but didn't look happy.

"Relax. I can handle it. Bausch deputized me for this operation. We go way back." He swirled the ice cubes in his tea. "How 'bout a drink?"

"Beer sounds good."

So far Hamlin hadn't shut him down, but he hadn't bought in, either. Mike motioned to the waitress and pointed at his glass. "Another one of these, and my friend wants a beer. What's on tap?"

She rattled off the list, and Hamlin ordered a pint.

Mike kicked back and took a loud slurp. "What's Morrison like?"

"Sharp operator, runs a tight ship." Hamlin rubbed his nose with broad fingers and lowered his voice, "But he's got a temper, and like I said, a long memory."

"How'd you wind up working for him?"

"Fell into it. When I left the service, a cousin hooked me up with Morrison's uncle." He flexed the arm with the tattoo.

"Marines? Thought so. Bausch and I did a hitch together." He stared into his glass then looked sideways at Hamlin, slipping deeper into character and embellishing the yarn. "Rangers. Can't go into detail, but we survived a couple dangerous assignments."

"Ah." Hamlin nodded, scratching his ear absently.

"When we got out, I took over the family ranch, and he went to the FBI, but we kept in touch."

Hamlin gave him an approving look.

The waitress sashayed back with their drinks and winked. "Here you go." She bent and set his glass on the table.

Hamlin's gaze fixed on her cleavage. "Thanks, cutie."

"No problem. Anything else you guys need?"

"Maybe later."

Hamlin watched her walk away, gaze tracking her swaying hips. "Anyway, I started doing special deliveries for Louie Souza, Morrison's uncle. Delivered packages, if you know what I mean."

Mike cocked his head to the side. Maybe the guy would blab some incriminating details.

"The kind where you don't ask what's in 'em. And I, uh, helped him maintain discipline."

His pulse raced, but he kept his expression blank.

"Busted some heads, you know? I never got uptight about the details when I did favors for the boss."

Hamlin might be a small time crook but he was being straight now. Mike gave him a calculating grin. "Rewards loyalty?"

"Yeah. You know, I kinda like you, Mickey. You're sharp, catch on real quick." Hamlin's fingers stopped twitching. "Morrison moved me out here six months ago, when he took over SVV."

Mike gulped his drink and crunched a piece of ice, his every sense on full alert. "Any, uh, anybody else I should watch?"

Hamlin drew on his beer. Then he shook his head. "Everyone else is harmless. The other drivers keep their ears closed. They don't trust Morrison, but want to keep their routes. Office girls are a bunch of airheads.

Morrison makes sure they're loaded, but not with brains."

Mike leered on cue.

"There's Morrison's tame lawyer at Atlantic Partners." Hamlin sneered. "Worked back east for the family. The candy-ass thinks he's hot shit, but I ain't seen him around SVV much."

"He in on the deal?"

"That turd. No way. Other than bragging about the money, Morrison ain't said squat to me, and I been with him for six years."

Mike narrowed his eyes, sweeping the man with a sharp gaze. What was the guy's motivation? "Sounds like you have a sweet set-up. Why rock the boat?"

"I was okay until that foreigner surfaced. Some things a man can't stomach." Hamlin's lips thinned, and he rubbed a knuckle across his broad chin. "I listened when he talked to the boss about that 'bug' thing, but I was real subtle. They never knew I heard 'em. Pissed me off. That's when I called the feds."

His heartbeat echoed in his ears, but he kept his face impassive. That jerk-off, Bausch, was right. Bug? They were after Dragonfly, and Liv could be their target.

Mike set down the glass to keep from crushing it. "That's why I'm here. How do I worm my way in?"

****

4:40 p.m.

Morrison shoved Sid Sylvester into the chair and stomped across the marble floor to wind his grandfather clock. He inserted the key and cranked the spring, watching the weights rise. "Time to hit a stationary target."

Sid cleared his throat. "Gordon's been with her a couple nights this week."

A surge of excitement pulsed in his blood. Tapping his finger on his lip, he closed the glass and turned to Sid. No time for a personnel change. He was stuck with this stupid fuck. "Then you'll have to be more careful. No more screw-ups. Grunt work or not, you're responsible."

****

4:46 p.m.

Fourteen more minutes. Standing behind the classroom podium, Liv slipped her shoe off and on. She usually enjoyed teaching her entrepreneurship seminar, but this afternoon her muscles were knotted, and she flinched at every odd sound. Mike was working a stakeout again today, and her nerves were frazzled.

She scanned the fifty-some students seated around a three-tiered semicircle. Cara sat in the last chair on her right engrossed in a computer math game. Liv had brought her along instead of leaving her at daycare. No way she'd let her daughter out of her sight right now.

Liv adjusted the post on her earring. No matter how she'd badgered Mike this morning, he'd refused to explain his assignment. But she could tell he felt guilty from the edgy, almost frantic way he made love to her before she left to pick up Cara this morning.

After dinner tonight she'd wheedle the details out of him. She blinked and returned her focus to the classroom.

"This case illustrates how leadership skills and an ability to understand market forces and roll with the punches are the keys to entrepreneurial success," Miriam Kazan summarized her study group's conclusions. Her full lips smiled broadly, her dark eyes shining with intelligence under her hijab.

Liv nodded. "Excellent analysis."

A hand shot up. She sighed. Him again? "Mr. Mustafa?"

"What about your own business? How did the international terrorist threat shape G-Tech's product choices?" Ahmed Mustafa, her other student from Krzystan leaned across his laptop with his hands drawn into clenched fists. Bright and intuitive, he seemed almost too intense.

She blinked twice, damping down her impatience. "Broad question. Current tensions around the world affect the entire market."

"But what about your technology?"

A crazy, sick feeling churned her stomach, and her mental alarms went bonkers. What was this guy doing? "I'm sorry. I can't comment."

"The products in today's case were military drones. Did you choose this case because they are similar to what your company makes?"

A cold thread of anxiety twisted through her. "In a word? No. I'm sorry. G-Tech products are classified. Please don't mention the subject again." Would she have to report this conversation to the FBI? She ignored his waving hand and threw him a withering look.

His features hardened with frustration. Then something else surfaced. Fear?

He looked terrified! Her heart drummed in fast, ineffective beats, crowding her breath into shallow bursts. Had the week's events made her paranoid or could Ahmed be a threat?

Chilled, she rubbed her hands together. Maybe he

was after info for a venture in his home country.

Her intuition pinged again. No, that couldn't be right. There was more to his desperate expression and dogged pushiness. He made her hair stand on end.

Drawing a slow, fragmented breath, she forced a smile. No question. She'd report the joker to the DOD. "I'll see all of you Tuesday. You have the Jet Blue case to prepare."

The students left the auditorium quickly. Kathy Linden waited near the door while Liv gathered her lecture notes.

"Time to go, sweetheart," she told Cara. "Hungry?"

Cara grabbed her game. "Can we get take-out?"

"Why not? We girls deserve a treat. Do you like Chinese, Kathy?"

"My favorite." Kathy winked at Cara.

"We can get enough for Daddy. He's coming over for dinner, isn't he?" Cara clapped her hands and wiggled.

"He promised to come by and tuck you in if he could." With her arm draped around Cara's shoulders, Liv led her daughter from the room. She was fed up with feeling the back of her neck prickle like someone was spying on her. Fed up with feeling clueless.

Chapter Fifteen

Sereno, Saturday, April 24, 12:00 a.m.

Monster sized American flags flapped overhead, spotlighted against the night sky. Mike drove the panel truck into the third car dealership of the evening, with Hamlin riding shotgun.

Midnight. So far his only chance to call Liv had been while he was working on his disguise, but she'd been teaching at that time, and she always turned her cell off while she was in class. He couldn't risk leaving the details on her voice mail, but he needed to warn her tonight. He'd skate as close to Bausch's orders as he could and still give her a heads-up.

Fuck Bausch. The sneaky bastard had read his mind and confiscated his cell phone, insisting Mike shouldn't carry any traceable electronics. He'd pocketed a secure prepaid phone from the department's stash anyway, even though Bausch had dogged his steps.

Climbing out of the truck, Mike hurried toward the loading gate. Maybe there was a men's room here. Since he'd made contact with Les, he hadn't had a moment alone to call Liv. She needed to watch her back, even with Nate on the job.

Mike made an angry grunting noise. If she thought he'd gone undercover without any explanation, he could kiss their marriage and his family goodbye. She'd never listen again.

Effortlessly, Les stacked six cases on a trolley and wheeled them off. He turned to Mike and chuckled. "I love repair waiting rooms. There's nothing for customers to do except eat junk and watch daytime TV."

Les filled the machine and then keyed open the moneychanger. Coins clinked into a canvas bag. Bundling bills from the stacker with an accounting slip, he tucked the haul into a leather backpack and slung it over his shoulder. The heavy bag jingled with each step.

"Nice take."

"Even more from charge cards, but those receipts go straight to the office."

Les locked the vending machine and tossed him a chocolate bar, unwrapping a second. "You wanna stop for food soon? Murphy's Place is just up the road," he mumbled, his mouth full of chocolate.

"Sounds good, but let me hit the head first." Mike sighed and masked his frown. Instead of making things right with his wife he was stuck watching this dude wolf candy bars.

"Sure. Meet you at the truck."

"I'll catch up." Mike pocketed the candy bar and headed for the john. By now Liv would be wondering where the hell he was. One FBI Agent had tried her damndest to destroy his marriage. A second one might succeed.

He secured the door to a stall, pulled the phone from his pocket and dialed. The phone rang once. Pick up, Liv. He flushed so Les wouldn't overhear the conversation.

The door slammed open. "What's taking ya so long, Mickey?"

Mike jumped at the sound of the marine's voice and dropped the phone. Damn. He wanted to kick the stall door open and strangle Les, but instead watched the electronics fry in the swirling water.

****

12:15 a.m.

Liv's eyes snapped open. She hitched in a deep breath and glanced at the angular metal wall clock behind the family room sofa. She must have dozed off. Past midnight already, and she hadn't heard from Mike.

She shrugged off the red and black throw, grabbed the phone from the coffee table, and punched in his cell number.

Four long rings and his voice mail kicked in. She loved the sound of his rumbling message. "Mike. Where are you? Cara waited up for you. When you have a chance, call and let me know what's happening."

Facing the floor to ceiling windows, she stared into the darkness. Hopefully, he'd call back soon and then she'd learn what was going on.

A faint scraping noise and a muffled thump came from the rear of the house. Her stomach plummeted as if punched by an invisible fist. Shutting her eyes, she concentrated. Had she imagined the sounds? She chewed on her lip for a moment, remembering the patrol Nate had ordered when he dropped by earlier. Probably just the cop on duty.

Goose bumps prickled her arms. Rubbing at them, she draped the throw around her shoulders. With everything that had happened, it made sense she was jumpy. Should she check in with Sereno PD anyway?

She stood and padded toward their bedroom. Unable to shake the nagging fear creeping over her scalp, she sat on the edge of the bed and lifted the receiver. Better to be safe, even if Mike's buddies did razz her.

Dispatch took her name, but halfway through giving her address, she heard Cara's bedroom window break. Chills tore through her spine, freezing her for an instant that seemed like an eternity. "It's a break-in! Hurry!"

Terror streaked through every cell in her body. She rushed to the gun safe for Mike's twelve-gauge. Her hands felt cold and stiff, almost detached, but she managed to pocket a handful of shotgun shells, slammed two into the magazine, and racked them into the chamber.

Could she pull the trigger? She banged her door open. Damn right, she could.

Desperate to protect her daughter, Liv ran down the hall. In the glow from Cara's nightlight, she saw the shattered window. A burly man balanced on the sill with one leg poked through.

Cara cowered in her bed.

Blood rushing in her ears, Liv planted her feet flat on the floor and braced for battle. She raised the Browning, propped it against her shoulder, and shrieked, "Get away from my baby or I'll shoot!"

Cara rocketed from the bed toward her, screaming, "Mommy!"

The man straightened and hooked an arm around the window frame as if to pull inside.

His features, blurred and flattened by a stocking

mask, jarred her memory. The carjacking creep with the tire iron.

Liv fired.

Buckshot sprayed his leg and the bedroom wall.

Her ears rang, and the recoil slammed her on her butt.

The burglar's ragged scream pierced her near deafness and touched off a satisfied thrill.

He dropped off the windowsill, and a second voice shouted obscenities from outside.

Scrambling to her feet, she pulled Cara into the hall and poked the old pump action Browning out the window.

She fired again.

The thunderclap jerked her head, but this time she kept her footing.

She peeked outside. Nothing close, but shadows retreated in the distance. She chambered another shell, aimed, and fired.

Sirens wailed in the distance over the ringing in her ears. Thank God.

Jagged rushes of fear shook her body as she hurried to her daughter.

Cara climbed into her outstretched arms and hid her face against Liv's neck, sobbing and clutching a lock of her hair.

Liv dragged her gaze away from the shattered glass and gaping blackness of the window. She struggled to swallow the terror and rage rising inside her, struggled to reassure her daughter, but her voice refused to cooperate.

She cuddled Cara's warm body closer and buried her nose in the child's hair, inhaling the comforting scent of baby shampoo.

The sirens screeched closer.

She stumbled along the hall, carrying her daughter on one hip and Mike's shotgun in her other hand.

Through the sidelights, she saw three Sereno PD cruisers speed into the driveway, following Nate's black-and-white SUV.

She threw open the front door and stood, shivering, on the threshold. "Backyard," she croaked.

Cops she knew, Mike's buddies, friends of hers, poured from their cars wearing unfamiliar, grim expressions. Weapons at ready, alertness telegraphed by their tense muscles and set jaws, they peeled off and flanked the house.

Nate jogged up, gun in hand, and threw an arm around her. "You two okay?"

Liv nodded, trembling violently, her breath coming in shaky, rasping sobs.

He took the Browning, then held them both until Liv got control of her breathing. He ushered them inside. He ejected spent casings from the shotgun, dropped them on the counter, and set the gun out of sight. "Tell me what happened. You fired this tonight. Hit anything?"

Angry heat raced up her neck and over her cheeks. "I sure as hell did. The creep who carjacked me. I hit his leg. He was climbing in Cara's window."

"He was inside?"

Liv nodded.

"You warned him?"

"Yeah."

A wolfish grin split his face. "Good girl. Hope you broke his leg. That'd make him easier to find if he escapes. We'll send alerts to ERs in the vicinity."

A savage jolt of pleasure arced through her, and she grinned back.

"If I remember right, there were three carjackers. Spot anyone else?"

"I heard at least one more guy outside. Couldn't be sure what I saw in the dark. I fired two rounds through the window, but I don't think I hit anyone else." Ragged shudders shook her. "Nate, where's Mike? I know he was on a stakeout, but why didn't he call me?"

He looked at her long and level, but the corners of his lips were tense. "I need to tell you something important, Liv."

She froze, heart pounding in her throat. "Cara, sweetie, you're cold. Can I put you on the couch with the comforter?"

The child shook her head and clung harder.

"Okay, then we'll stay together. I'll be right here." Cara begrudgingly curled next to her, but soon closed her eyes and relaxed.

Continuing to stroke Cara's soft hair, she looked up. "What's wrong, Nate?" She hoped her voice conveyed a calm she didn't feel.

He pulled up a chair and perched next to her. "Relax for a minute."

Liv clutched Cara's blanket, but leaned against the cushions. "You're not making me feel better. Spit it out."

He winced and gulped air. "The timing sucks, but Mike went undercover."

She sat there for a long moment. Disappointment, worry, and anger at Mike jumbled together with her terror and rage. "He promised! How could he disappear without any warning? Without even a call?"

"I'm sorry. He didn't want to, believe me."

Cara whimpered.

"What's going on?" Liv loosened her clenched arms and patted her daughter, pretending nonchalance in the middle of chaos.

Nate avoided her gaze. "My hands are tied. I'm under specific orders not to brief you."

"Damn it!" She gritted her teeth. "You're joking."

"I'm asking you to trust Mike. He wanted to refuse the assignment." Nate held out his arms to Cara, and she crawled into his lap.

Liv stomped across the room, but returned with a warmed quilt to wrap around her daughter. "How can I trust him?"

"Then trust me." Rising to his feet, Nate added, "If it helps, Jana's about ready to strangle me, and she hasn't heard about this break-in."

"How long is the assignment?"

"A few days."

She crossed her arms and screwed her mouth into a question mark. "Give me something."

Nate released a haggard sigh. "I'll be as straight with you as I can. Sereno PD isn't in charge."

"FBI?"

He nodded.

"Will you get permission to brief me?"

"I've tried, but I'll try again. Remember Mike's a top-notch undercover officer. He had no choice, but he'll finish and come home safe."

The remains of the adrenaline jag peppered the brew of terror and frustration bubbling in her stomach. Liv leaned back and rested her head against her arm.

Had she ever felt so alone? She glanced at her friend.

Nate's feet were planted, his hands fisted. No flex there. "Grab what you need for tonight. You and Cara are coming with me. I promised Mike. I was getting ready to come by when your call hit dispatch."

"Nate, why were you still at the station that late?"

His expression hardened, carved from a solid block of obsidian. "Pack right now. I should have had a team inside before, blanketing the freaking place."

Cara patted her arm. "Mommy, I want to go to Auntie Jana's."

Rubbing the back of her neck, Liv looked at the fear on her daughter's tear-streaked face. She smoothed the blonde curls from Cara's face with a shaky hand and kissed her damp cheek. "Let's go get our toothbrushes. We'll let Uncle Nate track the bad guys."

****

1:45 a.m.

What a pit. Mike shut the door behind Les, flipped the deadbolt, and glanced around the bleak, furnished apartment he was stuck with, courtesy of the FBI.

He paced on the worn shag carpeting between the tiny living room and tinier kitchen. Much as he hated to wake Liv, he had to get through to her fast, before everything went from sugar to shit. He flexed his hands, trying to loosen the tension.

Too bad he drowned his freaking prepaid cell. He stared at the old phone that hung on the wall. Should he call Liv on the landline? Nope. Too risky. No doubt the FBI had the damn thing tapped. Bausch would bust his ass if he warned her with the feds listening in. He didn't know how explicit he'd have to be before she understood.

Okay, so how long should he wait before he sneaked out to call? He peeked through the dingy blinds, trying to rein in his impatience. He'd give Les another minute and then hoof it to the all night liquor store a couple blocks away. Odds were he could wangle a phone call there.

He sighed and scrubbed his hand through his short hair. Wouldn't that be a fun conversation? After Liv exploded, she'd demand an explanation. Wouldn't do anyone much good for him to get hauled in on federal charges, but bottom-line was he had to warn her, had to explain, even if Bausch threw his sorry ass in jail.

Screw Bausch and his tactics.

Mike swapped his boots for running shoes and headed out the door. No sense second guessing things he couldn't control. Better get it over with, and then see what he could salvage.

He clomped down dingy, littered stairs that stank of urine and jogged onto the sidewalk. It felt good to run off the kinks after sitting in the damn delivery truck with Les most of the night.

Scanning the layout, he approached the store. A solitary spotlight cast a wavering, yellowish circle over the parking lot. Weeds poked through cracks in the disintegrating asphalt. The lights were still on inside, but there were no customers in sight. Good.

He pushed open the heavy front door of pockmarked, bulletproof glass reinforced with black steel bars.

The proprietor, dark haired and dark complexioned, laid his smoldering cigarette in an ashtray, and dropped one hand under the counter. "Help you, buddy?" he asked, a ghost of Biloxi in his voice.

Mike held his hands waist high, empty palms facing up. "Got a pay phone?"

"Who's asking?" He gave Mike a gimlet stare, signaling years of experience with winos, crooks, and late-night scumbags.

Mike met his gaze and spoke calmly, "Gonna grab my ID. Okay?"

The guy's head bobbed sharply.

Slowly, Mike reached inside his pocket and pulled out the federal badge. "Mickey O'Neil. FBI."

The guy behind the counter checked it, unasked questions flickering across his face. "Employee john is through that door. Use the wall phone. I'll buzz you in," he offered in slow, molasses-laced tones.

"Appreciate it." Mike strolled toward a painted steel door, waited for a buzz, and stepped inside. Metal shelves covered two walls, and an old-fashioned black wall phone hung opposite the sink.

He grabbed the ancient receiver and started dialing. Nobody answered at home. His heart revved.

Ditto the cabin.

Jiggling the change in his pocket, he grimaced and tried Liv's cell.

That came up empty. Listening to her voice mail greeting, he breathed in short, choppy bursts. "It's Mike. Can't get home tonight and my phone's toast. Until I have a chance to explain, watch your ass."

Pulse erratic, he paused before adding, "And watch Cara's. You can trust Nate. Your best chance is do exactly what he says. I love you, Livy. Never forget that."

Leaning against the grimy wall, he dialed Nate's cell, cursing each slow ring. He didn't know what his former partner would think about a two a.m. call and didn't much care.

Priority one: find Liv.

"Kapulani."

When Mike heard Nate's voice, part of the tension seeped from him. His heart still thumped a marathon inside his ribs, but he could breathe again. "I can't get hold of Liv."

"She's here."

Finally. "Put her on the line."

"Can't."

The tiny, windowless room closed in on him, and his sweat stank of fear. His hand gripped the receiver until his fingers grew numb. Screwing his eyes shut, he braced for the details. "What the hell do you mean, can't? She hurt?"

"Hold on, partner, don't you lose it too. She's okay. Cara too."

"Good."

"Let me catch you up. The creeps who tried to hijack her car broke into your house a couple hours ago."

"What?" Mike interrupted. "Where the hell were you?"

"Bausch and his idiot feds had me jumping through hoops. I'd just wrapped up with them when her call came in to dispatch. They ambushed the patrol I ordered. Frost is in the hospital with a concussion."

Afraid he'd pass out, Mike sank onto the toilet and listened in silence to Nate's quick run-down.

"When I brought them here, Liv put Cara to bed. Then she lost it. Never thought I'd see her hysterical. Shocked the crap out of me. Jana had to sedate her."

His gut turned over at the chilling image of Liv in such misery. Sharp pain stung him between the eyes, and he rubbed his forehead. "Jana watching her?"

"Yeah, but she's zonked. Finally stopped sup-supping in her sleep a while ago."

"I'm coming in. I'll tell Bausch where to shove this assignment."

"This is important, Mike."

"Yeah." He let out a long breath. "I gotta tell you I'm proud of her, shooting my dad's old Browning. Did you nab the asshole she wounded?"

"No. Marino found a trail of blood and footprints, plus tire tracks at the end of the road, but no perps. We have APBs posted. We'll catch 'em."

"When? Before or after they snatch Liv?"

Chapter Sixteen

Sereno, Saturday, April 24, 9:30 a.m.

"Damn that stubborn, macho cop! Mike's undercover making the world safe for everyone else while Cara and I face low-life burglars." Liv set her favorite wedding picture back on her dresser with a thump and turned to Jana. Tears burned her eyes and throat. She blinked hard to keep them back and took a shuddering breath. "I can still see that creep hanging over the windowsill."

"Stop," Jana said firmly, using her best bedside manner. "You had a rotten time, but you need to calm down. You don't want more sedatives tonight."

"Got that. I'd rather not feel like a zombie again tomorrow morning." Liv cleared her voice, still chain-smoker-raspy from last night's terror. She stretched and tried to shake off the cold, flat feeling that encased her.

"The fogginess should wear off soon. Can I get you more water?"

She shook her aching head. "Water? No, I need a quadruple espresso, but first I want to finish packing and get out of here." Yanking open another bureau drawer, she hauled out a handful of underwear and stuffed it in her suitcase. She zipped the case, hefted it, and draped a garment bag over her shoulder.

"Hand me that bag." Jana raised her eyebrows

pointedly, extending one hand. "Is this everything you'll need for a week?"

"Who knows? But there are worse fates than retail therapy." She forced a grin.

"Now that's my friend Liv." Jana winked and followed her into the hall.

Liv set the suitcase next to the door and looked out the sidelight at the cop standing guard nearby, assault rifle in his hands. Her stomach hitched. A chilly wave of nausea climbed her throat and sent shivers pulsing over her skin. The unmarked sedan that had followed them from Jana's house was parked at the end of her long driveway. "More shadows."

"What?" Jana peeked around her shoulder.

Rubbing at the dull pain behind her eyebrows, she tilted her head toward the agents in the beige sedan. "After the break-in last night, Bausch apparently decided to increase security. Wish he'd told me."

"You know they're here to keep you safe."

"But a heads-up would have been nice, so I wasn't scared when I spotted them tailing us." Liv released her hairclip and ran her fingers through her mane. "And don't forget Kathy Linden's watching the kids. Perky, blonde, and armed to her French manicure." With a dismissive wave, she turned her back on the window and stepped into the sunken living room.

Jana followed. "At least Cara enjoys Kathy. And better Sergeant Marino at the front door than creeps crawling in the window."

She shivered. Her head pounded without mercy. "My husband disappears undercover. My life is crazy-out-of-control-scary. And I only have a sneaking suspicion as to why."

"Nate's very tight-lipped. I couldn't squeeze anything out of him, but it must be important." Jana's nose wrinkled. "I know Mike didn't explain, but maybe he couldn't."

"Maybe it doesn't matter." She flopped onto the sofa and rested her cheek against her balled fist. "I can't trust him to keep his promises. He lied before. He could lie again."

"Don't waste your energy imagining scenarios like that. Mike knows the consequences. Nate does too. He's not happy about whatever's in the works, but he's not frantic, either. He would be if Mike had done something really stupid."

Exhausted, Liv closed her eyes and massaged her neck. "But I need him to help me figure out what's happening."

"I know you'd feel safer with Mike around, but you can stay with us as long as you need to." Jana rested an arm around her shoulder. "Want some tea before we leave? It'll be easier on your system than espresso."

She couldn't summon even a half-hearted smile, but followed her friend into the kitchen. She stared at her hands and tapped out "Chopsticks" with her nails on the granite counter. "I need to drop by work later."

Jana turned and shot her a disapproving look, her lips pursed. "You should rest."

She opened her mouth to object, but Jana held up a hand and continued, "Doctor's orders. We'll be out late tonight, and your job will still be there Monday."

"Maybe not." Liv pressed her fingertips over her eyelids and worked to swallow the tenacious boulder lodged in her throat. "One of the lead investors came by

G-Tech yesterday. Brought his pet Navy SEAL with him."

"Pet what?"

"The board's threatening to replace me with a gun-toting, mail-order-MBA."

Jana lit the flame under the teakettle and shook her head. "Never happen."

With a shrug, Liv opened the slider to let in the cool morning breeze. Kathy Linden stood on the back lawn guarding Cara, and Jana's son, Michael. The boy, solidly built like his father, had Nate's deep brown eyes and dark, wavy hair. Cara was tall for her age also, but small-boned. Her blond curls glistened in the sunlight.

Cara waved and then punched her fielder's mitt. "No, Michael. Don't toss the ball easy. I need practice. My team plays their first game this week."

Liv's heart warmed, and she found a small smile.

Jana set the tea on the breakfast bar. "Kids doing okay?"

"They're fine. Thanks for bringing Michael. Cara adores him." Liv lifted the fragrant mug.

"How's she holding up?"

"When I talked to her about Mike going undercover, she was so angry she practically vibrated. Said maybe she'd rather be divorced if he kept leaving without saying goodbye. He could just stay in stupid V'ginia with stupid Sam. Then the tears started to flow."

"Yikes. She understood that much?"

"Scary, isn't it?" Liv shrugged and sipped her tea. "I'm ready to give up. I'm so tired of trying to find a way to live with Mike. What would he do if I packed all the stuff he left here and had a bonfire."

"Or a garage sale?" Jana asked with a teasing gleam in her eyes and a wait-'til-you-hear-this-one lilt in her voice.

Hoping for an upbeat distraction, Liv asked, "Garage sale? Must be a good story."

"Family scandal. My cousin Beth got sick of her husband's antics. Good ole boy, Hank was running around with his eighteen-year-old receptionist."

"The rat!"

"Hank supposedly went fishing, but actually, he'd shacked up at a local motel. Beth sold everything he owned for pennies: motorcycle, trophies, sports gear, everything."

"Everything?"

"Yep, even his briefs. Then she had the locks changed and called her lawyer. When Hank rang the doorbell, she handed him twelve dollars and fifty-three cents."

Liv chuckled, her heart lightening. A mischievous grin crept across her lips. "My worst self loves the idea, but can you imagine if I sold Mike's college baseball trophy?"

"I'd send flowers to your funeral."

She squeezed Jana's hand. "Thank you. I needed to blow off steam."

"What are friends for?"

Liv picked up the tuxedo jacket Mike had left draped over a chair and smoothed the fabric. Emptiness flooded her, and she cuddled it close. "I miss him. I miss that sexy, romantic adrenaline-junkie-of-a-cop."

****

3:30 p.m.

Her oversized, men-in-black bodyguards sat with

their knees around their ears on the delicate, gilt and burgundy velvet couch. Their large noses wrinkled at that acrid, catch-in-your-sinuses perfume of permanents and beauty products.

With her chin firm, Liv walked through the elegant salon toward her stylist's station. Retail therapy worked. The slinky new purple dress she'd bought had certainly helped her mood and the designer stilettos were killers, but she planned a complete transformation before she faced the world at the benefit tonight.

She untwined her heavy hair from its clasp and stared resolutely into the mirror. She needed this change, and if she pissed off Mike, so much the better. She twisted her lips into a smile. "Cut it all off."

Her stylist, Sue, lifted a strand of the waist-length hair. A worried expression flickered across her heart-shaped face. "All? Really?" Petite and full of energy, Sue shook her head, and her soft brown curls bounced.

"I want it short." Liv swung into the chair. "Short and sexy."

"You sure? That's such a big step. What if we try shoulder length first?"

"I'm sure." She gripped the arms of the chair. "Give it to Locks of Love."

"That's a great cause. My sister got her wig from them during her chemo." Sue twisted a rubber band around her long hair but hesitated. "Liv…"

She squeezed her eyes closed. "Do it." The scissors sliced through her thick ponytail with a strange rasping sound. She winced. No turning back now.

Half an hour later, Sue swiveled her around. "What do you think?"

The stranger in the mirror stole her breath. "Wow."

She drew her fingers through her short, spiky hair, and a slow smile bloomed.

"Shows off your cheekbones." Sue grinned. "I've always wondered how mahogany highlights would look. Your natural color goes that way in the summer. Do you have time?"

"Sure. Why not?"

Liv settled under the dryer, her head studded with aluminum foil. She leaned back under the swirling heat and willed her body to relax.

Bausch had insisted she stick to her normal schedule. She frowned. But why did he care? Probably just liked ordering her around. Special Agent Dan Bausch thought he was emperor of the universe. The guy needed an enema.

Over the racket of the dryer, she thought she heard her phone buzz and dug it out, but missed the call. The log showed unknown. Was it Mike this time? She'd gotten a few anonymous hang ups today.

Her heart beat faster. A message? Wiggling in her seat, she dialed voice mail and listened.

Click.

Then nothing.

Chapter Seventeen

Sereno, Saturday, April 24, 8:20 p.m.

Liv identified a dozen government agents scattered through the chandelier-lit ballrooms, despite their rented formal wear. They stood straighter, looked more aware than most guests at the benefit.

A swing band played while waiters plied the glittering crowd with champagne and hors d'oeuvres. But she wasn't excited about schmoozing tonight, although Bausch had assured her she and Cara would be safe.

Draining her flute of bubbly, Liv ramrodded her spine and headed toward a small knot of black-tie donors, determined to carry off the evening with style.

Tom Morrison's eyes widened, and his mouth puckered for a soft wolf whistle. "I didn't think you could get any prettier, Liv. That's some outfit."

"Thanks, Tom. Seemed like a good night to celebrate."

"You know, I always thought your long hair was the sexiest thing going, but, wow." He moved closer and brushed his broad fingers over her spiky hair.

Suddenly chilled, she ducked back a step and ran her thumb over her finger where her wedding band had been. "It was time for a change."

Tom gestured at the shoppers swarming a crowded

silent auction table and chuckled. "Everyone seems to be having a great time tonight."

She clenched her hands together in front of her. Good. This time, he'd kept his distance. It gave her the creeps when Tom crowded her. "Your donation's a big hit. How did you manage to get the tickets to that Las Vegas show?"

"Trade secret." He winked.

Jana approached, willowy and elegant in a mossy, gold-flecked sheath, and kissed her on the cheek. "You look beautiful in purple."

Liv grinned at her friend and relaxed. "I'd like you to meet one of my committee members. He did a super job of soliciting donations."

"Just twisted a few arms for a good cause." He laughed, extending a hand.

"I'm Jana Kapulani. I didn't catch your name." When her hand touched Tom's, Jana gasped.

His smile evaporated, and his gaze shifted around the room. "Sorry, need to talk to someone," he mumbled and hurried away.

Liv made a puzzled face and shrugged, studying his back as he approached a cluster of men at the bar.

"Liv, I don't—" Jana broke off. Her hazel eyes were huge and glassy. Every freckle on her pale face stood out.

"Are you sick? You look like you've seen a ghost."

"His laugh was sinister." Jana shuddered, leaning heavily against Liv. "When he touched me, I felt so cold."

A shiver crawled over Liv's skin, leaving a trail of prickles in its wake. "What are you talking about?"

"That man gave me screaming chills." Jana's voice

sounded distant and shaky. Spooky.

Stomach pitching like a rowboat in twenty-foot waves, Liv shook her head slowly. Her friend's intuition was uncanny. What was going on with Tom Morrison?

Chaffing her arms, Jana huddled close to Liv. "I've seen him before, some place scary. His eyes are hard as flint."

"Can I get you some water?"

"I'm better. Give me another minute. The spots are almost gone." Jana trembled, color slowly returning to her cheeks. "What's that man's name?"

"Tom Morrison."

"Yes!" Jana smacked the heel of her hand against her forehead. "The man in the picture. I need to find Nate now." She searched the crowd and then pulled Liv by the hand.

Her feet stuck to the floor. "Slow down and tell me what's going on!"

"I didn't recognize him right away because his eyes weren't visible in the photograph. But the name's right."

"What are you talking about?"

Instead of answering, Jana bolted across the ballroom.

Liv hurried behind her. "What's wrong? Tell me."

"Nate, we need to speak privately!" Jana called.

He glanced up at them and smiled. "Hey gorgeous. What's up?"

"I've been trying to get her to stop and explain," Liv complained.

Nate frowned. "Come outside."

On the deserted terrace, Jana grabbed Nate's arm.

"Do you remember the photograph Agent Bausch—"

Liv's jaw went slack. "Dan Bausch? How do you know him?"

"Careful," Nate warned.

Jana grimaced. "Are you kidding? Liv needs to know what's going on. It's her company and her ass on the line."

Nate drew a long, slow breath but nodded.

After making a disgusted grunt, Jana continued. "Remember the photo he wouldn't explain? Thomas Morrison is here. He was on Liv's committee, but he gave me the screaming willies."

Nate started. A look of controlled alarm flashed across his features, followed by an angry red flush. "Here?" He scanned the ballroom windows. "Man, oh man. I'm gonna kill that fucking fed."

Her heart tap-danced, and her blood thundered in her veins. Liv studied Nate's fierce expression, and exhaled in exasperation. "I'll bet you can't explain either."

He acknowledged her frustration with a tilt of his head. "Question is what can I get away with telling you?"

She glanced nervously over her shoulder. When she turned back and looked at Nate, her stomach did a nosedive.

Eyes closed, jaw locked, he banged his fists together in front of his chest. Then he looked at her, gaze dark and solemn. "I have to ask you to trust me."

Liv hissed.

"Ask Bausch if you want answers." He stomped away.

****

11:30 p.m.

Mike found Les Hamlin crouched outside Morrison's office door. "Hey man. What are you doing?"

"There's no one here." Hamlin wiggled the knob. "There's usually someone around until late on Saturday, but we have the place to ourselves."

Was opportunity pounding on the door? "Will Morrison come back tonight?"

Groaning, Hamlin rose to his feet. "Don't know. He's at some charity thing. Griped about it all week."

Mike swallowed the baseball wedged in his throat. Liv was there too. Alone, but Bausch had half the feds in the state on duty, so she'd be safe. He slammed the door on his doubts and focused on the job.

Almost midnight. At least half an hour before the benefit was over, and he needed to know what Morrison was doing. He needed to know now. He was sick of this farce and wanted to bust the freaking case open and go home. Setting his jaw, he squared his shoulders. To hell with the chain of evidence. He crept down the hall and scanned the parking area. "Keep an eye out."

"What are you doing?" Les asked.

"Unlocking Morrison's office to check around. Does he have a safe?"

"Yeah. No idea how you'd get into it, though."

Mike knelt and examined the lock. "Whew! Pretty fancy set-up for an office. Medecos are almost pick-proof, even under the best conditions."

"Worth a try."

Mike unzipped a small inside coat pocket and pulled out his lock picks. "What have you got hidden in there Tom?"

For several minutes, Hamlin watched from the end of the hall. "How long is this gonna take?"

Mike grunted in response, but kept his breathing even and his hands steady. Kept the tension tool exactly right and shifted the lock pins by feel. "I need time. The mechanism is crazy complicated. I'd already have popped a regular set-up."

"Hurry, man. I don't like this."

"This was your idea." He had raised the pins, no sweat, but couldn't clear the diagonal sidebar. Morrison had paid big bucks for this lock set. "Not much more I can do, at least with you breathing down my neck. There's another tool at my apartment I could try."

"Yeah, but he'll kill us if he finds out we broke in, and he'll know if we come back."

"How?" Mike wiped the doorknob clean. "No prints."

"He's got surveillance cameras on the entrances." Hamlin hurried away, face shiny with sweat.

Mike's stomach did a back dive into an empty pool. "Anywhere else?"

"I dunno. But he's plenty paranoid."

****

Sunday, April 25, 4:45 a.m.

Unable to escape what he knew came next, Mike tossed and turned in his sleep, restless and struggling.

The room felt like a sauna and smelled of greenery and rich earth overlaid with the stink of chemicals. He blinked, squinting into the glare of dozens of fixtures. Row upon row of marijuana plants stretched toward the artificial sunlight.

Tomasini kicked Nate's Glock six feet to one side. He had Mike's 9mm tucked in his belt, and waved a

.357 at them with a shaky hand, blocking the only exit. With their arms raised in the air, he and Kapulani confronted their snitch.

Mike cursed silently. How did that scumbag get the drop on them? If only he hadn't holstered his weapon to climb the ladder.

The trapdoor was ajar. A faint shuffling noise came from the garage below. A rat? Mike held his breath, cocked an ear, and heard it again.

Jana's bright auburn hair peeked through the opening.

His eyes widened, and his pulse flip-flopped. Well, shit!

She climbed into the room with a length of galvanized pipe in her hands. They never should have brought an intern on patrol tonight.

Nate's face paled, and he twitched sideways a step, drawing Tomasini's gaze.

Tomasini hadn't spotted Jana yet, but drew a bead on Nate. "Stand still or I'll shoot. I know my rights. You idiots came in without a warrant," their snitch ranted, his eyes bugging out in his sweat-covered face. "You'll never pin this on me."

Mike's heart jammed, but he said casually, "You got us there, Tomasini, but one way or another, we'll shut this place down. You had a nice set-up for a while."

Nate slid another step sideways and the snitch's gun tracked his movements.

Fear climbed through Mike, chilled him to the marrow, but he kept up the line of patter, drawing Tomasini's attention. "Drop the gun, man. An operator who does a little gardening is different than a fool who shoots a cop."

With shaky hands, Tomasini kept the gun zeroed in on Nate.

Jana crept to within a few feet of the crook, and Mike cringed with her every step.

Nate twitched to his right.

"Damn it, cop. I swear. Move again and I'll kill you where you stand," Tomasini shouted, retreating.

She raised the pipe and slashed it toward Tomasini's weapon, but he must have seen the movement. He squeezed the trigger as he twisted, sending a round into the floor.

The pipe smashed his knee, and he cried out, but kept hold of his gun.

Falling to his knees, Mike rolled to retrieve the Glock. He came up in a crouch, but froze, staring at the gun pressed to Jana's temple.

Tomasini had grabbed her, his left arm around her neck. He growled, "Drop it. Drop it, or she dies right now!" He backed away and limped toward the trapdoor, dragging Jana with him.

An icy heaviness fogged Mike's brain like a slow motion mudslide. He eased his gun to the floor and immediately wanted to twist time backwards. Christ. What an idiot!

Tomasini aimed and fired, and Nate hit the floor clutching at his chest. Blood seeped through his fingers.

Cold spasms of fury seized Mike by the balls, cramped his lungs and paralyzed his heart mid-beat.

Mike's heart broke free and screamed into agonizing motion. Drenched in sweat, he took a deep, shuddering breath, trying to ward off the remembered smell of blood and fear.

Seemed like years since the last time he dreamed about the night Nate was shot. Funny he replayed it tonight.

Wishing Liv was sleeping beside him so he could cradle her, he took another deep gulp of air and willed his racing heart to slow. The numbness started to fade.

That creep Tomasini had vanished while Mike called the Medevac chopper. He'd dogged that case for months, locked away the crook's cohorts, and broken up the drug ring, but never uncovered any trace of the ringleader. He'd always figured Tomasini was dead or at least wouldn't cause more trouble.

Past time he made sure.

Chapter Eighteen

Sereno, Sunday, April 25, 8:30 a.m.

What was the big, fuckin' deal? Liv Gordon wasn't dead. Wasn't damaged. She wasn't even wrinkled.

Dan sat on a bench outside G-Tech's main entrance, sucking down an espresso. At three a.m. Kapulani had bellowed into the phone, ripped him a new one for exposing her as bait at the benefit. But where did a local police captain get off dictating procedure in a federal investigation? Pushy bastard.

Dan rose and stomped around the nearly empty parking lot. Asphalt expanses edged three sides of the single story building and a narrow delivery lane ran behind the warehouse, backed by a twelve, maybe fourteen-foot brick wall. Trees from the building behind stuck up, and branches spilled onto the barbed wire that topped the barrier.

Mouth drawn tight, he shook his aching head and winced. Security and access control sucked. Yeah, the main entrance was locked, with an armed guard station and metal detector inside, but no checkpoint hut or entry control existed at the two front drives.

Instead, the edges of the G-Tech lot melted into the other parking areas on each side, with no more barrier than a cement curb and change of pavement striping. Across the wide street, another line of buildings mirrored these.

Adrenaline twanged his raw nerves like an old steel guitar. He chucked his cup into the trash and stuffed his hands in his pockets. He'd hate to have to defend this place after a security meltdown.

Dan released an exasperated sigh. His contact at Interpol was playing it cagey, refusing to give him anything. He'd wasted yesterday chasing his tail, and he had to nail this case down. G-Tech must deliver the drones on time. No leaks. No thefts. No fuck-ups.

Barb Chandler's big yellow delivery van nosed into G-Tech's lot and parked straddling two spaces. She jumped down from the seat, with her ponytail bobbing, and a beautiful smile curved across her face. Snug jeans and a bright yellow polo hugged her luscious, toned body. "What do you need, FBI?"

Ignoring the awareness walloping him, he leaned close. "I need your experienced eyes to check this place."

"What exactly are you looking for?"

"Wish I knew." He grimaced, flipping his hand against his leg. "My hunch is there's surveillance hardware hidden in one of the vending machines."

"Ah hah. That's why you called me." She looked up at him through her lashes.

Dan made a noncommittal noise and tucked his tongue back into his mouth.

Before they reached the entrance, another truck whipped into a reserved spot. Liv Gordon exited from the passenger door of the big, red SUV and marched toward them, trailed by her driver, a Sereno PD uniform. She stopped toe-to-toe with him, obviously annoyed. "Agent Bausch, I had a message from security to meet you, but they didn't tell me why. What's this about?"

His headache cranked up a notch. "I'd like you to meet Barb Chandler." His words were clipped, but as polite as he could manage.

"Good morning," Mrs. Gordon bit out and slid her key card through the reader. The scanner automatically unlatched the door. Moving through the entryway, she ushered them to the guard station and opened her purse on the counter for inspection. "Hi, Frank."

"Morning, Mrs. G. You brought company?" Frank Johnson, a stocky, almost bald, former army master sergeant, now FBI agent, was stationed near the metal detector.

"You know Agent Bausch." Liv dipped her head in his direction.

Dan flashed a quick salute.

"He and Ms. Chandler are my guests. Officer Linden can wait here with you."

"Sure thing. Good morning, Special Agent. I'll need your badge number and a thumb print from Ms. Chandler."

Dan waited impatiently while the formalities were concluded. Then they followed Liv through the secured doors.

He tried to iron the knots from his forehead with one hand. "Sorry to disturb your weekend, Mrs. Gordon, but I'm following a suggestion from local law enforcement."

Her eyes gleamed under winged brows. "Should we start in the break room?"

"As a matter of fact, yes."

"This way." A trace of smugness colored her

words.

Dan's jaw tightened. He held the door and his comments, allowing Barb to survey the room.

She turned to him and shrugged. "I see the latest model soda, snack, and juice machines, coffee service, and calories in boxes."

"See anything unusual? Anything a small tech company wouldn't ordinarily have, or hardware that doesn't come standard."

Liv gave a quiet snort. "Your agents swept the building Thursday and you're looking for extra hardware?" Sarcasm frosted her words.

"We're taking additional precautions." He rolled his eyes. The woman was a pain in his butt.

Barb shook her head, glancing around the room. "There's nothing unexpected here. Nicer set-up than usual for a start-up, though. How much does he charge you for the cookies?"

Liv named a figure and Barb whistled. "He's selling them below cost, assuming his accounting is accurate. You might want someone to audit deliveries."

Liv's eyebrows hiked again. "I'll do that."

Three cups of espresso sloshed acid in Dan's stomach. Big effin' deal. He'd already proved Morrison was a small time crook. What he needed was hard evidence of espionage.

Barb walked in a circle, scrutinizing the equipment. "I don't see any signs of tampering or alteration. Everything looks stock."

"Surveillance?" he prompted. "We already checked the ceiling fixtures."

"No point to installing cameras in the machines. They get unplugged all the time."

Liv tapped her chin with a curved index finger. "They replaced the juice dispenser a few weeks ago, just before I found the first bug. Of course the machine didn't work most of the time and the bill changer looked like a retrofit."

He blew a frustrated breath. Too bad Morrison had pulled the sucker, but he must not have everything he needed. "Too bad the machine's gone."

Barb sighed and fisted her hands on her hips. "Nothing catches my attention. This place looks like a hundred other start-ups in the Valley."

"It was a long shot."

"In my office. Now," Liv ground out the words one by one. She crossed her arms in front of her chest and clenched her jaw. "You're withholding important information, Agent, and I'm sick of your obfuscation."

"Certainly." Any second, she'd start tapping her toe. She'd been a thorn in his ass from day one, questioning every move he made, trying to wrestle control out of his hands.

Barb shot him a questioning look, but remained silent.

Given a little time, he could get Liv canned. The Pentagon had recruited an MBA-packing former SEAL to take over G-Tech. But she wouldn't surrender without a full-scale boardroom war, and he couldn't afford the time.

Liv ushered them past the security doors and through the warren of cubicles. She opened the door to her office, a sunny room with modern furniture set on a high-end Oriental rug. She chose one corner of the sleek leather sofa and waited for them to settle.

"Great office, Ms. Gordon," Barb offered.

"Thanks." Liv glared at him.

Barb started to rise. "Should I…"

Bausch shook his head.

Liv shrugged and continued. "There's a threat to G-Tech, and I want the details now. We're scheduled to ship the first sensors in a few days, but your crap has sucked up all my time. I'm fed up. You have five minutes to explain."

The silence lengthened, but he felt the laser point of her glare bore a hole through his aching forehead. No question it'd be better if she didn't know the details. An innocent should be safer, but more important, he wanted to catch Morrison red-handed, not scare him off. "Mrs. Gordon, I understand your concern—"

"Quiet!" Barb's hand gripped his arm, stopping him mid-sentence.

Putting one finger to her lips, she indicated a large, chrome cappuccino machine, then moved closer and checked it. Barb pointed to the clock-timer. Without a word, she gestured at the door and led them into the hall.

Liv slammed the door behind her and swiveled to face Barb. "What on earth?"

"Has to be that cappuccino machine. It's the commercial model, top of the line, four-figure price tag. How long have you had it?" Barb asked.

"Not long, three weeks, maybe a month." Liv paused, and then her eyes widened. "The vending company gave us an upgrade since we're good customers and my assistant snagged the machine for my office."

Barb's expression glowed with excitement. She touched a warm finger to his hand. "The clock's an

196

add-on. Never seen one on that model. The machine would be a great place for a surveillance device, because it's likely to stay plugged in."

Liv's lips tensed into a frown.

"You want hot water, when you want hot water."

Bausch blew out a stream of relieved air. "Plus, the heavy metal construction would shield the electronics." Pay dirt. Pleasure surged. Energized him. Erased the pounding in his head. "I'll get a team in and check it right away." He pulled out his phone.

Liv flushed with anger. "Wait a minute, hot shot. Brief me first. Then you can explain how your sweeps could miss a bug this obvious."

"Can't. Need to know."

"Bullshit! Why does she know more about what's happening with my company than I do?" Liv jabbed a finger at Barb.

"I think I'll go wait by security. I'm sorry to have met you under difficult circumstances, Ms. Gordon."

Liv nodded crisply at her, then turned and fixed a defiant stare on him, eyes tracking every movement. Her foot tapped, twitching like a tiger's tail.

Tension oozed back, redoubling the pain behind his eyes. How little could he get away with? He arranged his features in an inscrutable expression. He hoped. "The current investigation is extremely sensitive."

She examined her fingernails, then glanced at him, her eyebrows arching. "So I understand, Special Agent. But you need my continued cooperation. I can and will shut G-Tech down."

He rubbed his hand behind his neck, and then straightened his tie. Shit on a stick. She had him by the *cojones* and knew it. "We have credible information about the source of G-Tech's security leak. Your technology is the target and the buyers aren't allies."

"How did your clones miss that bug? Are your sweeps that worthless?"

"Embedded in metal and wired like that, we'd have to catch a device actually transmitting to ID it. The new ones are all intermittent, but that is wicked."

"I see. Do you suspect one of my employees?"

"Not our main avenue of inquiry."

"Then there's an informant."

"I'm not at liberty…"

"And Mike's investigating?" Liv fired back.

Dan's brows lifted. He couldn't control the automatic reaction. Clearing his throat, he sighed and leveled his gaze.

"You have an informant, G-Tech's the target, and, Jesus, I'm the bait."

"I didn't say that," he spat through gritted teeth.

"Not in so many words." Her hand ruffled through her ritzy new punk-chic hairdo.

"Stay aware of your surroundings and close to your bodyguard." He took her elbow and herded her toward security.

She jerked her arm free, but said, "My head of security will facilitate access."

"Appreciate it." About fucking time.

Screwing his lips into a grimace, Dan watched her exit. He couldn't depend on Liv to behave normally anymore, and Morrison wasn't stupid. Time to prod him. Jump-start the action.

****

11:45 a.m.

Ahmed slammed out of the library and rushed

down the stairs ahead of his study group. Suliman, the prince's cousin, would arrive soon. How would he explain his failure?

At the bottom of the steps, he ducked into a shaded alcove and slumped onto a cement bench. In class on Friday, he hadn't gleaned any new information from Professor Gordon. Again. And there had been no news from Morrison. He cringed at the thought of further dealings with the amoral American.

Miriam took the last few stairs and turned into the courtyard.

He shrank against the wall, trying to avoid her notice, but she adjusted her headscarf and approached him.

"Sunday study sessions in the library aren't that painful." Miriam sat gracefully beside him, the corners of her wide mouth turned up.

"No, we completed…" Ahmed began earnestly and then stopped and smiled back.

"Much better." She laughed. "Want to go to the barbeque? I can smell it from here."

He debated, then stood and squared his shoulders, holding out a hand to help her rise.

"Yes. I am hungry."

They loaded up on grilled chicken, salad, and bread. Holding two colas, he asked, "Where shall we sit?"

"Let's find a quiet spot under the trees," she suggested and walked toward the oak grove. Her bright scarf fluttered in the breeze.

He followed, footsteps crunching on the gravel path.

She chose a table near the center and sank onto the

bench. "You are hungry." She pointed at his overflowing plate.

Heat rose on his cheeks. "I had soccer practice all morning." He took a big bite of the juicy chicken and the barbeque sauce dripped down his chin. He swiped at it and licked his fingers, smiling at the spicy sweet tomato flavor.

Laughing, she handed him a stack of napkins. "Practicing kicks? Or working on your endurance?"

"Both." He gazed into her glimmering dark eyes. She had helped him once. Could he confide in her?

Her expression innocent, she asked, "Why did you ask about Professor Gordon's drones again?"

His stomach plunged and for a moment he stared at her blankly. Then he shuttered his face, rose, and said coldly, "No reason. I'm curious."

"I don't believe you. Who made you ask?"

Gooseflesh crawled over his body. He pivoted and hurried away. His apartment wasn't far. If he ran, he might reach it before he was sick.

Why had Miriam questioned him? How much did she know about the plot? About the tasks he had been given?

Fighting to keep lunch from rising in his throat, he unlocked the door.

A tall, hawk-faced man with a piercing gaze sat at the kitchen table.

All the blood drained from Ahmed's cheeks, and he lowered his gaze submissively.

****

4:35 p.m.

Every single muscle in Mike's body was wound tight. He jumped up and checked the Judas hole in the door again. Les was five minutes late, and Mike itched for the threat to materialize so he could get this freaking assignment over and buried six feet deep.

Hauling snack food felt too much like sitting on his ass. He cracked his knuckles. Had Bausch planned it all along to keep him from interfering?

Mike leaned against the threadbare cushion and propped his feet on the scarred coffee table beside his aviator glasses. He tugged at wayward hairs in his droopy false moustache, straightening them.

His new, FBI-issued cell phone vibrated in its belt carrier, and he pulled it out.

"Gordon? Bausch here."

"What's going on?"

"Update on the investigation. Everything quiet there?"

"Nothing's changed. Morrison hasn't made a move. I haven't gotten within twenty feet of him," Mike said, disgusted. "When he's at SVV, he stays hidden away in his locked office counting his money or spying on the warehouse from the upper level. You make any progress?"

"We located unauthorized hardware at the target company. Unfortunately, we found it in the CEO's office."

Mike jerked up straight. "What did you do?"

"We disposed of the sophisticated hardware creatively. Our sweeps never caught it. These guys are resourceful."

"No surprise there." He paused. Bausch's glib explanation worried him. "Think they'll catch on soon?"

"Probably tomorrow morning. Time to poke

Morrison and see which way he jumps."

His leg jiggled to a staccato beat. "Why screw around? You have enough to haul him in and hold him until he caves."

"This is bigger than Morrison. The trap is baited." Bausch's glee oozed over the phone line, grating his nerves.

"Yeah? Then let's talk about the important part, pal," he spat out, venting a sliver of his frustration. "What about protection for the target? Or should I say the worm hanging on your hook? She's still exposed."

Bausch hesitated and Mike wanted to shove his fist through the phone.

"No problem. Her new car has the GPS system and transponder, makes it easy to trace. I ordered the tail you requested, two agents, twenty-four seven, plus her driver."

"And my daughter?"

"Yeah, yeah. I'll place a team at her school tomorrow."

"I want guards at both gates," Mike demanded, pacing.

"Fine. Don't need them in the classroom. Better if they keep a low profile."

His forehead wrinkled. "Bausch? Hang on a minute. I have a hunch. Can you lay your hands on another transponder?"

****

11:45 p.m.

Morrison had learned the hard way to pay attention to the details. Better check and see nothing happened here while he wasted last night at that fucking benefit.

He locked his office door, set the alarms, and

clicked on the audio from the cappuccino machine. So far, he'd gotten zip from Sid's brainstorm. Nothing worth the big bucks he'd sunk into the damn thing. The bitch never worked in her office.

Cycling through the recording on fast-forward, he screened for voices. Saturday night scrolled through silently, but Sunday morning got interesting.

Liv Gordon's angry voice came through the speakers, "...I'm fed up. You have five minutes to explain."

Morrison grinned. The bitch had the fed by the balls today, twisting hard. And the suit was sucking ass. "Mrs. Gordon, I understand your concern—"

"Quiet!"

Barb Chandler? He listened to the silence for another minute. Shit. That bitch clued them in.

His gut burned with anger. Morrison shut off the machine and slammed his fist on his desk. He was way too smart to get caught by Keystone cops trailing after a brainless fed.

He limped to the door, grumbling. Taking out the agent would cause a backlash, but long term, it didn't matter. Bausch was probably a grunt anyway. He'd get Barb Chandler too. About time he had a good excuse.

Chapter Nineteen

Sereno, Monday, April 26, 7:45 a.m.

"Do I have to go?" Cara whined.

Frowning, Liv studied her daughter. "There are burritos for lunch today, and you don't want to miss art."

Kathy Linden drove the SUV through the gates of Highbrook Country Day School and stopped in the carpool lane.

Liv got out, opened the rear door, and unbuckled her daughter. She'd feel better after Cara was safely in class, and she could concentrate on maneuvering her company back on track.

"I don't want to go to school."

Liv sucked on her lip, searching for options. Funny how ordinary stuff still demanded her attention. What had Cara so upset? The break-in? Her daddy?

Feeling guilty, Liv glanced at Kathy Linden. "I think I'll walk Cara to class this morning."

"No problem. I can watch you girls from here," Kathy said. "See you this afternoon, Cara-bear."

Cara scrambled across the seat and gave Kathy a hug.

They started along the tree-lined path, but Cara stiffened and stomped her foot, yanking on Liv's hand. "I'm mad at you, Mommy. It's your fault Daddy went undercover. You should have let him move back with us where he belongs."

Liv's heart twisted in her chest. "I'm worried about him too. I want him to come home safe."

"But why did you make him go away after you let him sleep over?" Cara's blue eyes flashed with anger. Her teeth were clenched and red streaked her cheeks. "Don't lie to me, Mommy. I saw his truck."

Heat flashed up Liv's neck, and she blew out a loud breath. Busted. So much for knowing what was going on in her little girl's head. "We both love you. We didn't want to get your hopes up until we were sure."

"Well I don't want to play T-ball today. I want to come home after school and wait for Daddy." Cara gave a sharp nod.

Liv tunneled her fingers through her short hair.

"Ple-e-e-se, Mommy. I don't like T-ball. Coach always puts me in right field. It's boring." Cara dragged out the vowel with her lower lip nudged forward.

"You made a commitment to play on the team. Practice is important while you're learning to play."

"I'm out there all by myself with nothing to do. No one hits the ball that far."

She glanced at Cara shuffling footsteps and said, "We have a few minutes. Let's go listen to the creek. You can tell me what else is wrong." Liv pulled Cara down beside her on a rustic bench and curled an arm around her shoulders.

Cara huddled close, and Liv smoothed a hand over her daughter's soft curls and kissed her forehead.

"I'm the worst player ever. I never hit the ball. Please don't make me go today, Mommy."

"Sweetheart, sometimes good things are hard work, especially at the start. Someday, you'll hit a home run."

"I don't know." Cara grabbed a pebble and plunked it in the creek.

She touched her daughter's shoulder and took a wild guess. "Does this have anything to do with Peggy?"

Cara's mouth pinched into a frown, and her brief shrug answered the question.

"You need to ignore the things she says."

"She's really mean."

"I know it's tough."

Cara turned her face away, sulking. "I'm mad and I'm scared and I hate stupid T-ball."

The lump in her chest swelled. "Okay. I'll talk to your coach after practice." She hated to see Cara so unhappy. "Can you tough it out just for today? I'll come get you early from work."

****

10:30 a.m.

Morrison swaggered along the hall with car keys in one hand and a plastic bag in the other. He found Sid Sylvester outside his office, checking his watch.

"Guess what, Sylvester?" Morrison turned the key, yanked Sid inside, and shoved him onto a chair. "Your big idea flopped. They spotted the last bug."

Sid frowned, and he paled to pasty white. The douche bag had realized he was in deep shit. "Who found it?"

"The FBI grunt. He's testing us." Livid, Morrison stared into the one-way glass and watched the coins cycle through the money counter. Good thing he'd heard the conversation last night and upped his

206

timetable.

Anticipation made his mouth water. He rubbed his jaw line with his knuckles and studied the skinny little weasel. The feds hadn't left him any other choices, and Sid could handle a kid.

Sid flinched. "If the cops found the bug, how'll we get what we need? Can we snatch Frau Gordon?"

"No. She's got too much protection. It'd take weeks to find her alone again and we don't have the manpower or the time. The feds are too close and my customer's all over me like piranhas on a gator."

Sid remained quiet, but his eyelid twitched.

"We can't get her directly, but I got a kick-ass plan to turn up the heat on our little CEO," he said, his voice rising with excitement. "Gordon has a daughter. I've been checking the surveillance cameras at her school for a couple weeks."

"A kid?" Sid shrieked, in a tone so shrill Morrison's fillings vibrated.

"After your fuck-ups, I'm out of options. The kid will give us a handle on the bitch."

Sid popped to his feet, puffing out his chest like a bantam rooster. "Bullshit. There has to be a better alternative. No way I'll get involved in kidnapping."

"Shut up and listen, asshole. The snatch happens this afternoon and you're handling the job."

"No fucking way," Sid bellowed.

"I'm not risking this on creeps like you hired before. They fucked up again, even when you were on the spot, so I paid 'em off and sent 'em out of state." He loomed over the pervert, gloating. "Louie would dump you in the river if he knew he had a queer in his organization."

Sylvester deflated and parked his pansy-ass in his chair.

"These fit Chandler's van." He tossed Sid a key ring and dug in his drawer for a sheet of paper. "Here's her schedule this afternoon. I figure you can tail her and boost the van while she's inside with a big delivery, no problem."

"Steal her van?" Sid's eyes widened like a flashbulb had gone off. His mouth flapped a couple of times, but no sound came out.

"You got it."

"Where'd, uh, how'd you get her keys?"

"Uncle Louie's organization. With the vehicle ID number, it's a snap. You got a couple hours to find a disguise."

"What do you mean, a disguise?"

"Your ears plugged today? Or your brain?" Morrison blew a hiss between clamped teeth. "Start with a wig and elevator shoes. You don't want them feds to ID you right away, do you?"

"ID me? No!"

"You sound like a fucking parrot." Morrison pulled a yellow polo shirt and a matching baseball cap from the plastic bag and shoved them in Sid's hands. "Wear these. I had 'em copy the Chandler Vending logo down to the lame canary."

****

3:55 p.m.

Stupid batting practice! The ball had dribbled off the tee every time she swung. Cara kicked the chain-link backstop and tried to forget Coach Susan's unhappy looks.

Peggy cut in front of her, steely gray eyes daring

her to complain. Cara clamped her jaw shut and studied the outfield.

"Why don't you quit? You can't catch. You can't hit," Peggy taunted, her mouth pulled into an ugly frown.

Cara shrank away from the other girl and counted to ten, twice. She remembered all the giggles when she had swung with all her might and the ball had landed at her feet. This was too hard. She'd never be any good.

"That's why Coach sticks you in right field. You can't mess up anything," Peggy said, looking really mean.

Cara's face burned, and her shoulders hunched. She poked the backstop with her foot and wished she'd never started T-Ball. Why wouldn't Mommy and Daddy let her quit now?

She could hit the ball at home when no one watched. Mommy chased balls for her, and she hit lots of them really far. But at the plate with her heart thumping wildly, she always missed.

Coach Susan was taking forever working with Trudy. Cara felt bored and thirsty, and her tummy rumbled. They'd fixed veggie burgers for lunch instead of burritos. Yuck. But maybe the snack shack was still open. It was just down the hill.

She jingled the quarters in her sweatshirt pocket, pulled them out, and counted them. Mom would be mad if she had a soda, but she'd never know. Cara wrinkled her face. And she was really, really mad at Mommy. Could she sneak away again today? Nobody ever caught her.

"Where are you going?" Peggy demanded.

"I want to get a drink of water." She stuck out her

lower lip.

"You'll get in trou-ble."

"I'll be back before my turn." She slid the quarters together in a neat pile. "Coach won't care. She's still helping Trudy. 'Sides, I need to use the restroom."

Cara hurried toward the snack shack, but noticed the counter was closed. She shrugged. She could still get a soda from the machine, but maybe she should go to the bathroom first, so she could tell the truth. Relief rushed through her, and she started to skip.

A few minutes later, she stepped out the restroom door, squinting into the afternoon sun. Pausing, she cocked her head. Funny. There wasn't anybody around the soda machines. But the big kids didn't practice on Mondays.

Didn't matter. In fact, it was better. She'd pop in her coins and be back on the field in no time.

Behind her on the hill, she heard footsteps and turned to see a man wearing a pretty yellow shirt and baseball cap walking toward her.

"Hi, kid," he said, a crooked smile on his face.

She hadn't seen him before, but he wore gloves and a uniform like the delivery lady did. Cara remembered the funny yellow bird on her shirt. He probably worked on the machines, but when he touched his moustache, he almost looked scared.

The way he watched her made her itchy, and she took two steps backward, hoping her plan wouldn't be spoiled by something dumb like a stuck can. "Is the soda machine broken?"

"Yeah. I'm changing it." He pointed at the red one parked nearby.

She felt cheated. "Today's not a good day."

"You want a drink, kid?"

"Yes, I'm thirsty." She held her quarters so he could see them.

"I'll get you one. You can even have it for free."

"Thanks." Maybe he was a nice man after all, but she stayed back.

"Let me open this. I'll get you a nice cold one."

The man took a ring of keys from his pocket and opened the side of the machine.

It swung wide and Cara crept closer to peek at the magic inside. A shiver swept through her. It was empty.

He grabbed her from behind and stuck a cloth over her nose that smelled like a hospital.

A scream stuck in her throat, and her stomach heaved at the stink. With her heart pounding, she struggled against his strong hands, gasping for breath. Daddy? Mommy? Help!

But she couldn't wriggle free.

Couldn't make a noise.

Couldn't keep her eyes open.

Through a dark, foggy tunnel, she heard the door snap shut.

Chapter Twenty

Sereno, Monday, April 26, 4:27 p.m.

Damn Dan Bausch for grilling her again! She'd planned to sneak away from work early to pick up Cara. Production was ahead of schedule. Security was top-notch. So why wouldn't he back off and just let her run G-Tech?

Liv rubbed her hands over her thighs. Dr. Holden might give her crap because of her control needs, but Liv couldn't count on anyone else in this impossible situation. Not power grubbing, rule-book-up-the-ass special agents. Not flaky nannies. Not even her AWOL save-the-whole-world-except-for-his-family husband.

Kathy Linden pulled into the Highbrook parking lot and shoved the SUV into park. "Want me to walk with you?"

The sprawling, rural campus was beautiful, but negotiating the woodsy grounds in heels was a killer. "No, T-ball practice is nearly over. I don't have enough time to hike up the hill and watch. I'll talk to the coach when she brings the girls to carpool."

With a few moments to spare, Liv dragged her phone from her purse to review the production schedule.

Five minutes later, Kathy asked, "Wasn't practice due to finish at four-thirty?"

Liv checked the time again. "Yeah. Wonder where she is? Cara's not one to rush, but she should be here by now."

"I've been watching. Lots of kids appeared over the last ten minutes, but I didn't see Cara or a coach."

She tossed her work aside. "Guess I'd better go and get her moving. Be right back."

A tan car was parked just outside the office with two men in the front seats. Another FBI tail? No, she'd noticed them when she arrived, so they couldn't have followed her.

One man flagged down a car exiting the school lot. Liv rubbed a hand over the shivers crawling along her arms. The FBI must be watching Cara's school.

Why hadn't Bausch warned her he'd placed guards at Highbrook? She glared at them. What would happen if she hiked over there, rapped on the windows, and demanded their identification? She huffed and hurried along the walk. No, poking a watchdog wasn't smart.

From atop a small bridge, Liv scanned the playground and the path ahead. Had Cara lingered to talk to her coach? Maybe she'd asked for extra help.

A pang of guilt stabbed Liv. Unfortunately a bully had focused on Cara. Her daughter had been so miserable this morning, but right now there was so much to juggle. Watching practice had to wait.

Liv hiked to the baseball diamond, her stilettos punching into the turf with every step. She passed the snack shack and noticed the headmaster and coach. They both looked up as she approached, but the coach hurried away.

She frowned. Weird.

"Mrs. Gordon. So glad you're here." Mr. Blevins

scrambled down the slope to meet her. His graying hair looked windblown, and his bow tie was crooked. "Mind coming to the office with me?"

"I can't today. I'm behind schedule. Where's Cara? I should pick her up."

Ignoring her question, Harry Blevins took her arm and chatted about the current building project. He pointed out recent progress on the new school gym as he rushed her toward the quaint redwood frame office.

Struggling to keep pace with his long strides, she noticed a clump of teachers dispersing from in front of the office and heading in different directions. A cold tickle on the back of her neck disturbed her thoughts.

Sweat broke out on her palms, and she rubbed her hands against her skirt. Something was very wrong. "Is Cara in the office?"

The headmaster's usually affable face was lined and gray. He rushed on without a word.

Her pulse rocketed, blood pounding in her ears with sickening force. She grabbed his arm and planted her feet, facing him squarely. "Mr. Blevins, you didn't answer my questions. Was my daughter hurt?"

"Please come with me." He ushered her inside the building.

She didn't see Cara at the nurse's station or in the waiting room. The secretary's strained expression deepened her suspicions.

Wrenching away from his hold, she shouted, "I've had enough. Tell me what's going on! Now!"

"Mrs. Gordon—"

"Where's Cara?" she asked, but didn't recognize her own high, panicked voice.

"We don't know. She's missing."

The blood washed from her face, and she swiped a hand across her forehead, trying to clear the spots clogging her vision. Her head whirled dizzily.

Time stuttered and emptiness rose beneath her heart.

Mushroomed.

Exploded a ragged hole in her chest where her heart had beaten.

"Sit for a minute. Please? I insist."

Twisting her hands together in her lap to keep them from shaking, she slumped into a chair, her mind muddled from shock. Her throat constricted. She couldn't swallow. Couldn't breathe. Couldn't think.

"Do you need to put your head down?"

Reining in her panic, she met his gaze. "No, I need my daughter."

Blevins knelt before her. "Coach Susan missed Cara about twenty minutes ago. After searching the fields, she alerted us."

"Did you check all the classrooms?"

"Teams of teachers are combing every building. They'll check in immediately when they find Cara. I bet she got distracted and forgot the time."

Impotent rage flared, curling her fingers into fists. He was babbling, trying to pacify her. But guilt spilled over, diluting her fury, and her fists went limp. "Cara didn't want to play ball today. Why did I make her?"

Blevins patted her hand. "That's good news. Maybe she's having a little fun at our expense."

With her heart beating like a barrage of machine gun fire, Liv rose halfway out of her chair.

"The FBI has been watching both gates. Cara must be somewhere on school grounds," he continued, patting her again.

She yanked her hand away. "Stop treating me like a hysterical female and find my daughter!" Shouting cleared her foggy thoughts for a second. She remembered the phone in her purse. "I'm calling the police."

"No need to involve the authorities. We'll find her any second."

"Nate? It's Liv. Thank God, you're still there." Tears burned behind her lids and a sob caught in her throat. "I think…I think…Oh, God, Nate, I have to find Mike. Someone's kidnapped Cara."

Kathy Linden barged through the door trailed by two men in dark suits. The men from outside the gates.

One shouldered in front of Kathy and held out his badge. "FBI. What's the problem?"

****

4:40 p.m.

Morrison paced his office, chewing on an old cigar. Sid should have pulled off the snatch by now. He chuckled, thinking about that weasel's terrified face, disguised by an artificial tan and a fake moustache. Pansy'd even worn that idiotic yellow cap.

On the surface, his plan was falling seamlessly into place, but worry still ate at him. Unless this operation worked, and he covered his tracks, he'd have to hightail it out of Sereno. The enforcer from Krzystan wasn't the type to leave loose ends.

Good thing he'd planned ahead. The storage room at G-Tech was crammed full of "earthquake supplies" sealed in plastic. No skin off his ass if the place blew up with all the geeks inside.

He ground the butt into an ashtray. Les and the new

guy, O'Neal, had taken too long to load the rig today. He didn't like Les making friends so fast. They were both ex-military. Maybe there was nothing to it, but it bugged him. What was it about O'Neal? Had he run into him before?

Time for a look. On impulse, Morrison stuck his head out to check the hall and locked his office. Reaching behind his desk, he pulled a concealed lever and a hidden mechanism slid a display case sideways.

He checked the tapes from the hidden motion sensitive cameras. Sure enough, on Saturday night Les and O'Neal came in and loaded up. No big deal. Les always worked a Sunday run.

Squinting at the images, Morrison watched O'Neal stoop in front of his office, then try to pick the lock while Les stood by, dancing from foot to foot.

He slammed his hand on the counter. "The filthy traitor. Les musta blabbed to the feds." Shit. He couldn't even trust muscle he'd bought and paid for. His lips curled in disgust. "More assholes to eliminate. But how?" He sank back into his chair and leaned on his elbows.

A few minutes later, the alarm on the electronic gate buzzed, and his head snapped up. He paused the tapes to watch the monitors while he drew a gun from his desk drawer. He watched Les sneak through the back entrance, and his hands shook with rage.

Morrison checked the load and shrugged into his jacket. He pointed the muzzle down and shoved the weapon under his belt at the small of his back.

On the screen, Les crept along the hall and peeked into the warehouse.

"Son of a bitch." Morrison slipped out of his office

behind Les. "What a surprise. Whatcha doing?"

Les jumped a foot and did a double take. "Hey, Boss. I, uh, was checking to see if you was still in."

He snickered. The jerk was puffing like a train engine climbing a grade.

"The new guy, Mickey, wants to know when he can meet Sid. He's real anxious to sign the contract, so's he can start raking in the dough." Les smiled broadly, nodding.

Morrison smelled fear on the big lug. "Interesting. He helped you load this morning. Why'd it take so long?"

"I showed him how it works, you know? Doing it the right way." Sweat had broken out on Les's brow, and his gaze jumped around like a jackrabbit. "Mickey's real anxious to get started."

"Yeah. You already said that." Morrison clapped him on the shoulder. "You're nervous tonight, Les. Something going on I should know about?"

"Uh, no, Boss."

"You're acting like a three-legged cat in a room full of attack dogs."

Les's mouth twitched, and he licked his lips. "Don't know why you think so."

Morrison checked his watch. He'd give Les what he deserved and solve another problem too. O'Neal could wait. "Reminds me, speaking of dogs, we need to go for a drive. I got a job for you at Sid's place." He pulled the gun and pointed it.

The big idiot's fat face paled.

Chapter Twenty-One

Sereno, Monday, April 26, 5:40 p.m.

Liv stared at the mute phone. Her brain felt disoriented, paralyzed, like it had been soaked in liquid nitrogen. Huddled on a stool at her kitchen breakfast bar, she planted her elbows on the counter and cradled her aching head in her hands. "Where's Cara? Why don't the kidnappers call?"

Jana hugged her. "We have time on our side. I know it's hard, but hang on."

"How can I?" Liv hiccupped and rubbed her swollen, burning eyes.

"Sereno PD is tearing up the valley, following every lead, and the FBI field office mobilized the tender years kidnapping task force." Jana's face was pale and drawn, but her tone was firm. "Cara needs you to focus, and Mike does too. No one has given up yet. You can't."

Liv sniffed, swiping a soggy tissue across her nose. She had to stay strong. She dredged up a feeble smile. "You're right. Thanks."

Jana smiled back. "What about dinner? The team is ordering in pizza. Want to split a veggie special?"

A bundle of vice-like knots writhed in her stomach. No way she'd keep anything down. "I'll eat later."

"Then let's get you some tea." Jana poured the last

drops from the pot and spooned in sugar. "Drink up, girlfriend."

Liv wrapped her hands around the warm cup, stood, and wandered toward the refrigerator. She blinked and sucked in a breath to fight off the next round of tears. With one finger, she traced the happy family Cara had drawn in crayon. Mom, Dad, and Cara, with a smiling, orange polka-dot cat.

Kathy Linden hurried into the room. "Mike's on his way."

Liv froze. Her numb fingers trembled, and her heartbeat thundered like a kettledrum in her ears. She grabbed the counter and closed her eyes to steady herself, terrified that he'd bring bad news.

The front door slammed.

She rushed into the living room with Jana close on her heels. His darkened hair and fake moustache didn't fool her for a minute. He'd joined Nate in the circle of uniformed police officers standing near the phone tracing equipment.

"Mike! What happened?" Her voice sounded strange to her ears, almost frantic.

He turned. "Livy."

Melding into his strong arms, she clung to him and released a gasp of pain, but a spark of hope kindled in her insane, desolate world.

"I love you, Livy. You know that, right?" He kissed her and held her gently.

She shuddered, leaning against his warm, solid chest. His words helped, but not enough.

He smoothed his thumbs down her cheeks and met her gaze. "You and Cara were in danger and I had to protect you, had to go undercover. Forgive me?"

"I love you too, Mike, and I understand. But I can't even think about us right now. Nothing matters except Cara."

"We're doing everything we can." He tucked her head under his chin. "I went through the security tapes from Highbrook and we have a couple leads."

Liv frowned. "The school has security like that?"

"They were vandalized a few years ago and installed outdoor cameras. The FBI techies pulled together some clips and we need to show you the pictures. Can you handle it?"

Ignoring the fear, she set her shoulders. "Yes."

"I need to tell you something." He shifted to the side, but kept his arm around her waist.

Reading the regret and the love in his deep blue eyes, she forced in a steadying breath.

He gave her a quick kiss. "You know the tender years task force? Since the West Coast team was appointed, their track record has been phenomenal."

"What's the bad news?" Bracing for the impact, she searched his expression.

Mouth pinched, eyes narrowed, brow lined, he looked almost guilty. "The team will be here any second. The bad news is Sam Blackthorn is Agent in Charge."

Raw cold washed over her like a rogue wave and her jaw dropped. "Great." Her gaze darted between the tall blonde moving through her doorway and Mike's face.

Fury attacked the dull ache smothering her heart, and vaporized the fear that had kept her immobilized. She'd do whatever it took to get Cara back, even be civil to Special Agent Samantha Blackthorn. Pasting on a frigid smile, she shrugged off Mike's arm and went to meet the skinny slut.

Sam's eyes widened fractionally. "Hey, Liv. I'm sorry about your daughter, but we'll find her soon," she said in a hollow, overly hearty voice.

Liv pressed her lips together, aiming for control, but her harsh intake of breath had probably given her away. "Yeah, thanks."

Sam's cheeks reddened, and she laughed, a forced yap of obvious discomfort that died into nothingness. She shifted back a step. She cleared her throat. "Guess I owe you an apology. Mike probably told you he and I, uh, we never actually…"

You scheming, manipulative liar. Liv focused the electric current sizzling along her nerves into a clear, crisp stream of strength she could draw on. "Yeah, he did. So make it up to us. Bring our daughter home."

****

5:50 p.m.

Felt like a fucking volcano rumbled under his belt. Mike blew out a disgusted breath and grimaced. He tapped the DVD case against his palm, wishing his gut would give him a break.

How would Liv react to the images of the kidnapping? Could she cope? The dark circles under her swollen eyes gnawed at him.

Nate hurried in, a thunderous scowl on his face. "I ordered Agent Blackthorn to brief her team in the living room."

Mike grunted. "She better leave my wife alone."

Nate glanced at Liv and Jana seated on the family room couch. "I know how you feel, but we need her expertise."

222

Forcing down the rage and sense of impotence that clogged his throat, Mike shook his head. "Liv won't hold her temper forever. Neither will I."

He crossed the room and loaded the disk. His back and shoulders and jaw ached with unrelenting tension. Dan Bausch had dangled Liv and Cara as bait and then failed to protect them. Mike pictured ripping off Bausch's arrogant, smirking face and running it up a flagpole.

He buried the image in an obscure corner of his brain and swallowed the bucket of rusty nails in his throat. Facing Liv, he kept his own voice and emotions shackled. "Ready?"

Jana took Liv's hand and smiled supportively. Thank God for Jana.

"We put together clips showing Cara or unknown people on campus near the time she disappeared." Mike clicked the remote and grainy, black-and-white pictures of children playing ball flickered on the screen.

Liv gasped. "It's so…so normal, but Cara looks unhappy."

When Mike froze the frame, his stomach seized. Even after seeing the video several times, the pictures pumped revulsion into his gut. He moved a firm hand to Liv's shoulder, as much for his comfort as hers. "Cara was with her team at three fifty-eight." The time stamp at the bottom of the screen confirmed his statement.

Cara stood inside the dugout, looking away from the action on the T-ball field. In the next few jerky images, she moved past the dugout and beyond camera range.

"She left practice just after four. There isn't a camera on the back quarter of the field, but we caught her again by the girl's bathroom. When she came out she continued toward the snack shack." The screen showed 4:06.

"The snack shack wasn't open when I came up the hill."

Mike drew her cold hand into his. He stopped the action again when Cara approached the shuttered snack bar. "The volunteers closed up about three thirty-five. The camera is positioned above a classroom about a hundred yards away," he said, advancing the recording one frame at a time.

A dark-skinned man wearing jeans, a light-colored shirt, leather gloves, and a baseball cap appeared, following Cara across the scene. While he walked, he fiddled with his large moustache.

"My God, Mike, he doesn't look like a monster, but I hate watching him."

She was holding up better than he expected, but seeing her suffer while he kept his cool ate a hole through his insides. A hole the size of Wyoming.

"Who is he?" Jana asked.

"Don't know," Mike continued in a controlled, flat tone, "I'd say he's close to five-nine, under one sixty. Possibly Hispanic or Middle Eastern."

"Do we have pictures of the next area?" Nate moved closer and stood behind Jana.

"Should have, but someone shut down that camera about ten minutes earlier," Mike explained.

Liv turned to him. "How?"

"Cut the wires. They also incapacitated the two other cameras covering most of the athletic fields. The three they took out were all a couple years old, but a different company installed new ones earlier this month and none of them were touched. That's how we got these shots."

"So whoever planned this knew about the old cameras," Liv said.

"Looks like it." Mike squeezed in next to her and hugged her. "Blevins and I searched through all their video footage. This guy was the only person on campus this afternoon we couldn't identify."

"They checked all the parents," Nate said. "The front gate guards did their job. Every other adult left with their own kid."

"How about older tapes? Does this creep appear anywhere else?" Jana asked.

"Bausch's team is combing through them now, but that'll take time."

Liv straightened her shoulders. "Do we need cash in case there's a ransom demand?"

Damping down the fierce anger that stirred his gut, he wished he didn't have to respond. "Got it covered, Livy." He kissed her forehead.

"The agents installed a surveillance cam at the back gate this morning. This was the kidnapper's vehicle." Mike showed footage of a light-colored panel truck. "Came in at three forty and passed back out through security at four twenty-one."

"With guards on duty, how the hell did the kidnapper get through?" Jana demanded.

"That part makes sense." Mike swiped the back of his wrist across his mouth. "It's Chandler Vending's truck and their regular delivery day. Vehicle was reported stolen about two forty-five, but no one connected the theft to this case before it left Highbrook."

He sped up the film, and Liv's car pulled into the front lot at four twenty-seven.

"Practice should have ended about four thirty. I wanted to come earlier, maybe watch, but Bausch was in my face about security and wouldn't let me leave work. If I'd been there, maybe I could have—" Her hand gripped his hard.

He returned the squeeze. "You can't think that, Livy. Doesn't do any good."

Her lips quivered, tearing at his self-control. Berserker rage flared in his brain, made him want to strike out at everyone who'd hurt his family. Including a short list of FBI agents. He twisted his mouth into a painful sneer. Letting the anger help him focus, he exhaled slowly and found the dark, ominous center of the storm.

He handed Liv a grainy photo of the suspect. "The FBI lab enhanced this blow up. No luck yet with the databases. Do you recognize the guy?"

She shook her head, one hand covering her lips.

Nate moved around the couch and squatted in front of her. "Someone who worked for you? Maybe way back?"

"Look at his face, Livy. I know the baseball cap and moustache are in the way, but study his profile, his chin and what you can see of his bone structure." He watched her struggle. Guilt twanged for pushing her so hard, but she was their best shot to ID the suspect.

"Remember, he could have changed since you knew him. Different weight, different hair," Nate prompted.

Liv leafed through the photos again and squinted at the clearest shot of the kidnapper's face. "No. I'm sorry."

"It's okay. I don't know him either." He fought his disappointment and frustration.

"He's not from Silicon Valley Vending? Or Atlantic Partners?" Nate asked.

"No one I've come across." Mike held Liv against his chest. "You're still in shock, Livy. If anything comes to you, let me know right away."

She nodded.

He tipped her chin and brushed away the tears streaking her cheeks. When he kissed her he tasted salt. "The Amber Alert went out thirty minutes ago. We'll have his face and a photo of the van on every news station for the six o'clock news. We need the public involved."

"The van is bright yellow, pretty distinctive, so someone must have spotted it," Nate said.

"Brace yourself, Liv. The alert will bring the press down on us like a ton of fertilizer."

Nate paced in front of the sofa, his mouth turned down. "Bothers me he only disabled some cameras. We should explore that angle."

"Yeah." Mike stood and scrubbed his forehead with both hands. "I'll get it rolling."

"How did he get Cara out?" Liv asked, her voice a bare whisper. "Wouldn't she have fought? Wouldn't someone have noticed? Heard her scream?"

Ducking his head, Mike dug his fingers into the palms of his hands. "That was the real fuck-up. When the van reached the back gate, the agent didn't inspect the inside of the vending machine."

"Shit." Nate groaned. "Those feds are useless. Talk about a waste of air."

Mike watched the implication hit Liv. All the color in her face drained away, and her hands flew to cover her mouth. "Oh my God, Mike. Our poor baby. She was inside the machine, wasn't she? They must have drugged her. How could she breathe in that metal coffin?"

His heart stuttered, and his eyes burned. He paused and blinked several times. It wasn't fair to keep the truth from her. "The truck was dumped in the parking lot behind an abandoned building. The soda machine inside was hollow. Crime scene guys found a curly blonde hair caught on the latch."

Chapter Twenty-Two

Sereno, Monday, April 26, 6:55 p.m.

Trapped by the image on the wide screen, Liv slumped on the family room couch with Cara's cat curled beside her.

A handsome, well-dressed man gripped a microphone, his strong chin turned toward the camera. Lights glared from the news van rack behind him, setting off gold highlights in his tousled hair. "Roger Kirby, broadcasting breaking news from the home of millionaire entrepreneur Olivia Gordon, G-Tech's CEO."

The camera panned the driveway and focused on her home. Liv shivered. Warm light glowed from the windows, but barricades and police tape flanked the drive.

"You don't need to watch," Jana said gently and sank onto the couch beside her.

Liv shook her head once and raised a finger to her lips.

The flat screen television flashed this year's school picture. Pain, like a dull-edged knife cut through Liv, and she balled a fist against her chest. Cara looked so young in her blue plaid jumper.

Warning blasts sounded and an Amber Alert scrolled across the screen.

The bottom of Liv's stomach dropped and the strange buzzing returned to her ears.

Jana gasped, covering her mouth.

"If you spotted this yellow van today between two and five p.m., or have any information related to the kidnapping of Cara Gordon, call nine one one."

Liv tried to look away, but it was impossible not to rivet her gaze on the screen. The unknown man's photo flashed again, and she shuddered, nausea rising in her throat. This wasn't really happening. She rubbed her hands together, fighting the numbness.

The doorbell rang. She rose to answer it, but had to pass through the living room, where Kathy Linden stood exchanging fierce whispers with Samantha Blackthorn.

Much as she hated seeing the agent in her home, Mike had insisted Sam was Cara's best chance. Liv took a deep breath and skirted the two women with an I-don't-trust-you smile.

Sam stuck a hand in front of her and barked, "Stay back."

"Keep your hands off me."

"Let us handle this. Go sit with your friend in the other room."

Liv bristled. "This is my home, and I'm not under arrest." She snapped off the last word, just barely restraining herself from calling the woman a bitch.

Palms up, Sam drew in air. "Liv. Please. My job is to rescue your daughter and I promise to do my best, no matter what you think, but if you don't want to be tossed in jail for obstruction, stay out of the way."

Eyes narrowed, Kathy moved to Liv's side and Jana slid next to her.

Sam glanced at the women and retreated a step, glowering.

Liv let out a short huff. "There are three manned cruisers out front. I should be safe enough answering my own front door."

Kathy Linden checked the sidelight and cautiously opened the entry door. A familiar looking man waited on the front step.

"He's the guy on the evening news," Jana said.

Liv's pulse rate doubled.

Several television vans parked at the curb. The camera crews jostled for position behind the barrier. Telephoto lenses pointed at the door, filming the encounter from beyond the yellow tape. A deep sense of invasion made Liv shudder.

Kathy shifted in front of both women, shielding them. "No statements, Mr. Kirby."

Roger Kirby dangled an envelope enclosed in a plastic bag. "The kidnappers contacted the TV station, Mrs. Gordon. This arrived a few minutes ago."

"You vulture. You're enjoying this, aren't you?" Jana asked, her voice loaded with revulsion.

Expression set in a somber mask, Kirby ignored her, but posed solemnly for the cameras. "My instructions were to hand the note directly to you, Mrs. Gordon."

Her heart fluttered like a fledgling's wings as she grabbed the bag. "Then you did your job."

Kathy slipped outside the door and closed it behind her.

Liv turned and tore open the plastic.

"Wait," Sam commanded. "It needs to be dusted."

Finding fingerprints seemed unlikely, but Liv

couldn't chance destroying a potential clue. Scowling, she surrendered the bag.

Samantha pulled a pair of latex gloves from her pocket, tugged them on, and eased open the cheap envelope.

"It's addressed to me," Liv reminded her.

"Do you want to wind up in custody?" Sam threw her a withering look and held out a half sheet of paper with bold block letters.

"Your daughter in exchange for the plans."

Light headed, Liv slumped onto a chair and turned to Jana. "No surprise. They want the sensor."

"But why go after Cara?"

"Because Dragonfly's so well-protected now, they can't get what they want any other way. They tried." Liv rose and stared through the back windows at the last hint of sunset in the western sky. All this was her fault. She'd endangered Cara, and now she had to save her. But how?

"Will you give it to them?" Jana asked anxiously.

Sam stood motionless, listening. Her pale blue eyes glittered.

Liv's heart hammered fiercely, and her cheeks burned. She flicked a glance at the agent. She needed to be extremely careful.

Forcing her eyes open wide, she covered her mouth with a hand and shook her head innocently. "I can't. That would be treason. Dragonfly is top secret. I have to let the authorities handle everything." She let a sobbing breath escape.

Sam snorted derisively and secured the note and envelope back inside the bag. "I didn't think I'd ever see it, but you finally got something right. We can ID the perps from the TV station security cameras, or worm Kirby's source out of him. Trust me, I'll recover your daughter."

As if she would trust that woman with anyone or anything she loved. After Sam left the room, Liv whispered, "Jana? Come out on the patio with me. I need a favor."

"Sure. Should we check with Nate? Or Mike? I have no idea why those two idiots left that woman in your home."

"They didn't have much choice. Shush. Come with me."

Liv herded Jana through the kitchen, through the door, and onto the deck. "I need you to sneak me out of here."

"What?"

"I have to go to G-Tech." Liv grabbed her arms and pleaded, "Your car's in my garage. If I hide in the back, you can drive me to my office without anyone knowing."

"What do you need there?"

"I need the specs so I can trade them for Cara. It's my decision, not that pit bull, Sam's."

"Liv. That's crazy. There has to be another option."

"Don't you see? It's my company. My fault." Liv took a quick breath to steady her nerves. "I'll do anything to get Cara back."

Jana looked appalled, face pale and eyes huge. Through thin lips, she hissed, "It's exactly what those creeps are counting on. And there's no guarantee Cara will be safe, even if you give them what they want."

"Don't worry, I have an idea."

"But the task force—"

Liv narrowed her eyes and pointed one finger toward the house. "Who's heading that task force? Would you trust Michael's or little Molly's life to Special Agent Samantha Blackthorn?"

Jana stood silent, staring into the night.

"Will you help me?"

"Only if you talk to Mike first and tell him your plan. Then I'll take you wherever you want."

"But he'll try to stop me."

"Frankly, I think he'd understand and find a way to keep you safe. After you talk to Mike, I'll do whatever you need me to. I'll even deliver the plans to the kidnappers myself. Okay?"

"You're right. Let's go to the station first. I have some info I need to share with Mike, anyway." Liv chewed on her lip a moment more. "But let me take the lead when I talk to him."

"I can do that."

The frantic pounding of her pulse had slowed. It felt good to be acting, not waiting. She dragged Jana through the kitchen. "Get your keys while I grab something from my bedroom. Sam's still on the phone, and we have to leave before she's finished, or I'll end up in jail."

When Liv returned, she found Jana standing by the garage door. "All set. Are you ready?"

Kathy Linden walked in the front door, looked at the two of them and frowned. "What's going on?"

Liv met her gaze straight on. "There's evidence I need to show Mike. We're going to the station."

"But I can't drive you now," Kathy argued.

"It's okay. Jana can drive her car and I'll hide in the back seat so the press doesn't know. Just give me a minute before you call Mike and let him know we're on the way. Then Sam won't figure it out until we're gone."

"But..." Kathy's frown deepened. "What if the kidnapper calls?"

"On a land line?" Liv said. "They already sent the demand. If they did call, they'd call my cell."

Kathy looked more worried.

"I'll be safe. The kidnappers already have Cara. They've done their worst."

Chapter Twenty-Three

Sereno, Monday, April 26, 7:30 p.m.

Crouched on the floor of the back seat, Liv adjusted a corner of the blanket and peered at her friend. "Calm down. You're shaking like a 6.0 quake."

"Sam isn't stupid. We'll be caught the moment we leave the garage," Jana said in a jittery voice.

"Then hurry up. If we give her half an excuse, she'll arrest us." Liv ducked her head. "Can you see me?"

"No. In the dark, the beige blanket blends with the upholstery. Tuck in your shoe and you're almost invisible."

"Good. Let's go."

Jana's door opened and closed and a seat belt snapped shut. The engine turned over and the garage door cranked. "There are reporters all over. Why can't they give you some privacy?"

Liv let out a sarcastic little snort. "Wouldn't pull in ratings."

"Rush hour traffic is still pretty heavy. Oh, damn. There's a news van following us. I'll try to get away."

Liv braced as the car accelerated.

"I can't shake the tail. Hold on. Maybe I can fake them out and run the light." Jana's car slowed, then zoomed forward and made several quick turns.

Liv curled into a ball, rolling with each jerk and swerve. She had no control. Her stomach heaved and under the blanket, her breath felt hot and moist against her face.

"Lost 'em." Jana cheered. "It's not far to the police station now."

Desperate for fresh air, Liv peeled back the throw and peeked out over the seat.

The car turned a corner and Jana groaned. Media vans littered the parking lot in front of Sereno PD. "Quick! Cover up. I'll go in the back way."

Liv huddled on the floor and waited, her heart pounding. The tires crunched onto the long, graveled alley leading to the officers' entrance. She threw off the blanket again and slid onto the seat.

The guard raised the gate, waving them through.

When Mike opened the steel door and smiled, the weight in the pit of her stomach eased.

"Kathy Linden let me know you'd left. Guess Agent Blackthorn wasn't happy," he said with a snigger.

"Too bad."

His strong arms closed around her, quieting her racing pulse.

He folded Jana under the other arm and escorted them through the secured door. "It'll be fine, Livy. We have a hundred people looking for Cara right now."

Jana paused in the lobby. "Go ahead. I'll catch up."

"Are you okay?" Liv asked.

"I just need to sit and think for a minute." Jana squeezed her hand and sank onto a bench. "Really. Show Mike your info."

He guided Liv through the station. She put one foot

in front of the other, fighting the guilt and fear turning somersaults in her stomach. She dodged his gaze and peered between the metal blinds into the conference room, now the command center. A dozen people worked the phones and more concentrated on computer screens.

"We need to talk." Mike opened his office door and followed her inside. His mouth brushed her nape, his fake moustache tickling her neck. "Forgot to tell you before, but I love your sexy new haircut."

She turned and smiled at him. "I can't think when you do that." She found a chair and sat, holding her knees so they wouldn't shake. "Did they identify the guy in the van?"

He perched on his desk. "No luck on the suspect. Hat and moustache made an ID tough. We ran him through every database the FBI has, but we don't even have an ear to go on. And we dusted the entire school. Zip so far."

"You said it was a long shot." She failed to hide the disappointment in her voice, but straightened her spine. "There's something I forgot to tell you. Can I use your computer?"

"Sure. What's up?"

She slid into his desk chair and logged on to the Biz school website. "Last Friday, a student in my class made me suspicious, but with everything that has happened, it slipped my mind."

Mike swiveled, his eyes focused on the screen.

"It might be a coincidence, but he tried to worm details about Dragonfly out of me. He's from Krzystan, so his behavior might be cultural."

Mike's jaw dropped, and he leaped off the desk.

"What? What's wrong?"

"Krzystan? They're at the top of the terrorist watch list right now. What's the student's name?"

She tapped the screen. "Ahmed Mustafa." She queued the file and the printer hummed. She passed Mike the page. "Here's his info: bio, home address, all the details."

"Even pictures!" He dragged her to her feet and kissed her.

She buried her face against his chest and drew in his strength, letting it seep through every pore and recharge the numb parts of her mind and body.

Nate cleared his throat from the doorway. "Gordon, what's going on? Agent Blackthorn just blistered my ear."

"Look what Liv found. Her student from Krzystan pumped her for details on their new drone." Mike handed him the printout. "That's Shorty, the suspect I saw at Hakone with Morrison. He's the right size, and his profile's a match."

"I'll take this to Bausch." Nate grabbed the papers and headed for the door.

Jana burst into the room, her fingers splayed on flushed cheeks.

"What's wrong?" Nate asked, steadying her.

"I-I finally remembered!" Jana stuttered. "I know who's behind the kidnapping! Morrie Tomasini."

Liv had never seen her friend look so frantic and moved to her side, frowning.

"Tomasini escaped. Remember? He's long gone," Nate said.

"No, he slipped into the shadows for a while, but I suspect he's back." Mike nodded slowly.

"What connection does Morrie Tomasini have to Liv or Cara?" Nate asked.

"Thomas Morrison is his name now. I saw him at the Hospital Benefit," Jana said, her voice strong with conviction.

Liv shivered. "I remember. You looked like you'd seen a ghost."

"Morrison doesn't look anything like Tomasini." Nate scratched the back of his neck. "It's not only Morrison's weight, his nose and jaw line are different. He even has hair. Tomasini was bald and fat."

Liv touched her husband's forehead. "Look at Mike's hair line right now. And Tom had hair transplants. I noticed the tiny round scars."

"Never got within twenty yards of the creep," Mike groaned. "But why didn't I recognize him and make the connection?"

"He's had a face lift and a nose job too, but his flinty brown eyes didn't change. I saw them when he held the gun on me all those years ago," Jana said.

Mike's brows rose, and he slapped his hands together. "Had a hunch and started tracking Tomasini yesterday. Turns out his prints vanished from the FBI database. No wonder Morrison had a clean slate when we ran his fingerprints."

Stomach twisting, Liv asked, "How could that happen? Agent Bausch claims the FBI is infallible."

Mike snorted. "Right. But he refused to brief you in the first place."

"He what?" Liv gasped.

"Yeah, Bausch's orders." Mike waved the computer printout. "Could have used this earlier."

She let loose a deep growl. "Damn the FBI."

"That's my tiger." Mike pulled her into his arms, drawing a gentle finger down her cheek.

Her breath caught. "Then this is about revenge. Tom can settle his score with you and protect his new identity," she finished in a rush, her mouth drawing into a brief, tense smile.

"But Flynn was outside Morrison's office at the time of the kidnapping. He never left." Nate pursed his lips. "Hard to find a tighter alibi."

Mike frowned. "Who says he does his own dirty work? That's not the Tomasini I remember."

"True," Nate said.

Mike crossed his arms. "Feels like old times. Better order Flynn back on stakeout."

"Silicon Valley Vending has the G-Tech contract." Liv paused. "Even the second bug, the one in the conference room fits in. Sometimes they bring breakfast service in there."

"Man, B and E aside, I wish I could look around Morrison's office." Mike rotated his shoulder blades. "And I have to find Hamlin. Can't get through on his cell. I'm worried Morrison broke my cover and has Les tied up with a gun to his head."

Her throat seized, but Liv braced herself and asked, "Does Cara have a chance?"

"Yes. We're finally on the right track, Liv." Mike drew her close, and she nestled her head in the hollow of his shoulder. "Jana, leave your car here. I'll assign a uniform to escort you two home."

"A squad car would draw the press." Liv frowned at the floor, brushing a hand through her hair. She'd given Mike an important lead, but she was running out of time and couldn't force herself to reveal her plan.

Since she planned to skirt the law, maybe it'd be better if he didn't know.

Jana aimed a piercing glare at her and jerked her head toward the two cops.

She caught the signal, but flashed a determined look and shook her head. Teamwork was great in theory, but who could she really trust? No, she had to pull off the next step solo.

To cover the twitch tugging her left eyelid, she blurted, "Can you imagine the pictures on TV? The two of us in the back of a black-and-white, plastered all over the screen?"

Chapter Twenty-Four

Kings Mountain, Monday, April 26, 7:30 p.m.

Cara refused to open her eyes. If she did, the nightmare would start again. Shivering, she curled into a ball and pretended she was safe in her own bed.

Except she was sick to her stomach and hungry at the same time and this stupid room didn't smell like home. It smelled funny and the thin blankets were stinky and scratched her bare legs. She whimpered, and her tummy twisted again, leaving a nasty taste on her tongue.

She stuck her nose out and squinted, head throbbing. Everything in this room was ugly and brown. Not pink and happy like her room. The dogs barking outside didn't sound like home, either. She curled up as small as she could on the lumpy bed.

Metal clicked and the door hinge squeaked.

She dove back under the blanket.

"I brought you some food," a deep voice said.

She hid, holding absolutely still. A shadow moved. Something icky rose in her throat, and her breath came in little puffs, warm against her face.

"Come on, Cara. I know you're under there. I made macaroni and cheese." The light came on and the door closed.

She studied the man through the thin cloth,

watching him set a plate on a small table in the corner. He wasn't the man who had grabbed her. He was much bigger.

"Come on. I ain't gonna hurt you," he coaxed, soft and low. "You'll feel better if you eat. I brought you some juice too."

A familiar cheesy smell made her tummy rumble. When she peeked, the man backed away and stood by the door.

"What time is it?"

"After seven. You slept."

"I want my mom and dad," she pleaded, her voice shaky.

"I know. I think we can get you back to them real soon, but some things have to happen before you can leave."

"My daddy's back in California. He'll be real mad at you. And he's big too."

"Eat your dinner, Cara."

She rose to her knees, pushed out her chin, and made her face look like Peggy's. She could either act mad or cry, and she wouldn't cry in front of him. "Let me go now."

"Can't."

"Why not?"

He pointed at the window. "See those dogs in the yard?"

"I heard them barking." She hung her feet over the bed and funny gold spots swam behind her eyes. She sucked in a breath and held still. Slowly the dizziness went away.

"You can't get to the gate without the dogs seeing you, and they won't let anyone go."

Cara moved slowly to the window. She rubbed her fingers over the big nails pounded through the wood. "You could make them sit and stay while I run away."

"They aren't my dogs. I can't make them mind." He shook his head, frowning. "They would hurt you."

"I could run fast."

"No. We're both stuck here."

She studied the big man for a moment, then walked to the table and grabbed the juice box. The cool drink slid down her raw throat. Her stomach felt better. Maybe she could eat. The macaroni looked like the kind her dad made, sticky orange cheese and shells.

She picked up the spoon, but the man stayed by the door. Maybe he'd help her. "Why can't you tell the dogs what to do?"

"They're trained in another language."

"Like Spanish?" She waved her spoon. "I know how to say sit in Spanish. Mommy taught me. Siéntete!"

"Won't work." The big man shook his head again. His eyes looked sad. "They only obey certain people."

She scrunched her forehead, studying him. "You're not mean like my babysitter. Mrs. Rose is a troll."

The man chuckled deep in his belly.

Cara's heart had stopped jumping. She took a bite of macaroni. Maybe he didn't want to be here anymore than she did. "What's your name?"

"Les. Do you know how to play cards?"

Twenty minutes later she had a huge pile of cards, and he only had a few left. She yawned again, hoping he noticed. "Go fish. I still don't have any kings. But I'm tired." She stood and stretched.

How could she escape? Before, she'd seen nothing

but dark trees around the house. Now lights had winked on far away. And that meant there were people who might help her.

If she got outside, maybe she could get away from the dogs. Uncle Nate had an old police dog named Bruner. One time he'd put a treat on the big boxer's nose and told him to stay. Bruner sat until Uncle Nate snapped his fingers. These dogs were trained too. If she found treats for them, could she make them sit still?

First, she had to figure out how to get outside. "I'm thirsty, Les. Can I have another drink?"

"I'll get you one." The big man grunted as he rose from the chair and moved toward the door.

"Can I come with you and call my mom?"

"There's no phone. We're really stuck here."

She pouted like she did with her dad and blinked until a tear dripped down her cheek. "It's scary up here alone."

"You need to stay in the room." His voice sounded firm, but his eyes moved from side to side.

She gave her best sob and let her lip quiver. "Pretty please?"

"Come on." He waved a hand, and she followed, smiling to herself.

Cara trailed him down the wooden staircase. Two ugly chairs, a banged-up table, and a leather sofa filled the dark room. The stone fireplace was cold and empty. Beyond, she saw the lighted kitchen through a swinging door.

He dug in a funny old fridge for another drink, while she wandered over and checked the door. It was the only way out. Above the knob, she saw a big, shiny lock she was tall enough to reach. Her heart didn't feel so weighted down. All she had to do was turn it, and she could get free.

"Do you want a cookie?" Les asked.

****

8:45 p.m.

Cara leaned against the window, staring into the darkness. She didn't dare lie down. If she fell asleep, she'd never get away tonight. She put her mouth near the cold glass and blew, making a foggy spot. Why hadn't she been nicer to Mommy this morning even though she was mad? She drew a daisy and swallowed hard to keep from crying.

Close to the house, a twisted old pine tree stood out in the moonlight. A row of tall trees grew in the background. Blinking her dry, sandy eyes, she stared at the lights far down the hill. She'd reach those lights and find help.

Downstairs, Les had been quiet for a long time. Cara pulled a cookie from her pocket, broke it, and put the pieces back in.

She had asked Les for a deck of cards, fibbing that she wanted to play with them. She took one and walked to the door. The lock looked like the same kind she had on her bedroom, only backwards, so it kept her in. She had watched Daddy open her door once with his bankcard, slipping it in the crack and nudging the latch.

Cara eased the card into the gap, but it bent. She frowned. She hoped she was being quiet enough, and tried two cards, but they crumpled too.

Three cards worked. Her heart pounded fast, and she was breathing like she'd run a race. She opened the door and peered into the hall.

She stood still and listened for a long time, but

couldn't hear any noise so she tiptoed toward the stairs. Each time Les came up or down, the steps had squeaked, so she sat next to the wall and scooted down, one at a time.

The living room was dark, but light spilled in through the half-closed kitchen door. Les lay on the sofa with his eyes shut. She stopped on the third step and peered through the railing to study him. His breathing was deep and slow, like her dad's when he napped in front of a football game.

Cara took off her shoes and sneaked across the rough wood floor in her socks. She slipped into the kitchen. Her heart still pounded like it might explode.

She couldn't make up her mind. Should she close the door behind her? She pinched her lips together. No, it might creak and wake Les. The lock would be noisy, but once she was outside she could run fast.

Cara took a moment and caught her breath, trying not to be scared. Her hands shook as she retied her tennis shoes, but she reached on tiptoes, turned the deadbolt with a loud clunk, and jerked open the door.

She bolted into the darkness. Leaping off the porch, she dashed through the tall weeds. They scratched at her bare legs, but she ignored the pain. They grabbed at her shoelaces, tangling her feet, and she struggled to keep her balance on the steep slope.

With her breath whooshing in her ears, Cara reached the tree she'd seen from her window upstairs. She leaned against the trunk and let her eyes adjust to the darkness around her.

The pine smell reminded her of Christmas. She listened for the dogs, but heard only the wind in the trees. A slice of moon hung low in the sky, filling the path with scary shadows. She took a sneaky step away from the tree and crept along the driveway, leaning backward on the hill.

Suddenly bright lights turned on. She yelped and skidded on a patch of the gravel. Her feet flew out from under her. Far away, dogs began to bark as she slid down the hill.

Cara smashed into something. "Ouch!" she yelled, rubbing her sore knee. Behind the stand of trees, a giant rock wall she hadn't seen from her window surrounded the yard.

She brushed off the dried grass and stood on tiptoes, reaching high. How big was it? Could she climb over using rough spots in the stones? If she followed it, would she find a gate?

She heard growls close behind her, and her neck prickled.

Feeling like a cornered baby rabbit, Cara froze against the wall, hoping the dogs wouldn't notice her. But all four moved in slowly with their white teeth gleaming.

She remembered the cookie. Would the dogs fight over the pieces? She'd climb fast, if only they'd let her start. She tossed the chunks.

The dogs ignored the treats and growled again.

A cold shiver shook her. Using her loudest, most grown-up voice, she shouted the Spanish command, "Perro! Siéntete!"

They circled closer. They were so big their eyes were level with hers! The biggest one snarled low in its throat and then barked, making her jump backwards. She whimpered and bit her lip. The others joined in, with ears laid back and teeth bared.

She turned and groped for a handhold on the wall, scrambling as fast as she could.

The dogs closed in, barking. One snatched her shoe.

She screamed and wet her gym shorts like a little baby.

"Cara, stay still," Les yelled. "Don't move or they'll bite."

Toe on a ledge, she reached higher. This was her chance.

One of the dogs attacked, but Les grabbed her around the waist and pulled her off the wall. He kicked the dog, and it howled and fell.

He threw her over his shoulder and lashed out at another one. The two dogs crashed together. But the last one bit his arm, and Les bellowed. He flung it off and charged up the hill.

Cara could see the pack closing in from her spot on his shoulder. She wanted to be back in the house, safe from the dogs. "Hurry! They're gaining on us."

Les tripped on the porch step, but jerked upright, lunged through the door, and slammed it.

The scary dogs snuffled and dug at the door, howling.

Chapter Twenty-Five

Sereno, Monday, April 26, 8:45 p.m.

Liv buckled her seat belt, feeling like she had a bomb strapped to her belly. The timer ticked with every thudding pulse beat. She ground her teeth together until her jaw ached. She'd be ready when that twice-damned kidnapper called.

Composing her features, she turned to Jana. "They'll be busy for a while with those leads. We can swing by G-Tech, get the specs, and be home before they check on us."

Jana's eyes glittered angrily. "You're crazy, attempting this alone." She stabbed the key into the ignition and the engine roared.

"Who else can I trust?"

"Me, damn it. I kept my promise. I kept quiet, but you didn't tell Mike your plan," Jana said, jagged shards of broken glass in her tone.

Liv cringed, dropping her gaze to her lap. "I'm sorry. You know that's not what I meant. I was afraid to tell Mike, afraid of what he'd do. You heard what he said. He wanted to send us home under armed guard."

"Mike wants to protect you. We can still go back inside and talk to him."

Liv spiked her fingers through her hair. "He'd go ballistic and stick me in a cell."

"At least you'd be safe and the cops could do their jobs." Jana gestured a hand at the door, her jaw set in a grim line.

"Do their jobs? Think Samantha Blackthorn will do her job any better than the FBI did guarding my daughter at school? Cara was kidnapped from under their noses."

"Mike isn't Sam Blackthorn. Won't you give him a little more time?"

"But he isn't in charge, and I'm sure now that the FBI has other priorities. I don't know what they want, but I was just bait to them." Liv twisted her fingers together in her lap.

"Shit. Cara was too," Jana said in a slow, creepy voice and gazed at her with huge, stricken eyes.

"Now you understand why I can't afford to delay. I need to be prepared."

"I'm terrified both you and Cara will be hurt. Morrie Tomasini is evil."

"I believe you, but it's strange. Tom has always been so charming to me."

"He's a classic sociopath. Think Scott Peterson or Ted Bundy." Jana's face scrunched. She opened her mouth again, but didn't say anything more, just shuddered.

"I know I'm asking for more than a simple favor. I know I'm asking my best friend to risk her reputation, maybe her career. Will you take me to G-Tech?"

"You're determined to keep this from Mike?"

"You can pull off plausible deniability, but he can't. If this blows up on me, Cara will need him."

Jana paused, but shoved the car in gear. "Nate's going to kill me."

"Thank you." Liv stared at the crescent moon dangling low in the eastern sky, mind churning with worry and hope. She was tired of playing Blind Man's Bluff. Bausch and even Sam were more concerned with their plots and their egos than Cara's welfare. Well, she wouldn't cooperate anymore.

After a silent ride, Jana pulled in across the street from the G-Tech parking lot. "Where to?"

Two men sat in the front seat of an American sedan parked at the entrance to the driveway.

Liv sucked in a breath, leaning forward to get a better look. "Damn. More FBI. Use the alley and drive around the back of the building. Let's see who else is here."

Jana nodded silently.

"The engineering team is still working. I see Manchester and Nguyen's cars."

"Is that good?"

"Yes, but it means I won't keep what I'm doing secret for long. Pull into my spot. You're coming in with me. We'll brazen it out together."

"Can't we just..." Jana's gaze locked on hers. "Fine. What's the plan?"

"We can't sneak into my office with no one the wiser. The special agent inside will challenge us. We'll need a story." Liv rubbed her forehead, but her mind was blank.

"We could tell them you need to check in with your team on a special project. It's almost the truth."

****

9:12 p.m.

Dan Bausch slammed his hand on the gleaming stone counter in the television station's front office. He glared at Roger Kirby. "Who delivered the ransom note?" he demanded through clenched teeth.

Kirby raised his sculpted chin and cleared his throat. "As a journalist, I must protect my sources."

"A little girl's life is on the line, a cop's daughter." Dan's phone vibrated, but he ignored it, and dragged a set of handcuffs from his pocket. He shook them in front of Kirby's plastic-surgery-perfect nose.

The newsman's eyes hooded.

No way this news anchor wannabe would impede his investigation. The stakes were too damn high. Dan set his jaw. What kind of leverage would motivate this prissy jerk?

He stepped closer and frosted his glare and his voice, "Look, bozo, here's the warrant. Tell me who delivered the note, or I'll throw your ass in jail. What shape do you think your pretty face will be in, when the cops have finished booking you?"

Kirby gaped at him, and covered his nose with his hand.

****

9:15 p.m.

Morrison answered the call and recognized the Krzystani enforcer's posh accent. A cold tendril of fear tugged at him. "What's going on?"

"The target just entered the building with another woman," Suliman reported.

"Must be the doctor."

"They circled the factory before they went inside."

Frustration tightened his jaw. "You're armed. Why didn't you snatch them?"

"Because I am not a fool like you. There are at least two special agents between my location and the entrance, and undoubtedly several more inside. Assuming they would let me even drive into the parking lot, the slightest commotion would have them on high alert instantly."

Fool? Morrison pulled at his lower lip and enjoyed the spurt of rage shooting through his gut. That camel jockey was skirting pretty close to his limit. Guess Suliman didn't realize he was dealing with another badass.

A faint smile twitched at the corner of his lips, and he let the insult slide, for now. "Watch the cameras. Call again when the light goes on in her office."

"Agreed. But remember, fools who don't deliver on their promises die."

****

9:19 p.m.

Liv slid her key card through the reader and waited while Jana hurried past the interior security door.

"An armed guard, palm and retinal scans, and my thumbprint for this?" Jana raised her guest badge. "Now I understand why the bad guys resorted to kidnapping. It would be easier sneaking into the OR."

"We do what we can."

Jana's expression sobered. "You lied to an FBI agent."

"Yeah. Thank goodness, he wasn't suspicious. Frank's used to me coming in after hours." She hurried past the electronics lab. "Now we have to run the cubicle gauntlet. I can break away more easily since you're with me."

Two minutes later they were alone in her office. Her fingers flew across her keyboard, and she ignored the nagging guilt. She had set her plan in motion and booby-trapped the data with a vicious, homegrown virus.

She reached into her purse and pulled a thumb drive off her key ring. "One minute to download this and we're gone."

"You were tough on Alyssa, assigning that new project tonight."

"Recalibrating the sensor? You never know when we'll need it. There! Done!" Liv shook the kinks from her hands.

"What's next?"

"Now we sneak this puppy past the guard." She ejected the drive, keyed in the sequence to overwrite the keystroke tracker and shut down. That would delay the FBI when they came snooping, but not for long. Slipping the tiny drive into her bra, she shrugged her jacket into place.

"I have an awful feeling. This is..." Jana bit her lip, frowning. "This is so wrong."

"I know you're caught in the middle." She took her friend's clammy hands in hers.

"My intuition is hammering me over the head. This is a disaster in the making. You need Mike's help. Won't you reconsider?"

A spark of foreboding swept her nerves. Liv shivered. She trusted Jana's hunches. Suddenly, her plan seemed foolhardy, and she hesitated. Was teamwork the answer? Should she ask Mike for help? "Maybe doing this on my own is dumb."

Jana strengthened her grip. "Call him."

Liv picked up her cell and stood. Before she could hit speed dial, it rang. She dropped it on her desk and scrambled to retrieve it.

"Who's calling?"

"The number's blocked. Hello?"

An electronically distorted voice squawked at her. "We have your daughter. She's safe—so far."

Panic rose, clogging her throat. "Who the hell are you?"

"That's not important. We know you're in your office with Dr. Kapulani."

Alarm shot through her, lifting every hair on her body. Liv couldn't speak.

"Bring complete specs for the explosives sensor. They'll be checked on the spot, so don't try a fake." The frigid, soulless voice enunciated each word. "Unless you do precisely what I say, the kid dies in one hour."

"One hour? But—"

"Listen carefully. If you contact the authorities, your daughter will die. Armed agents are watching you. We're monitoring your cell phone and your office phones."

Fighting rolling nausea, Liv sank back on her chair. "I understand."

"We're also monitoring Dr. Kapulani's cell."

She flicked a horrified glance at Jana. The caller had thought of everything.

"Go to the vista point rest stop on 280, north of 92, at the base of Father Serra's statue."

She sucked in much needed air, and repeated, "The statue."

"Park in the last space at the far end. Come unarmed. You have five minutes to leave the office, starting now. If you wear a wire, we'll kill you." The connection broke.

"The kidnappers?" Jana's shaky voice rose to a squeak.

Liv nodded and frantically gathered her purse. "No time."

"What did he say?"

"I have to bring the specs. Give me your keys. They'll kill her if I don't leave in five minutes."

Jana held her arms against her body. Her face was filled with concern. "Where?"

"I can't tell you. They know you're here with me."

"How?" Jana gasped, and followed her from the office.

"Probably have more bugs or cameras the FBI didn't find. They even know I copied the specs." She locked the door. "Give me an hour before you call Mike. Promise?"

Jana's lips opened with a noise of protest.

Liv unclasped her purse and touched a tiny, tissue-wrapped bottle for reassurance, but her hands shook as she pulled out a sealed envelope. She had to calm down. There was still a chance. She had a good plan.

Stepping in front of her, Jana blocked her way, phone clutched in one hand. "No. I'm calling now."

"You can't." She seized the phone and stuffed it in her jacket pocket. "I won't risk it. If I contact the police, he'll kill Cara."

Jana's arm shot out and caught hers in a vise-grip. "What if it's a trap?"

"Then at least I'll be with Cara."

"You want to get yourself kidnapped?"

"No, but they have my daughter. At least I can protect her, maybe get her away."

"Liv—"

"They'll kill her. One hour. Promise me?"

Jana heaved a sigh. "Okay."

"Give this to Mike, but don't open it yet." Struggling to swallow the aching lump in her throat, she scrawled the details on the outside of the envelope.

"Be careful, girlfriend." Jana tucked the envelope in her purse. Her eyes filled with tears, and she hugged Liv.

"Now help me get away, fast." She headed toward the cubicles, hoping they'd avoid the engineers, but Alyssa stepped into their path.

"Liv, about the project—"

"Can I borrow your cell phone? My battery is dead."

"Sure, but…"

Liv reached for the phone clipped to the engineer's belt. "Thanks."

"About the special xerogel screens. We have all but four of the units ready to ship tomorrow. You sure you want production on hold while we finish this special project?" Alyssa asked.

"Yep. Get a move on. Stay all night if you have to." Liv took off, desperate to meet the caller's demands.

Before they rounded the last corner, Jana grasped her hand. "Promise me something? I know in my soul that you need Mike's help, or you and Cara won't finish this alive."

Her skin tingled and the hallway started to spin. She leaned against the wall and refocused her eyes.

"Promise me you'll use Alyssa's phone and call him? They can't have her phone tapped."

"What if they bugged your car?"

"Even if they did, you can give him a hint without alarming them. Wait until you're almost there. Promise me."

"Yes, I can do that."

Around the corner, the security station buzzed with activity. Frank was arguing with another man in a dark suit and shaking his finger angrily.

"Lousy timing," Liv said.

"Maybe now you'll listen to reason."

She trained her gaze on Jana's rigid face. "Okay. Here's what we'll do. You have to use the restroom before we leave."

"Christ!"

Ignoring Jana's eye roll, Liv slumped and leaned against her, sniffing loudly. "My poor baby."

The two agents' heads snapped around.

Jana slipped a hand around her shoulder, helping her toward the guard station. "They'll find Cara soon."

"Mrs. Gordon. Dr. Kapulani," Frank said.

Liv pulled on his sleeve, adding a layer of hysteria to her voice, "Have you found Cara?"

"Not yet. I'm sorry."

She stifled a sob with her hand.

The second agent looked her over. "We want to be prepared in case they contact you directly, so Bausch ordered me to set up surveillance here."

A chill shook Liv. Good thing he hadn't installed bugs an hour earlier, or she might be headed for jail. "Anything. Anything that might find Cara. Alyssa can help you with technical problems."

"Thanks." He squinted at them.

"I'm, ah, taking Liv home," Jana stammered, and plopped her purse onto the counter for a search.

Liv dug for a tissue and then shoved her own purse toward Frank, feeling pinned by his eagle-eyed scrutiny. She barely resisted the impulse to adjust the memory stick in her bra.

Her gaze darted to her friend while Frank rifled through her purse. "Jana, go ahead and use the restroom. I'll wait in the car."

"Would you excuse me for a minute, Agent? I'm worried about Liv. I don't want to leave her alone any longer than necessary." With a blank expression, Jana handed her the keys and rushed off.

"Hurry." She blew her nose. "I want to be home in case they call." Frank's communicator buzzed.

Dan Bausch's voice erupted over the speaker. "Johnson? You called me?"

"Hold on a sec," Frank said, handing back Liv's bag.

"Thanks." She fled.

****

9:37 p.m.

Dan's cell phone crackled back to life.

"Bausch? You get the info on the note delivery?" Frank Johnson asked.

"We're tracing the courier who left it here. Who were you talking to, Johnson?"

"Liv Gordon and Dr. Kapulani."

"What? The captain said they were headed to the Gordons' house." Suspicion nagged at Dan. Was Liv up to something?

"They are now. Mrs. Gordon is waiting in the car while the doctor takes a potty break."

Dan made a disgusted noise.

"I gotta tell you, they set off my bullshit indicator.

I've never seen Liv Gordon so emotional. She was frantic for her daughter."

"Natural reaction." He shrugged. Maybe that was all. Maybe not. "I'll be there soon, but it can't hurt for Harold to start with her office now. Give him your key. Who has access to her password?"

"I can log on for him. Dr. Kapulani is past the security doors. She'll let herself out."

Chapter Twenty-Six

Crystal Springs, Monday, April 26, 10:34 p.m.

Liv concentrated on breathing deeply and rhythmically, but nothing could subdue the fear clawing at her heart. Her knuckles ached from gripping the steering wheel with sweaty palms. She shook her head. The kidnapping had to be a nightmare.

She sped north along the deserted road, winding through a mountain valley south of San Francisco, above Crystal Springs Reservoir.

A river of fog blew between a break in the coastal mountains ringing the lake, and flowed across the road toward the bay, glowing eerily in the moonlight. She felt detached, like the fog had crept in and frozen her soul.

She slowed and moved into the right lane. Five minutes until the kidnappers' deadline. She could reach the rest stop in three. Jana was right. She had to tell Mike her plans and this was the time to risk a call. Even if they did have Jana's car bugged, the kidnappers were probably on the road too. She grabbed Alyssa's cell from the seat and keyed in his office number. "Mike?"

"Hi, Livy. We don't have much news yet," he said, his voice rough and gritty. He sounded exhausted.

"Mike, I need to tell you something."

"What's going on?"

She cleared her throat and braced for his reaction. "The kidnappers called."

"When?"

"Almost an hour ago."

He groaned. "Damn it, Liv! Why didn't you call right away?"

Her heart caught. "I couldn't tell you before."

"Why not?" Hurt shaded his voice.

"They bugged my office, said they'd kill Cara."

"Your office? Shit. What were you doing at G-Tech?"

"Listen! I only have a few minutes." She fought through her ripening guilt. "I'm taking Dragonfly to the kidnappers and trying to reach Cara. I won't stand by knowing she's alone with those monsters."

"That's your big plan? You want them to snatch you too?" A semi roared past, buffeting the car. "Where are you? Which highway?"

"I can't tell you. They bugged everything, and they'll know. I brought the information they want, but they can't open the files without an access code. I won't give them the code until I see she's safe."

"They're terrorists. They'll kill both of you without a second thought. Won't you let us help?"

"I don't trust the FBI to stay out of it."

"I can come alone. The feds don't have to know. Hell, I can bring the whole SWAT team. We'll protect you and grab the bad guys at the same time. Please, Liv. Trust me."

"It's too late now. If I'm not there in two minutes, they'll kill Cara. But if I'd told you before, would you have let me go?"

For a moment, she only heard his breathing on the

line, and her own blood pounding in her ears. "Mike?"

"I said we're a team. What did you think I meant?" His voice was riddled with pain and fear.

Acid burned her stomach, spreading to her heart. "I'm sorry, Mike. I'm sorry I didn't tell you before. I'm sorry it's too late."

"I can't lose you. I don't know how I'd survive without you." His tone softened, reaching out to her.

"I love you, Mike. Follow me."

He growled. "Turn the car around now!"

She hesitated.

"At least tell me where the hell you are!"

"In Jana's car. Follow me. We can rescue Cara together." Her eyes smarted with unshed tears. She disconnected the phone.

Liv steered onto the exit lane and said a quick prayer as she drove past the illuminated statue of the kneeling priest perched on the side of the hill. She backed into the last parking space. The overhead light was broken, probably vandalized by the kidnappers.

She was alone and vulnerable in the dark, empty asphalt lot high above the freeway. What had she gotten herself into?

A car drove in and aimed its bright lights through her windshield, stopping nose to nose with Jana's car.

Liv pried her damp fists off the wheel and swallowed the knot in her throat. Stiffening her spine, she stepped out, clutching her purse and precious memory stick. She squinted at the shadowy silhouette of the driver. Nerves dried her mouth, stole her breath.

"Bring me the specs."

Her knees quivered like gelatin. Liv lurched forward, surprised she could walk. She dropped the drive on the hood and stood back while he took it.

"The data files can't be opened without an access code. If you try, it'll overwrite with random numbers and fry your computer. You have to take me with you." She clasped her trembling hands behind her.

He waved her toward his car with his gun and chuckled. "That was the plan all along."

In the light she caught a clear view of her captor and gasped. "You creep! You took my daughter!" She resisted the impulse to rip out his throat. This asshole could take her to Cara.

"How'd you figure that one out?"

She faltered and ignored the question. He didn't know he'd been caught on tape.

"I'll take this!" He grabbed for her bag, and she jumped back. Searching it, he seized the cell phones and pitched them into Jana's car.

He tossed the purse back to her, but it slipped from her shaky fingers.

When she bent and fumbled for it, a bottle of perfume rolled onto the pavement, and she crunched the glass under her foot. "Damn."

"Klutz." He snickered.

She smiled secretly and lifted the broken bottle, spilling scent on her jeans and sweater.

"Stand up. Now turn around!" Pulling handcuffs from his pocket, he dangled them briefly and then secured her hands behind her.

She arched her back, struggling to ease the strain on her shoulders, but the cold metal edge bit into the tender skin of her wrists.

He opened the car door and motioned with his gun.

"I won't fight you."

"Right." He pulled a cloth from a plastic bag and held it over her face.

She choked on the sickly sweet odor.

****

Sereno, 10:35 p.m.

Jana was sick of sitting hunched on the toilet and staring at the green metal walls of the stall. Time to get help. Long past time.

Anger at her friend for pressuring her into this disaster, fury at herself for going along with Liv's idiotic scheme, and fear for everyone and everything she valued chased around her brain in a vicious whirlwind.

What an idiot. Why had she agreed? Had she jettisoned her life, along with Liv's and Cara's? How would an orange prison jumpsuit look on her skinny, freckled ass?

With her skin prickling like spiders paraded along her spine, she crept from the frigid restroom.

Turning the corner toward the security station, she barged smack into Dan Bausch and squealed. A guilty blush flamed her cheeks as he disentangled them.

"Sorry, Dr. Kapulani, I didn't see you." His head jerked, and his eyes widened. "Well, shit. I should have seen this coming."

Unable to meet his gaze, she shrugged, wanting to shrink inside her skin until she melted away.

With his face like concrete and eyes like glaciers, he asked, "Do you need to tell me something? To be honest, I thought better of you."

She checked her watch once more. Three minutes. Close enough. "I need to call my husband," she announced in a dignified voice, her back ramrod straight. "Perhaps I can phone from Liv's office? You can listen."

He escorted her along the hall. "I could kick myself. Nope. The SAC will handle that. He'll have my head on a pike."

She dialed, cheeks still flushed. "Nate? No, I'm at G-Tech. The kidnappers called Liv's phone, and she's taking them the drone."

Dan's head wilted into his hands, and he groaned. "Un-fucking-believable."

Her shoulders bowed under the weight of her choices. Jana winced and held the phone away from her ear. "Nate. Nate," she interrupted his tirade. "Please, I know. I already feel horrible. I couldn't stop her. Believe me, I tried."

She explained the happenings of the past few hours, responding to terse questions from her husband. Nate had every right to be livid.

Jana rubbed her forehead. "I know. Liv had no business doing this on her own. I tried so hard to talk her into getting help, but—"

"Apparently you didn't try hard enough." Nate's bellow carried through the phone, across the room, and made her flinch.

"You're right, I didn't. No, I can't even imagine what he'll say." She cringed, visualizing Mike's fury.

Dan stood and flashed his badge, glowering viciously.

She felt all the color drain from her face. "Nate," she broke in, "please let me finish. Liv left an envelope. She wrote on it before she left, Serra rest stop 280 past 92. That must be where she went." She opened it and unwrapped the plastic covered card.

Dan's nose wrinkled.

"Nate, it reeks of Liv's perfume."

****

10:38 p.m.

Steel bands of fear not even a crow bar could budge squeezed Mike's guts. His heart raced, jammed his lungs, and pummeled his ribs as he sprinted into Nate's office. "Do you know what my wife did?"

"Yeah." Jaw rigid, Nate stood, facing him straight on. "Jana just called. Liv had help."

Raw terror held his throat in a suffocating fist. "Well, shit. I should have known." He slammed his palm on the desk. Anger was easier than thinking about the barren wasteland his life would be if he couldn't rescue his girls. Liv had stabbed him in the heart, but Jana handed her the scalpel.

"Take a deep breath."

"What the fuck did Jana think she was doing? Aiding and abetting?" He glared, hands on his hips.

"You know Liv when her mind's set. Jana tried to talk her into getting our help."

He flung himself in a chair and combed his fingers through his hair. "Hell."

"We couldn't guess they'd pull such a stupid, reckless stunt, but Jana knows she screwed up. Dan Bausch is grilling her right now." Nate snorted, half grimace, half chuckle.

"What?" He glowered.

"Actually, it's kind of funny." One side of Nate's mouth lifted.

He surged from the chair. "Damn it! I don't see anything funny."

"Listen for a minute, will you? They not only

269

hoodwinked us, they pulled the wool over the FBI's eyes twice. First Blackthorn, then the two agents Bausch had on the spot. They talked to Liv right before she took off."

"Told Bausch all along he should brief the girls." Mike headed for the door. "Ironic, huh? First Liv brings in the critical info, and Jana identifies Morrison. Bet that bites his federal butt."

"Liv left a note with Jana."

"Where is she? Tell me what she said!" Mike demanded.

"Up the Peninsula, by Crystal Springs."

"Let's move."

Nate draped a companionable arm across his shoulders. "Hold your horses, cowboy. Let's check the GPS tracking equipment first. It'll only take a sec."

"That's right. Thank God I had them place a transponder on Jana's car. But why the hell didn't we monitor them to be sure they went home from here?"

They stalked into the command center together and Nate briefed the team.

Mike raced to the tracking gear and focused on GPS displays of ever-smaller sections of terrain, announcing, "The car is stationary, off 280, north of the 92 interchange. Squares with Jana's tip. Ready to hit the road?"

"I'm betting Liv is already gone."

The steel bands cinched tighter, and his pulse jerked. "But we don't know that. We need to…"

Nate raised a restraining hand. "The Highway Patrol can be there faster. Hopkins, place a top priority call to the CHP. Move it! McLean, get started searching the property records in San Mateo County for all

Morrison's known aliases. We were looking too far south."

Mike swallowed hard. Then he nodded sharply. "Makes sense."

"Come on. G-Tech's on the way to the freeway. Don't you want to see what Liv gave Jana?"

"Bet she had an ace up her sleeve. She said I should follow her so we can rescue Cara together," Mike muttered. "We're taking a squad car. Full lights and siren."

"You drive."

They tore through the quiet streets. Blue lights bounced off parked cars and businesses shuttered for the night.

Mike ran through all the evidence in his mind. One glaring omission nagged at him. "We need to haul in her grad student."

"Don't know why Bausch is sitting on his ass. He got the info hours ago."

"By now he should have cleared the inquiry through channels."

"When we get to G-Tech, I'll lean on him."

"Man, I'd love to strangle that fucking fed so we can take control of this operation."

"Hope it doesn't come to that."

He shot Nate a quick glance. "Who can we mobilize if we can't shift him off his ass? SWAT squad? Any of the undercover team from county?"

"They've all got your back." Nate tapped his shoulder. "Me too."

"Good to know, partner." He exhaled fiercely. "My crazy wife's facing the terrorists all alone and Bausch set her up."

"Jana ripped into me for leaving Blackthorn at your house. She was rough on Liv after we left. Must have been ugly."

He hit the siren, snarling. "If anything happens to Liv, I'll have Sam's badge."

"Don't panic yet. Liv's a survivor."

A delivery truck pulled over, leaving the road clear. Mike floored it and the squad car skidded through a turn. "Wish she'd trusted me. We should have tackled this together."

"Thought I could trust Jana to take Liv home." Nate shrugged. "I was wrong. But I figure Jana's suffered enough by now."

Mike whipped the car into the G-Tech parking lot and left the lights flashing. "Tempting to leave her on the hot seat."

Chapter Twenty-Seven

Kings Mountain, Monday, April 26, 10:53 p.m.

Les stared at the blood dripping on the ratty gold linoleum. He had to pull the damn bandage tighter.

Gritting his teeth, he braced his elbow against the kitchen table and jerked the adhesive tape. He ripped off a strip of hair and flinched, jarring his arm. Pain seared him to the bone.

The loose glass in the door rattled, and Sid clumped into the kitchen wearing platform shoes and a bright yellow get-up.

Even with a sore arm, Les almost busted a gut. "You're still wearing makeup?"

"It's my disguise." Sid stuffed his cap in his pocket and made a show of adjusting his holster. Posing, he pulled a dramatic hiss through his teeth. "Oh my! Looks like you had a rough night."

"Went out to feed your damn dogs."

"That was a stupid idea."

"They made a racket chasing a rabbit or something." Les shuddered, remembering the sight of that growling, slobbering brute attacking little Cara. "Didn't want the neighbors to hear. Mighta called the cops."

Sid shook his head and grabbed a drink from the beat-up fridge. "Told you not to go near them."

273

"Yeah, well they can starve next time." Les shrugged and finished taping his arm.

"Kid okay?"

"Out like a light last time I looked."

"I got the mom locked in the car."

"No shit?"

"She got a snoot full of the drug and hasn't come around. I checked her for wires. She's clean. But you'll have to lug her up the hill. She's too heavy for me."

Les levered himself out of the chair. "Pen the dogs."

"Fine. Wait inside."

When Sid reached for the door, Les hung back. The sight of the pack prowling near the steps made him queasy. Jiggling his foot, he watched through the window.

"Platz!" Sid ordered and the pack dropped to their haunches. "Fuss!" had them trailing him toward the kennel.

Les repeated the commands silently. If he could control the mutts, he could grab Cara and get the hell outta here.

Sid drew his piece and waved him onto the porch.

Les scowled. "No need for that."

"Orders from the boss." Sid shook his head again and chuckled. "You really fucked up."

The dogs flattened their ears, growling and snapping from behind the chain link fence. Les glared at the leader. Forget commands. "If I had my way, you'd get a bullet right through your pea brain."

"That's why I have the gun. It's a valuable investment. But we gotta get Frau Gordon." Sid minced through the weeds toward the gravel driveway.

Les trudged beside him, every step sending pain shooting through his arm.

Sid opened the car door and recoiled. "Shit! She still reeks."

"What's the stink?"

"Stupid broad dropped her purse and stepped on the perfume bottle. Instead of leaving it on the ground, the klutz dumped it all over herself. Had to open the window to breathe."

"Phew!" He hoisted the woman's limp body over his shoulder. "Not much of her, is there? Funny she's so tiny."

Sid shot him a dirty look. "Dump her in the other bedroom, not with the kid. Handcuff her."

****

Sereno, 11:06 p.m.

Hell of a shock when that queer's mug flashed across the TV screen. Morrison slammed a tire iron into the bag beside his desk. Sid had bluffed his way past the feds stationed at the school, but he'd missed a couple cameras.

He grinned. Now he had another reason to snuff the mouthpiece. Pleasant thought. He'd rid the world of another faggot. Those pictures of Sid in the San Francisco nightclub made his skin crawl.

He shoved in the big bills from the safe. Too bad he had to leave this business. He'd made a fortune in just a few months.

His fingers itching with anticipation, Morrison zipped the tool bag. He punched in Sid's cell phone number. "Sylvester?"

"I got her, Boss."

What do you know? The weasel had actually

pulled it off. "Did she bring the plans?"

"Yeah, but she put a security lock on the drive. She says it'll fry the computer and the info if you open it without the code."

"Fucking bitch. Beat it out of her."

"I would, but she's out cold from the drugs. Want me to wait?"

He swore and kicked over a chair. "No. Get your ass down the hill and bring the drive. I have a job for you. And set up the package before you leave. Don't forget."

"Okay. Okay, already. I'm not stupid."

Fighting off the blue-white sparks behind his eyes, Morrison disconnected and took a moment to regain control.

He dug in the open safe and pulled out a sleeve of photo-shopped pictures. A porn shot of Barb Chandler showed through the plastic. His plan to deal with her and implicate Sid would satisfy even the FBI idiots. Never hurt to be prepared when you're forced to work with screw-ups.

He wiped the sweat from his forehead and made the next call. "Suliman? We're on schedule. Meet me at one thirty. You can check the merchandise on the spot and pay me off." A sneer warped his lips.

****

Kings Mountain, 11:09 p.m.

Les peered through the cabin window, watching the candy-ass tromp down the porch steps. Sid hadn't relaxed his guard or dropped his gaze for a second, but had kept that freaking gun pointed at him the whole time he was on his cell with the boss.

Les pulled a face. He should have jumped Sid

anyway. Little creep probably didn't have the balls to shoot him. Just a couple minutes on the horn and he coulda given Mickey a heads-up, maybe got a ride outta this dump for Cara and her mom too. Shit, the feds woulda sent a freaking limo.

Sid turned the dogs loose and the beasts took off with their ears flattened against their massive black and rust heads.

He couldn't see what Sid got from the kennel. But when he returned to the porch and tinkered under the pipes, the heebie-jeebies buzzed up Les's spine, stinging like a hive of bees.

Les rubbed the back of his neck with his good hand, his brow wrinkled in concentration. After he checked on the woman, he needed some shuteye to give the aspirin a chance to work.

Nothing more would happen tonight. He'd make his move at first light and get Cara and her mom out of this death trap.

****

11:09 p.m.

Bitter fury oozing from every pore, Mike stalked into Liv's office. He planted his feet and glared at Jana with his arms crossed. "Were you in on this idiocy?"

Jana cringed on the sofa. "Did Liv call you?"

Ice burned through his heart and threatened to spread to his lungs. "Yes, damn it."

Nate appeared in the doorway and Jana's cheeks flushed. She lurched to her feet. Something metallic rattled as she faced him and blurted, "I knew her plans, and I helped her get away without the FBI realizing it."

Nate reached her in three long strides and turned her, despite her muffled protest. "They cuffed you?" he roared.

She gave a frigid nod and looked away, but Nate cupped her face. "Oh, Jana. Stay with her, Mike. I don't have a key on me."

"Hold on. I got mine. I'll take care of her," he said gently and dug in his pockets.

"I'm gonna give that controlling bastard an earful." Nate stomped out the door.

Mike came up with a set of keys and bent over her wrists. "I think I can get this."

One cuff loosened with a clunk and then the other. Jana released a deep sigh. She rubbed her wrists, flexing her hands.

"Why the hell did you let Liv go?" he asked.

"She promised me she'd call you. It was the best I could do."

"Yeah, I know, once Liv makes up her mind…" He heaved a fragmented sigh. "The CHP found your car. Empty, but no sign of a struggle."

She laid a hand on his arm. "Liv has my phone and Alyssa's. Can you track them?"

"Dumped in your car." He took a smoother breath, and his eyes searched the ceiling. "She walked right into their trap."

"Liv believed her plan was the only chance to protect Cara. She didn't trust the FBI taskforce."

"No shit. Neither do I."

Bausch marched into the office and stopped in front of them, arms folded and expression menacing.

Nate followed, his face a dark, furious red.

"I didn't authorize Agent Blackthorn—"

"Sam did this?" Mike growled. His hands balled into fists. "Liv was right all along."

"Samantha flew in and sharpened her claws on me for a few minutes." Jana screwed her face into a grimace.

"She shouldn't have restrained you, and she'll hear about it." Bausch rolled his eyes. "You're not a danger to the public, but you're still under arrest. There'll be a guard outside." He pivoted and slammed the door behind him.

Nate extended his hand to Jana. "Come here."

Jana wound her arms around his waist and pressed her cheek to his chest. "I'm sorry."

"I know. I wish you'd trusted me." Nate tilted her chin with one finger.

Unable to watch the couple, Mike rubbed his hands over his face and turned away, slumping onto the couch. "With any luck, the kidnappers would have led us straight to Cara."

"Liv almost told you at the station, Mike. I think I finally had her convinced, but at that instant the kidnappers got through on her cell phone. She took mine, or I would have called you."

"Why didn't you use one of the phones here?" Mike asked.

She held out her hands. "Maybe I should have, but I couldn't get to one without catching the FBI's attention, and I promised Liv."

"What she did was wrong. Illegal. You both could end up in jail," Nate said in a low, weighty tone.

Trembling, Jana gulped, but Nate took her hand and chaffed her wrists. "Bausch will send you home under house arrest. One of the feds will stay with you and the kids."

"But—"

"Call your service and explain the situation," Nate warned. "If Liv contacts you, don't try to handle it yourself. Tomasini is dangerous."

Another layer of ice hardened over Mike's heart. "Tomasini spent years sitting on this, plotting his revenge."

Jana shuddered and pointed to the envelope on the desk. "Liv instructed me to give this to you."

Mike waved the envelope in the air, sniffed the familiar scent, and felt the ice jam crack. "Her perfume?"

"Before she left, she started Alyssa Manchester on a special project recalibrating their drone. Dan Bausch is working with the engineering team. They plan to track her with the sensor."

His eyes widened. "Liv set her own trap."

Jana blinked, mouth taut. "There's one thing I don't understand. The kidnappers called Liv's cell phone and Bausch thinks they had a GPS monitor on it, but how'd they know I was with her?"

"Liv told me the office was bugged," he said.

Nate frowned. "Has Bausch done a sweep tonight?"

"Yes, they ripped the place apart but they didn't find anything." Jana paused, looking puzzled. "Maybe someone was—"

"Watching."

Chapter Twenty-Eight

Sereno, Monday, April 26, 11:37 p.m.

"Absolutely not!" Dan kicked the lab wall and the window rattled.

"I want to inspect the car. See if the CHP missed a vital clue like your dim wits did." Gordon glared at him and shook a tangle of wires under his nose. "Like these cameras from the parking lot next door."

Dan's ears flamed, but he set his jaw. He'd can that screw-up Harold for missing the cameras and the watcher, but he wasn't about to give Gordon the satisfaction, even though he was right. "Relax. If anyone was watching, they're long gone."

"We don't know that, do we, FBI?" Mike spoke through gritted teeth. "I'm going to yank Morrison in for questioning and send a couple uniforms to arrest Liv's student."

"I'm still in charge of this cluster fuck. It's my call."

"Bring Morrison in or I'm going after him," Gordon snarled.

"No way. We're not as close as we need to be. They have your idiot wife, and she handed over the fucking technology. Every second counts." Dan widened his stance. "We stake out Morrison on the assumption he'll lead us to the hostages."

"Morrison's under surveillance. He hasn't budged." Gordon chopped off each word.

Dan jabbed a finger at the cop's fake moustache. "But Mickey O'Neal can get inside."

Kapulani cleared his throat. "Good point. When Morrison moves, we need Mike on his tail."

For once, the captain had taken his side.

"Shit!" Gordon slammed the wires on the floor.

"Sorry, Mike, but you're the only one with entrée to the vending company," Kapulani added. "Someone else can track Liv from the rest stop once Dragonfly is ready."

"Can you coordinate that operation from here, Captain? Alyssa says they'll have the unit ready to test by one a.m."

"I'll handle it. Now what about the student?" Kapulani demanded.

The captain's overbearing tone cranked Dan's raw nerves like a CD in a paper shredder. "I've contacted Interpol and the CIA. We'll have the warrants for him shortly." He pulled on his coat and straightened his tie as a distraction. Interpol had the student pegged, but their agent insisted he was nothing more than a minnow. She was waiting for the killer whale to blunder into her net. But that info was need to know, and the cops didn't.

"Don't need a warrant. We have probable cause." Eyes narrowed to slits, Gordon moved a step closer, crowding him. "They're stalling. If you can't pick him up, we will."

Jamming his hands in his pockets, Dan glanced toward the door. G-Tech had to ship those sensors. The timing was critical if they didn't want the East Coast from Orlando to Manhattan to go up in flames on May Day. He shrugged and tossed out a few clichés, "I'm under the hammer too. Red tape. Interagency investigations—"

"Bullshit."

"No excuses, Bausch." Kapulani's jaw tightened to stone. Anger simmered in his voice. "We need him in custody now. Give me one good reason why I shouldn't send a unit for him ASAP. From where I'm standing, this operation is fucked up beyond all recognition."

He studied his hands. The cops were focused on two lives, not the thousands at risk, but those two were Gordon's wife and kid. "Look, Interpol is shadowing every move he makes."

"Shadowing? Fucking arrest the bastard," Gordon exploded, face bright red, eyes bulging, fingers curled into fists. "Your asshole feds have bungled every step of this case. Jana identified Morrison. Liv fingered the terrorist in the plot, even though you locked both of them out of the loop. And now my wife and kid are paying the price for your bureaucratic shit."

Half expecting the guy to swing at him, Dan raised his palms. "You want Morrison?"

The cop blinked.

"Then let's roll."

****

Kings Mountain, Midnight

Liv leaned against Mike, savoring the feel of his tall, strong body supporting hers.

"Let's go to our hotel, Livy. How much sightseeing can a guy handle on his honeymoon?" He ran his fingers through her long hair, smoothing it to her waist, and tucked her head under his chin.

Delicious warmth mushroomed low in her body.

Grinning, he caught her left hand and touched her shiny new wedding band. Then he kissed her palm. "Come on, Mrs. Gordon. It's been three hours."

"Mmm." Electricity spiked through her. She ran her hands over his arms. The crinkly hairs tickled her fingertips, and she shivered. Turning, she kissed the cleft in his chin.

He tipped her face and kissed the end of her nose. "You know, Livy, we're a team. You can trust me with your life."

His smile dazzled her. Drawn irresistibly closer, she pressed her mouth to his: warm, welcoming, tasting of sunshine.

His tongue swiped her lips and entered her mouth, stroking the inside.

With each penetration, she trembled, her body melting in his arms.

Mike rubbed his hands down her back and broke the kiss, nuzzling her ear. "Just a kiss, Livy."

"Just a kiss," she repeated.

He wolf whistled. "Wow. Look behind you. There's one sexy lady."

Liv turned, and her eyes widened in surprise.

A voluptuous blonde in a skin-tight gown walked with a sensuous wiggle of her slim hips. Her face was Samantha Blackthorn's.

Liv's stomach clenched.

Sam touched one ruby-tipped finger to her lips and blew Mike a kiss.

He ran a hand along Liv's hip and cupped her rear. "She does get a guy thinking," his deep voice rumbled.

Her blood heated in a rush, but the twinge of jealousy swelled. Unsteady, she shifted, and her nails made half moon depressions in his forearms. "You don't need her on our honeymoon."

"True." He kissed the crest of her ear before trailing moist kisses to where her neck and shoulder met.

Her knees weakened, and her mouth went bone dry. "Come on, let's get a taxi."

His deep blue eyes turned to steel. "No. You have lessons to learn." Something hot and primal flashed in his expression, but when she reached for him, he disappeared in a flash of red smoke.

"Mike?" Baffled, she swung around in a circle, looking for him, but the movement made her queasy.

Samantha looked mournfully through her curtain of yellow hair, and waggled her index finger, making tsk-tsk noises.

Liv fisted her hands on her hips. "What?"

"You lost him, sugar. Don't look so surprised. When a girl's got a hero of her own, she has to trust him."

"What are you saying?" Liv blinked furiously.

Between one blink and another, Samantha vanished.

A huge, colorful music box appeared. The metal crank turned slowly and the twanging singsong of a nursery rhyme jangled, harsh and grating. The lid exploded and a garish clown burst out.

Liv cringed in terror.

Under a motley hat, Sam's pasty white face had red circles on the cheeks and purple-lined red lips. Bobbing up and down, Sam pulled out a rag doll with

Cara's blonde curls and pointed a huge revolver at the doll's head.

The doll squirmed and screamed, "Mommy."

Liv tried to grab Cara, but couldn't move. When she screamed, only a stifled squeal escaped her tight throat.

The ground buckled. Her vision reeled, and her stomach twisted with nausea.

The gun fired with a brilliant flash of light. The blast pierced her chest, tearing her heart to shreds in an instant of searing pain.

Liv jolted awake with a hoarse shout. Her head ached piteously, and her parched mouth tasted foul. Where was she? Where was Cara? She forced open an eye but couldn't focus. The room whirled.

Slowly, her surroundings came into focus. Outside the window, the sky was still dark, but faint moonglow filtered through the tweed curtains. The cramped room smelled musty and damp.

How long she had been unconscious? Liv tried to stretch, but her hands were cuffed to the bed frame. Her shoulders screamed with pain. Her wrists throbbed.

A paralyzing hollowness numbed her to the core. What had she done? What if Mike couldn't follow her in time? Or it took too long to recalibrate the drone?

A tidal wave of remorse broke over Liv. The security codes she'd locked on the drive would only slow Morrison. Eventually they'd disable the virus and discover the specs were useless because she'd omitted Alyssa's brilliant breakthrough.

Maybe teamwork would have been a better option. The kidnappers might have bugged her office or monitored her cell, but there was no way they'd have wired Jana's car. She should have called Mike as soon as she left G-Tech.

"Stupid, stupid, stupid." Why hadn't she listened to Jana? Why hadn't she trusted Mike? They were a team. Were. She'd ripped out her husband's heart and thrown away her own life. She would die because of her pigheadedness, but they'd kill Cara first.

Liv's throat clogged, and hot tears slid down her cheeks. She cried until she had no tears left.

Heaving a dry sob, she wiped her eyes on the pillow. She couldn't let Cara die. She had to find her daughter. Squeezing the pad of her thumb against her palm, she tried to slip free of the cuffs. She twisted and pulled until her wrists were raw.

Boots clumped on stair treads outside the door. Liv's heart thundered in her ears. Should she feign sleep? She closed her eyes and relaxed her body, but couldn't slow her frantic pulse.

She heard a scrape and the bedroom door opened. Rough hands grabbed her arms and released the handcuffs. She couldn't suppress a whimper.

Large, powerful hands hoisted her upright onto her seat. "Good. You're awake. Do you think you can stand?"

"Don't know," she admitted groggily. She peered through the darkness at a man she had never seen. He was tall and broad-shouldered, with a crew cut and a bulky bandage on one forearm. "You're not the man who kidnapped me."

"No. He just left." He helped her to her feet. "Better?"

"Think so." Her voice rasped. She rubbed her wrists, chaffing at the bruises. Then the room lurched.

Liv grabbed the bedpost, leaned over and heaved into the wastebasket beside the bed.

"Let me help you onto the bed."

"I want to see Cara. You didn't hurt her? He said you didn't hurt her," her voice sounded tight and high.

"Relax. Cara's fine, and I don't need no hysterics. She's asleep, okay? Sit down. I'll bring some water."

Liv sucked in air to keep from retching.

He returned and offered her a glass, looking stern. "The boss wants the access code."

"I'll give you the code after I see my daughter." She drank, but when the tepid water hit her stomach, the nausea roiled again. She cradled her head, moaning.

Chapter Twenty-Nine

Sereno, Tuesday, April 27, 12:04 a.m.

Nate glowered at the clock on Liv's desk. With every passing tick, danger increased for her and Cara. He stood and stretched, wondering how Mike was holding up. Had he strangled Bausch yet?

Alyssa rushed past the open door, running a hand through her mop of curly hair.

"Whoa! How much longer?" Nate yelled from the doorway.

She turned back to face him. "Don't know, but we're almost done. I'm headed to the lab."

"Can I watch?"

"Sure. They're finishing the new molecular pattern template for Liv's perfume." Alyssa hustled toward the lab.

"Great." Brow furrowed, he followed her along the corridor.

"Nguyen is about done reprogramming the unit, then I'll test it."

Nate rubbed at the twitch in his chin. "It's been a couple hours since Liv was kidnapped. Won't the perfume have dissipated?"

"Dragonfly can detect a minute trace from a hundred yards." She puffed with pride like a new mother.

"Clever of Liv to start you working before she left."

"She told us we were practicing for a demonstration." Alyssa cleared her throat. "You'll need someone who can operate the handheld unit. It'll be easier than installing the joy stick and readouts in a vehicle."

"Volunteering?"

She pushed her glasses back and nodded. "Yeah."

"Thanks."

Nate leaned against the wall, watching Alyssa Manchester and the other engineers work. He ran his mind over the evidence and hunches that made up this case. Grimacing, he loosened his tie. Had he forgotten anything?

Their search hadn't uncovered any property owned by Morrison or Tomasini in San Mateo County and the Interpol honchos still hadn't responded to their query about Liv's student.

Nate jammed his hands in his pockets. Much as he'd like to walk in and take over, he knew he didn't have enough background info. Unfortunately, no matter how hard he pushed, the damned fed wouldn't budge without an official okay. Bausch had tap-danced around one demand after another. Pity he hadn't tripped himself on his wingtips.

Nate's phone buzzed, and he slipped out the lab door, barking, "Kapulani."

"Captain, this is Lawrence Kirby, Channel 10 News."

"No comment, Kirby."

"We know Mrs. Gordon left, but nobody has seen her for several hours."

Nate clenched his fist. The self-serving-slimeball. "Got it covered, don't you?"

"We lost Mrs. Gordon between G-Tech and the freeway, but we did see Dr. Kapulani escorted home in a cruiser," Kirby gloated.

Nate paced the floor, fury building behind his eyeballs. "Back off. This isn't a game. You could do real damage."

"Do you need help?"

"We're doing fine, so long as we don't have to deal with the media." He pictured the news truck trailing in their wake, cameras rolling, while they searched for Liv and Cara. They didn't need this complication. He pinched the bridge of his nose. Think, Kapulani. How could he maneuver Kirby so the good guys had the advantage?

"How 'bout if I send everyone a red herring?"

"What?" He stopped dead in his tracks. Out of the mouths of slimeballs. "How?"

"Everyone knows I have the inside scoop. I'll send them in the opposite direction."

Nate scratched his jaw, considering the offer. His lips twitched. "Sure. Get them off my back. Send everyone south. In fact lead them over the hill toward Santa Cruz yourself."

"South? Like into the mountains?"

"Yeah. Let's say Old Soquel Road. We don't want anyone following us to the East Bay." He grinned at his intentional slip.

"I get an exclusive?"

"Only if you get everyone, and I mean everyone, away from G-Tech immediately."

"Deal."

He flipped the phone shut. Now he'd order a couple squad cars north on 880 and catch Kirby in his own snare.

Alyssa burst into the hall, her face beaming. "Captain? We finished a gel screen matching the scent. We're ready to test it."

Energized, he rubbed his hands together. "Perfect timing. Now we're getting somewhere."

"Want to watch?"

****

12:04 a.m.

Ahmed couldn't sit still. Jagged spikes of fear stabbed him and he twitched and started at nothing. Events had closed in on him. He was nearly out of time.

Skirting the room, he searched the campus coffee house for Miriam. In the corner, a jazz ensemble wailed through the last set of the night. The low ceilings, dark wood, and old bricks gave the illusion of cigarette haze hovering in the air.

He slumped into a corner booth and shucked his jacket, pillowing his head on his arms. Why had Miriam insisted on meeting here tonight?

She approached, carrying two coffees and a plate of baklava.

He greeted her wide grin with a perfunctory smile. The familiar smell of honey and walnuts sent pangs of regret through him for what he had been forced to do.

Miriam slid into the scarred wooden booth next to him.

Trapped. He squirmed.

The band concluded their final song, a mixed blessing. He didn't miss the loud insistent drums, but felt exposed, despite the soft chatter and the noise from the espresso machines.

She looked at him sideways through thick lashes and pushed back the fringed silk scarf covering her long hair. "Ahmed, we're friends. In time maybe more than friends." She traced a design on his hand.

He jerked away as if her fingers seared him. "I must leave."

"No! Listen." She placed her palm against his chest.

His head whipped around at the intimate gesture. "You don't understand." Could she smell his terror?

"You had me drop off that backpack. I understand more than you realize. You're involved in something dangerous."

"No!" A muscle in his jaw jerked with the strain of his terrible guilt. "Don't ask me. I can't say anything."

"People will get hurt."

"I know." He met her gaze. "My family—"

"Bastards," she hissed, lips drawing in a thin line. "They have your family?"

His stomach cramped. "If I follow orders, they promised to free them. My father is ill. If I don't obey, they will kill him." He touched her hand, beseeching. "Please, Miriam, forget what I told you."

Her dark eyes held his gaze. "They won't let your family go. They didn't release mine."

He blinked, thinking through the implications. "I believe you. I can see it in your face. What should I do?"

"Tell me everything."

"And my family?"

"As expendable as you are." She glanced around as if checking for interested ears and shook her head slowly. "I followed orders, but it didn't matter. My family was executed."

Fear gnawed at his bowels, threatening to turn them to liquid. "I'm sorry."

She faced him. "Tell me now. If we act soon, I might help them reach safety, but if we wait, we shall only grieve."

Wracked by doubt, Ahmed stared at the old brick wall, hung with faded portraits of writers and philosophers. "A drone was our first assignment. And some new sniffing, no, sensing equipment."

"Explosive detection?"

"Yes." He frowned. "I don't trust the American I must deal with. He kidnapped a child to extort the technology."

Miriam shuddered. "You're doing the right thing. Come with me. I know people who can help."

She led him from the coffee house and through the silent campus. California mist filled the night, obscuring the crescent moon.

He glanced at her and then folded his fingers around hers. He had to stop Suliman. But how? Thwarting the prince's emissary would be difficult. Dangerous. Maybe fatal.

"Is your contact's family also held hostage?"

"No, he is a zealot."

****

12:09 a.m.

With a first class ticket on the eight a.m. flight to New York in his pocket, Sid hurried across the Silicon Valley Vending parking lot. After he checked in, Morrison should stay off his ass for a while. He could drag his feet on any new orders or lie his way out. He'd be at the airport and on a jet before Morrison suspected.

He sneered. No way he'd work with that screw-up again. Once he was safely back in Louie Souza's territory, he'd make sure Morrison was toast. Forget the pictures. Morrison might think his blackmail was damning, but a clever lawyer could spin dirt a thousand ways.

"Get in here, Sylvester," Morrison shouted through his open office door. Sid stepped inside the warehouse.

Guarding his expression, he walked into the office and adjusted his cufflinks. Morrison looked him up and down. "Everything in place? You look like an alley cat that swallowed a canary."

Perceptive of the old crook. He looked around. Couldn't be too careful when he didn't know where the bugs were. He presented the memory stick with a flourish. "No sweat. Everything came off exactly as planned."

Morrison smirked and snatched the drive.

Although his pulse jumped, Sid asked nonchalantly, "Did you transfer the cash to my account in the Caymans?"

"Took care of it after I called." Morrison passed him a piece of paper with the confirmation. "I trust you."

"Thanks. I need to catch a few zees before I go back up the mountain." He'd check his account too.

"That can wait. I told you I got another job for you tonight." Morrison punched him on the shoulder.

"What do you need?"

"I'll tell you on the way. I'm in on this one."

"Uh, sure." Now what? Since when did Morrison operate hands-on?

"Let's use your car. Mine's parked in the loading bay."

"Fine." Sid hid his angry disappointment. Too late to make a break for it now. He should have avoided Morrison like a choirboy with the clap.

He glanced at his watch. Still plenty of time to make his flight. Maybe he'd finish the job and then split. He opened the car door, fuming.

Morrison slid into the passenger seat, chucked a black gym bag onto the floor and pulled a face. "What stinks?"

"Frau Gordon broke a bottle of perfume, the klutz." He grinned, chest puffing out, remembering how powerful he'd felt.

"You rattled the ball-busting bitch?" At his nod, Morrison chuckled. "Who knew?" Then his expression shifted, taking on a dangerous, predatory edge. He pulled a stogie from his jacket, clipped the ends, and lit it.

Sid choked on the foul smoke. Perfect. He could almost ignore the musky perfume, but the combination turned his stomach. Hoping the dimwitted schmuck wouldn't suspect, he tried to keep the resentment from his tone, "What are we doing now?"

"Drive over to that slut's office," Morrison demanded, his voice gruff and raspy.

"G-Tech? It'll be crawling with cops."

"No, you stupid sod. Chandler Vending."

"Okay." Stupid? Sid restrained a disgusted snort, but his resentment simmered. He had the law degree. Where did this asshole high school dropout come up with such crap?

Morrison faced him. Smoke seeped out his mouth

as he talked. "I listened to the whole G-Tech tape. Guess who helped the feds locate that bug?"

"Barb Chandler?"

"Bitch. The conversation had just gotten interesting when that two-bit whore piped up with an ID."

"How'd she figure it out?"

"Not sure." Morrison hacked a sloppy cough. "But we're gonna teach her some manners."

Shit. Bad idea. Very bad idea. One glance at Morrison's intense, vicious scowl and Sid's fingers clenched the wheel until his knuckles bleached white. Sweat trickled down his sides. "Uh, maybe we should avoid Chandler. What if the FBI's watching her place? If she helped them, they're probably hanging around."

"Nah, the place is deserted. She has an early route today, won't be in until four maybe five a.m. We got plenty of time."

"How will we get in?"

"No problem. You got a tire iron in the trunk?" Morrison rubbed his hands together, the edges of his lips turned up in a grin more ferocious than his scowl.

"No! I don't have anything like that." Sid brushed his forehead and wiped his damp palm on his leg. He couldn't let Morrison see his suitcases.

"That's okay. I got tools." Morrison nudged the bag at his feet, eyes glinting. "I feel like smashing things."

Sid tugged at the collar of his shirt. Better deflect his attention again. "You know, I'm surprised. You usually leave, uh, enforcement to Hamlin."

"This is personal." Morrison flashed his teeth.

Sid forced a smile.

"And not everything went exactly like I ordered,

297

you jackass. You missed some cameras at the school."

"I disabled all three. Those freaking FBI agents you forgot to warn me about must have taken a picture."

"No, they caught one of you snatching the kid and released a fucking Amber Alert."

Chapter Thirty

Sereno, Tuesday, April 27, 12:09 a.m.

Mike's pulse rammed through his muscles and thundered behind his temples. Any second he'd start boiling and the sweat beading on his brow would evaporate into little puffs of steam.

He couldn't follow Liv.

Couldn't storm the building across the street.

Couldn't reach over and strangle the lying, manipulative fed in the driver's seat.

Wedged in a nondescript beige sedan, they'd watched Silicon Valley Vending for eleven and a half minutes. Mike thumped a booted heel against the floorboard. His blood pressure had climbed so high his jaw ached and chest felt constricted.

He slapped his hand on his knee and glared at Daniel fucking Bausch. "You commandeered me so I could get you inside. Why the hell am I sitting on my ass instead of tracking my girls?"

Bausch returned the glare. "Put a sock in it, Gordon. Morrison's our strongest lead. It's worth the wait to see where he goes."

"No sign he's moving anywhere within the next millennium." Mike put on his aviator glasses, smoothed his fake moustache, and drew his weapon. "Give me forty-five seconds and I'll have a gun stuck in his ear and another one poked up his ass. He'll talk."

"Real subtle, Gordon." Bausch rolled his eyes. "Don't. Move."

"Why wait?" Mike dug his fingers into the denim covering his thighs to keep from punching the guy. "What aren't you telling me?"

"Nothing."

A green Mercedes signaled and pulled into the SVV parking lot.

Mike bolted upright. "Holy shit!"

The electronic gate slid open, but the angle made identifying the driver tough. He read the tags aloud and Bausch punched the license into the laptop.

A minute later, the screen flashed and Bausch turned to him. "It's a lease, registered to Sidney Sylvester, 1101 Hawthorne."

Mike felt sparks glint from his eyes. His mouth stretched into a fierce grin. "The lawyer. Now we're getting somewhere. Pull up his driver's license photo."

"Roger." Bausch poked the keys.

Waiting for a response, Mike cracked his knuckles to keep from snatching the laptop.

"What do you know? Add a moustache. Recognize him?"

He glanced at the screen. His blood pressure shot into orbit again and the urge to kill grabbed at his gut. "Well, hell. Doesn't that frost your ass? The one creep I never saw while I played Mickey is the scumbag who snatched Cara. I'm going in. Now."

Bausch held up a cautionary hand. "Hang on for another minute."

"No way."

"That's an order, Gordon. I'll have your badge."

"Deal." With a sharp nod, Mike pulled his federal shield, slammed it on the console, and grabbed the door handle. But as he put his shoulder into it, the electronic gate rolled to the side and the Mercedes reemerged from the back lot.

"Sylvester's driving."

"Looks like Morrison in the passenger seat." Mike tugged on the bill of his cap. "I never saw that son of a whore riding shotgun with anyone. He always drives."

After the car accelerated past their location, Bausch edged out onto the road.

The Benz crawled through the industrial park. With their headlights off they trailed from a few hundred yards behind.

"Where they headed?"

"Chandler Vending is on the right," Bausch said, worry shading his voice.

"I'll call for backup." Mike grabbed his phone. "Kapulani? Morrison's lawyer showed up. Sylvester's the ass-wipe who kidnapped Cara."

"Good work. What's going down?" Nate asked.

"Sylvester and Morrison are at Chandler Vending."

"Building empty?"

"Looks like it."

Bausch parked across the street behind scraggly oleander bushes.

"I'll call it in," Nate said.

"Right. Lights. No sirens."

"I want those creeps as much as you do, but we need to know where Liv and Cara are. Wait for the backup units."

Mike ground his teeth. Wait. Again. Been there.

"Sylvester pulled a bag out of the car. Morrison's

headed around the corner. Probably after the electrical panel." Bausch hesitated.

"Yep. There go the outdoor lights. They cut the alarm. They're inside," Mike added.

"Maintain your position," Nate ordered. "I'm at G-Tech now. They're finishing the tests. We should be on the road tracking Liv in the next five minutes."

Seconds crept by with nothing to show for his patience. Then minutes. Each one jacked his heart rate a little higher. "Where's our backup?" he asked Nate.

"Should arrive shortly. The drone performed great and we're headed out."

Mike whistled. "Hot damn."

"I ordered a chopper to the hospital heliport. ETA twelve forty-five. You and Marino are on hostage rescue."

"Roger. With the backup units, even Bausch can handle Chandler Vending." Mike threw a sideways sneer at the agent.

"Shit. It's Barb." Bausch pointed at a bright yellow pick-up.

His pulse spiked. "Chandler just drove up." The truck climbed the curb and moved into the driveway as the electronic gate slowly slid open.

Bausch drew his phone and his weapon.

"We're going in." Mike wrenched the door open and dashed across the street, crouching low.

Bausch tailed him five yards back. They wedged behind a power supply box at the curb. "Barb?" Dan shouted into his phone.

Blinds shifted and the front window shattered.

"Drop! Now!"

She collapsed sideways and bullets pierced the

windshield where her head had been.

"Stay put. We're right behind you," Bausch ordered and positioned for the run.

"I'll cover the building. Go!" Mike let loose a volley of shots across the entrance. His bullets ricocheted off the office blocks while he sprinted to the truck.

Bausch pounded on the door and wrenched it open. "Barb? You okay?"

She lay frozen on the seat. Safety glass fragments scattered all over the cab and pinpoint cuts blossomed along her arm. "T-Terrified."

Bausch extended a hand. "Get on the ground behind the wheel."

She slithered out, teeth chattering. "Who?"

"Your competition. Keep your head tucked and don't move."

"You got it." She curled into a ball.

In the deep gloom of the night, Mike caught the flash of blue lights behind them. "Help's here."

Two squad cars maneuvered into place, blocking the entrance. Four uniformed cops jumped out, taking positions behind open doors.

Jackson Marino shouldered a high-powered rifle. "Got yourself in a jam, buddy?"

"Turns out I did."

Half a dozen rounds pinged into the door of the nearest black and white. Mike winced.

A shadow poked around the corner and Marino squeezed off a couple shots.

"Morrison's fair game, but we need Sylvester alive," Mike yelled to Marino.

"Gordon," Morrison shouted from inside, "we got

your kid and your wife. Let us go, and they'll still be alive when the sun comes up."

Bausch elbowed him. "I'll handle this."

"No way, FBI. We don't know where he's holding my family. I'm not risking them." Mike bellowed, "You're lying, Tomasini!"

"So you figured that out, Gordon? Doesn't matter. Your pretty little señora will die unless I get away safe."

"What do you want?"

"Let us go. I'll tell you where they are. I swear. They're dead unless we drive away."

Gunshots exploded through one cruiser's front window and the front tires blew.

"We don't negotiate with terrorists," Bausch yelled.

Hands fisted, Mike glared. "Can it. They're my girls."

"Yeah. And one's headed for jail." Bausch glowered back. "You're trapped, Morrison. Come out with your hands in the air if you want to stay alive."

Silence reigned for twenty seconds, and Mike could hear his breath rasp in and out. "Tomasini? Drop your weapon and come out, now. We'll make a deal."

From the rear entrance, Sylvester poked his head out and shot rapid-fire rounds into the yellow pick-up. A bullet whizzed past Mike's ear with a piercing whine, and he flattened against the truck.

With a terrified gasp, Chandler rose to her knees. The next rounds hit her neck and shoulder. She spun sideways and dropped, bright red blood spurting.

His guts clenched, and his stomach hit bedrock. Arterial blood. "Shit!"

"Cover me!" Bausch shouted.

Mike returned fire, his shots pinging off the corner of the building as Sylvester ducked inside.

Kneeling, Bausch applied pressure to her wounds.

Mike shoved in a new clip, but when Bausch started to lift Chandler, a bullet hit his leg, and he went down, losing his grip on the woman.

Marino's squad laid down a barrage.

While Bausch dragged himself to safety, Mike hauled Chandler's limp body behind the truck.

Her clothes and hair were soaked through, sticky with copper-scented blood Her face was grayish-white and pasty.

Digging the heel of his hand into her wounded shoulder, Mike felt her collarbone give and poke through flesh.

He groped for a pulse, but couldn't find one. His heart lurched. His shoulders drooped. His breath quaked on the way in.

"What a fucking waste."

He gritted his teeth, trying to keep the anger and fear within him from erupting in a howl.

Bausch glanced up, his face contorted with pain.

Stripping off his jacket, Mike shook his head slowly and pressed the cloth against the agent's wounded thigh. "She didn't make it."

Bausch stared at the lifeless woman.

One more shot echoed.

An engine revved.

An old, yellow delivery truck roared through the gate and rammed the intact squad car, shoved it over onto its roof, and accelerated out onto the street.

Mike fired twice and the rear window crazed.

"Damn. Can't chase him in those wrecks," Marino shouted.

"There's still a shooter inside. I'm going after him. Bausch is hit, and we need the pick-up for cover. Lopez, call in the EMTs and report to dispatch. Marino, you and Flynn circle in through the front."

"We're on it." Marino waved a hand.

Every sense on full alert, Mike edged along the wall toward the harsh light spilling from the wide-open warehouse doors.

Fingers sticky, Mike held his weapon at high ready and crab-walked forward. He smelled blood and brains and bowel before he rounded the corner and almost retched.

Sylvester was propped up-right beside an old Coke machine. Smears of blood and gray matter dripped down the wall behind the body. His weapon had been jammed in his mouth and fired.

Mike didn't buy the set-up. No way was this suicide.

Flynn and Marino appeared. "Building's clear," Flynn reported.

"What happened here? Did you make the shot?" Marino asked over the racket of the arriving ambulance.

"Morrison must have."

Two more squad cars arrived, rolling code.

His lips drew in a grim line. "Marino, we're out of here."

He wound his way through the emergency medical technicians to check on Bausch. "Doing okay?"

Bausch's mouth twisted while the EMT worked on an IV, but he met Mike's gaze with narrowed, pain-glazed eyes.

"Sorry about Chandler."

"Her name was Barb."

He squeezed the agent's shoulder. "Tomasini is flying solo. He took out Sylvester before he left."

Bausch hissed. "Damn, we needed that location."

Sam Blackthorn grabbed Mike's arm and jerked him around, her expression blank. "Chandler's old van was abandoned in front of Silicon Valley Vending."

"Morrison's BMW?"

"Missing. I sent out an APB."

"Bet he's headed north on 280." Mike turned and ordered Flynn, "Start the search for real estate owned by Sidney Sylvester. Have Hopkins try every variation."

"I'll update the Captain," Flynn replied.

Mike inclined his head. "Let's move, Marino. Our chopper will land in ten minutes."

Sam elbowed in front of him and poked him in the sternum. "Forget it, Gordon. You're out. I'm in charge of hostage rescue."

A flare of angry heat clenched his jaw like a vice. His heart thudded with sickening force. He grabbed her wrist. "Fuck it."

Her face paled. Then a fiery blush blazed across her cheeks.

The sick feeling in his gut escalated, and he flung her hand aside. "Your FBI bullshit drove Liv to act solo. Anything happens to my girls..." He left the threat hanging.

Fists planted on her hips, Sam hissed. "Liv's a traitor. I'll have her locked up so tight she'll never see daylight."

"Blackthorn"—Bausch interrupted the tirade—

"Gordon's commanding hostage rescue. You ride with the SWAT team. That's an order."

"We'll see what the SAC says about that." She pivoted and headed toward a squad car.

Pulling keys from his pocket, Bausch turned his head and whispered, "Morrison already took out one innocent. Move. Not much time."

Chapter Thirty-One

Sereno, Tuesday, April 27, 12:28 a.m.

Reining in his impatience, Nate dumped his hands back into his pockets and paced beside the idling squad car.

Alyssa hurried across the dark parking lot, the Dragonfly hand-unit slung over her shoulder in a backpack. She clutched an open cardboard box filled with jumbled scientific equipment.

"Spare parts?"

She blinked. "Yeah. I have an extra power source and gel screens for explosives."

He quirked an eyebrow and yanked open the passenger door. "Good idea. Get in." He jogged around the car, hopped in, and gunned the engine.

She leaned back in her seat, tangling her hair into a messy bun. "I can't wait to tell the boss we recalibrated for a previously unanalyzed substance in three hours and six minutes. She gave us eight hours."

"Hope it works." He skidded around a cloverleaf and accelerated out of the turn.

Alyssa squeaked and grabbed the panic bar.

He pushed the squad car to triple digit, rolling code with lights flashing and siren blaring.

He checked his pale, wide-eyed passenger. "You okay?" Driving partway into the median, he swerved around a civilian vehicle.

She gulped. "Do what you have to do."

"Hold on." Pulse pounding, he punched the gas again. The clock ticked away the minutes. They roared past Stanford's enormous communication dishes and Linear Accelerator.

Spotting the illuminated statue in the distance, he swerved into the exit lane and climbed the steep ramp. At the far end of the parking lot, neon yellow tape framed Jana's car. He shuddered and a cold spasm ripped his insides.

He screeched to a halt and shoved the door open. "Get that freaking thing working!"

Alyssa hopped out, kissed her finger, and touched the ground. Aiming the hovering drone at the crime scene tape, she fiddled with toggles on the side and the apparatus emitted a stream of loud beeps. She shot him a huge grin. "Yep, the boss was here."

"Where?" About six feet from Jana's car, the beeps became a relentless scream. Nate winced.

"I'd say this glass was from her perfume bottle. Liv made sure we could follow."

"Can you get a heading?"

Alyssa had the tiny drone circle above them, scanning in all direction, until she determined where the scent was the strongest. "This way."

Nate followed, but ten yards away, the beeps slowed to almost nothing. "Think she got in a car?"

"Looks like it."

"Only one way onto the freeway from here. Let's roll."

Heart turning back flips, Nate steered onto the freeway, blue lights flashing.

Alyssa aimed the drone north and periodic, faint beeps echoed through her controls. "There's not much of a trail here. Lots of turbulence."

"But we're still following Liv. Right?"

She cleared her throat and fiddled with the sensors. "I don't know. I'm afraid we're picking up the CHP units."

The burn in his gut flared. "Why?"

"If they drove over the glass, their tires would emit a signal."

"That'll make our job tougher. Okay, think." He blew out a loud breath and gritted his teeth. "Let's assume the kidnappers picked this spot because it's convenient to where they're holding Liv and Cara. Then we can also assume they took a nearby off ramp." He glanced at the engineer.

"Reasonable hypothesis." She shoved her glasses back up her nose.

"So, we'll check each one."

Alyssa recalled the drone, and they drove to the next exit.

Nate pulled up to a stop sign and held his breath.

Stepping out, Alyssa raised the unit into the wind and rotated it. "Nada."

"Keep trying."

They raced to the next exit. As they pulled off the freeway and slowed, the drone, now sitting on Alyssa's lap sent a series of rapid beeps. Alyssa looked over at him and grinned. "We're in luck!"

Nate grinned back. "Can you tell which way they went?"

She maneuvered the drone above her head, back and forth in front of the car. "Tough to say. The sensor reading is strongest at the stop sign. Choose a direction and see what we get."

Nate made a right, but a hundred yards later, Dragonfly remained eerily quiet.

"Nothing, so far."

"Time to turn around." Nate doubled back toward the freeway.

Still silent, the drone didn't signal until they were within several car lengths off the exit ramp, but then gave out a first, lone beep.

****

12:46 a.m.

Mike raced up the interior stairs to the hospital roof with Marino on his heels.

The deputy stationed at the alarmed door widened his stance and dropped his hand to his weapon. "Lieutenant?" His voice echoed down the stairwell as Mike and Marino huffed up the last flight.

"Yeah." Mike flashed his shield.

"Chopper's due any minute." The deputy disarmed the door. "Go on through."

Hurrying across the flat, graveled roof, Mike heard a whoop-whoop in the distance and searched the night sky. "Sounds like our ride is here."

The streamlined helicopter descended onto a tiny wooden platform. Good. Nate had ordered the new, smaller chopper that could land in restricted spaces.

Marino ducked under the rotating blades and climbed into the seat behind the pilot.

Mike slid into the operator's seat and the tension in his shoulders eased. "Hey, Walsh. Glad you're at the controls."

He knew the pilot from SWAT, knew he could

count on Walsh to get him there, count on Marino at his back.

"Gordon," replied the pilot. "Sorry to hear about your wife and kid."

Shivers crawled over his skin, but he forced optimism into his tone. Thank God he was commanding this operation. "We're on our way to get them back."

"I hear we're starting at the Serra viewpoint." A hail from the San Jose International Airport tower caught the pilot's attention. "Roger, this is..." he responded.

Mike fought the stone cold fear crackling his nerves. With numb fingers, he fastened the harness and tugged on a helmet. He activated the GPS system and the bank of eight radios so he could monitor all the local jurisdictions. He'd check the spotlight and infrared unit once they were in the air.

Walsh turned to him. "Kapulani called in on his phone and dispatch connected him. He's headed west on 92 along the reservoir. Says he's having some radio trouble."

"Think it has something to do with the fed in Flynn's squad car?" Marino asked.

"Weirdest thing. Captain's radio cut out in the middle of her shouting orders at him." Chuckling, Walsh threw Mike a quick salute.

His grin was slow but fierce. "Get this bird in the air."

Chapter Thirty-Two

Sereno, Tuesday, April 27, 12:46 a.m.

Fighting the fear rippling under his skin like a viper in the sand, Ahmed collapsed onto the kitchen chair. What a naive fool he had been.

Prowling through his apartment, Miriam flipped light switches and examined every surface. When she knelt and ran her fingers along the underside of the table, her hand jerked. She ripped something loose and emerged, holding a transmitter and grinning widely.

His blood iced at the sight of the bug, but she danced to the bathroom and flushed.

"The Americans have been spying on me?" Ahmed sputtered.

"No. We believe it's the prince's organization."

His heart thudded, fast and hard. Had he made a mistake trusting her? "What do you mean, we? Who are you?"

"I'll explain when I can." Miriam knelt before him. Her dark eyes met his without wavering. "Where's your family?"

The knot in his belly twisted at her evasion, but she was his only hope. "El Amir, a village twenty kilometers from the capital."

"When did you hear from them last?"

"Two days ago, no, three. They are held at a

compound owned by the prince."

"When do you expect Suliman to return?"

"Before morning. After we collect the information from Morrison, he will take it to the prince." Exhausted, he leaned his chin on his hand.

"By private plane?"

Ahmed looked up and nodded. "Can you help my family?"

"I believe we can."

He searched her beautiful face for signs of deception, but her clear eyes showed only the truth. "Miriam," he murmured and drew her close.

The door slammed open, and Suliman stomped into the apartment.

Ahmed jumped to his feet. He tried to shift Miriam behind him, but she stood her ground at his side. "Your Highness," he stammered through a throat blocked by fear.

His expression blank, but rigid, Suliman set his laptop on the table. "Are you mad? I should kill you both where you stand."

Head held high, Miriam moved forward. "It's my fault."

He turned on her and screamed in Arabic, "Whore! You should be stoned!" His spittle sprayed her face.

Hands cold and clammy, Ahmed stepped between them and shouted, "Leave her alone!"

"Your family will suffer for your lust. The prince shall have what he needs, but your precious professor and her company will be neutralized."

"What do you mean?"

"The bomb is in place. All the sensor devices will be destroyed and the engineers will die in a firestorm."

Suliman wrenched open the computer.

A flash of clarity centered his thoughts. Ahmed swept his arm across the table and the laptop crashed to the floor. "No! This madness is finished."

"Fool! Your family will die unless you follow orders."

His lungs refused to draw air. "Miriam promised to help."

Suliman's fierce black eyes narrowed. "Did she? And you believed her?" He backhanded Miriam across the face. "Traitor!"

Her temple struck the corner of the wall, and she collapsed to the floor.

Ahmed froze.

Suliman stooped as if to retrieve the computer, but his right hand shifted to his hip.

When Ahmed saw the glint of metal, fury surged.

Suliman launched forward from the crouch, attacked, but Ahmed dodged the slash. Knife hand guarding his face, Suliman closed with a quick hook. "Filthy dog!"

Ahmed blocked, but the move threw him off balance, and Suliman swiped low, connecting with flesh.

Ahmed howled and grasped his wounded forearm. A red fog of pain blurred his vision, but he focused on the knife.

Telegraphing the next move, Suliman thrust again, striking for Ahmed's thigh.

Ahmed evaded the jab, staggered, and fought for breath. His heart pounded, swift and hard. He sidestepped, dodging a swipe at his face, and rammed an elbow in the man's gut.

The knife clattered to the floor. Wide-eyed, Suliman grunted, gasping for air.

Furious but terrified, Ahmed grabbed his enemy by the wrists, and they grappled, still on their feet.

Wresting free, Suliman punched Ahmed's wounded forearm hard and shoved him savagely.

Ahmed slammed into the wall, and his head whipped back. Disoriented and breathing hard, he rolled sideways and ducked a kick. He launched to his feet and whacked Suliman's knee with his heel.

His face crazed, Suliman grabbed the knife. He circled, bleeding and limping.

Behind them, Miriam wobbled to her feet and drew her pistol. She braced for a shot.

To cover her movement, Ahmed threw his fist at Suliman's face.

She leveled her gun.

Furious, Suliman head-butted Ahmed and drove him against the table, blocking her line of fire.

As Ahmed braced his hands to push off, his fingers closed on a pen.

Knife poised in both hands, Suliman screamed, "Die!"

Ahmed feinted a kick to the groin.

When Suliman twisted away, Ahmed plunged the pen into the man's neck and ripped.

Blood spurted, pumping into the fluorescent light. Eyes widening in surprise, Suliman's hands convulsed and grasped his punctured carotid artery. He collapsed, choking, and within seconds, he was silent. Dead.

Lungs heaving, heart racing, Ahmed stood immobile and stared at the body sprawled on the floor.

With hands covered in blood, his own and

Suliman's, he sank to his knees, and looked up at Miriam. "I did not mean to kill him."

"He'd have killed you without remorse. If you hadn't killed him, I would have." She tucked her pistol away.

"I will be executed," Ahmed moaned. Bile rose in his throat.

Miriam dragged him to his feet. "Come to my apartment. Now," she said, but her words echoed from far away.

He gazed at the blood dribbling from his arm, mesmerized.

"I can take care of you, but we must go now." She tossed him a kitchen towel. "Wrap it to control the bleeding. We can't leave a trail." She laid her palms on his cheeks and turned his face so his gaze met hers. "If we hurry, we might save your family."

A phone rang. "It's Suliman's." Shivering, Ahmed glanced at the limp body.

Miriam knelt and rummaged through Suliman's pockets. She found the phone inside his pullover, the cover sticky with blood. It stopped ringing. She wiped the phone and tucked it into her pocket.

Ahmed rushed to the kitchen sink and vomited.

"Come on!" Scooping up the laptop, she grabbed him by his uninjured arm and hauled him into the deserted courtyard.

****

Kings Mountain, 1:00 a.m.

Morrison cursed and flung his cell phone on the passenger seat. He sucked in a deep breath, but a red haze still fogged his vision. "Why the fuck doesn't Suliman answer? They should be on their way. Stupid foreigners," he muttered. "No sense of time. No wonder their country's still in the dark ages."

He whipped the car around a hairpin turn and skidded onto the shoulder, almost hitting a power pole. Dirt and pebbles flew. Unnerved, he slowed. "I'm still okay. They aren't due for half an hour."

The freeway had been the trickiest part of his escape. But he hadn't panicked when he saw flashing blue lights behind him. He sneered. Dumb-ass highway patrol didn't flag his old New Jersey plates, just drove right by.

Morrison cranked up the sound system and leaned back on the soft leather seat. The surprised look in Sylvester's eyes when he died still sent electric thrills surging in his blood.

Wait until Gordon checked his bank account and finds the megabucks he'd transferred in. Later, he'd call the feds with an anonymous tip and saddle Gordon with all the blame.

"Always pays to have an escape hatch." He chuckled. He'd packed money and a pouch of diamonds in the trunk of his car and an ocean-going yacht waited at Candlestick Marina. He could be in international waters before the sun rose.

That left the big oaf and the foreigners. The Gordon bitch was exactly where he wanted her, with her precious daughter for leverage. Anticipation speared through him. She'd give him what he needed after he hurt the kid. Once he had the technology, pow!

Suliman wanted the kid. A blonde girl her age would bring big money in that backward dump of a country. Wouldn't that frost Gordon? Wife dead, daughter married off to a fat old prince, and the damn cop helpless? Morrison cracked open the window and flicked his cigar ash.

He pulled in a long draw of rich smoke. But Gordon had recognized him tonight. He'd make the connections, and the cops would blanket the ports.

He pushed the car a little faster over the rough road. Maybe he should handle the transaction with the kid himself. A private plane to the Middle East might be the jackpot.

He blew out a thick puff, pleased with the twist to his plan. He'd leave enough evidence at the cabin so it looked like the terrorists killed Gordon's wife and blew themselves up by mistake.

****

Sereno, 1:04 a.m.

Ahmed fought the nausea churning his stomach and the throbbing pain from his wounded arm.

Helping him into her bathroom, Miriam grabbed the antibiotic soap and unwrapped the towel. As she exposed his wound, he let out a low hiss.

"Lean against the tank." Her voice sounded like it echoed through a long tunnel.

Jaw set, he looked away while she cleaned the oozing gash. She tended his injury deftly, but even her gentle touch was agony.

"You need a tetanus shot, but these bandages should hold."

He met her gaze. "You should ice your face. That bruise looks painful."

She touched her cheek and flinched. "After I make a call. Do you trust me to help your family?"

He blinked twice. "Yes, with their lives."

"I'm honored. My superior will want details of the

plan and information about the American."

"Make the call." He cooled his face, resting it on the porcelain cover.

She snapped open the laptop and browsed the files. "Suliman didn't encrypt his data. What a fool." She grinned at him and reached for her phone.

"The plan we suspected materialized. I secured a gold mine of information." She paused, listening. "Yes, his laptop and cell phone. But first, I need a clean-up squad at the university and an immediate rescue operation in Krzystan. We don't have one second to waste. They planted a bomb at G-Tech."

Chapter Thirty-Three

Kings Mountain, 1:13:30 a.m.

Through the Plexiglas nose of the helicopter, Mike scanned the mountainous landscape, his mind clear and alert. The pale crescent moon lit a solitary eucalyptus tree, turning it a ghostly white.

The radio crackled. "Gordon? Kapulani here. Sereno PD just patched a call through. Bausch is still in surgery, but the student Liv fingered is coming clean to Interpol in exchange for sanctuary."

A grin creased his face. "About freaking time."

"One foreign agent is dead, but they expect to have the other operatives in custody and the network smashed by morning," Nate said in a guarded tone.

"What else?"

"Just sent the bomb disposal unit to G-Tech. Morrison had the place set to blow today."

He whistled. "Close call."

"No kidding." Nate cleared his throat. "Flynn's about twenty minutes behind us, taking it as slow as he can. So far, he's holding up to Blackthorn."

"We come out of this okay, I owe him a beer."

"A keg." Nate chuckled.

Below him, Mike caught the silhouette of Father Serra's statue. His jaw clenched, and his gut churned. Headlights illuminated Jana's car, surrounded by yellow crime scene tape.

"What's your status?" Nate asked.

"Following 92 across Crystal Springs Reservoir," he reported over the roar of the chopper's engine.

"The drone's tracking the scent along Vineyard. It's a dead end road off Skyline."

"We'll get more elevation, then scout ahead." He relayed the instructions to the pilot.

The copter angled into a turn. His seat on the inside left him an unobstructed view of the dark, forested slopes below. They spiraled higher, closing in on the signal from the squad car.

He returned his gaze to the heat-sensitive FLIR unit. The captain's car appeared on the screen. Its headlights bounced all over the rough, narrow road. "We've spotted you."

"The perfume trail continues steady. She's here someplace."

"We have to find where he stashed my girls."

"See any place to set down?"

Mike tapped the screen. "GPS shows an old winery on the other side of the ridge. No vehicular access, but there's enough room to land."

"We shouldn't be too far behind. It's slow going because of the washouts."

"How far between the winery and the end of the road?" Marino asked from the seat behind him.

Mike rubbed a hand over his chin. "Less than a mile."

"Pick you up at the end," the captain said.

Mike's hackles rose, but his heart dropped a thousand feet. "Son of a bitch. We're pacing a large sedan."

"Has to be Tomasini," Marino's tense voice crackled over the headset.

"Walsh, hit that parking lot, now!" Mike shouted.

"Roger."

The helicopter veered sharply, but his guts forgot to follow.

"Where's the car?" Nate demanded.

Mike leaned forward to study the dark, tree-covered landscape below. "Stopped in front of the last house on Vineyard, four miles beyond your position." Something ugly clutched at his chest. "Shit. There go the gates. He's turning in."

"Describe the house."

"Can't see details without the spotlight." He frowned, trying to make sense of the FLIR images. "Small, two story cabin, lots of trees. Heat sensor shows animals, probably dogs roaming loose."

"Meet you there."

Mike gritted his teeth. "Move your ass. Liv and Cara are inside and so is that bastard, Tomasini."

****

1:18:10 a.m.

An icy shiver crawled over Liv's skin. She cradled her warm, sleeping daughter, but with every passing minute she found it harder to stay still. Help was on the way, but deadly danger approached too.

She eased Cara's head off her shoulder, sat up on the edge of the bed, and then crept barefoot to the door. With her ear pressed against the hollow wood she heard Les snoring, but no other noises came from downstairs.

Silently, she moved back to the bed, laid her hand over her daughter's mouth, and kissed her cheek.

Cara's eyes popped open, her pupils dilated with

sleep and fear.

"Shush. Les is asleep."

Cara nodded, and Liv shifted her hand. "We need to hide. What else is upstairs?"

"Only bedrooms and a bathroom."

"Where's the bathroom?"

"By the steps."

After helping Cara tie her sneakers, she grabbed her own.

"I can unlock the door," Cara said and pulled cards from her pocket.

"My smart girl."

Cara opened the lock and beamed a brilliant smile of triumph.

Returning the smile, Liv eased the door open and motioned for her daughter to follow.

They crept along the hall, pausing at the top of the stairs. In the dim light, she saw Les stretched out on the sofa, his bandaged arm resting across his chest.

The bathroom door was ajar, and they slipped in silently. Moonlight washed through the tiny open window.

She eased the door shut. Above the background night noises, she recognized the sound of rescue and hugged Cara. "A helicopter. Daddy's coming, soon."

She searched for a hiding place. The under sink cabinet was too cramped for Cara, but Liv pulled open the door and grabbed an armful of dingy white towels.

She pointed toward the tub enclosed by frosted sliding glass doors. After cushioning the bottom, she helped Cara inside. The towels matched the porcelain, almost invisible in the dim light.

Kneeling, she held her daughter's hand. "I'll cover

you and the towels will hide you while I look around. Maybe there's a window open or another way out. I'll come back and wait with you until Daddy arrives."

"Mommy, don't go outside. Promise? The dogs are really mean. You saw what they did to Les's arm."

She leaned in to kiss Cara. "Promise."

"But what about Daddy? When he comes, the dogs will bite him."

"Daddy knows what to do if he meets a mean dog."

"But there are four of them."

"We have to trust him." She laid her aching head against the cool tile. Tears of regret burned her throat. Good advice, she thought, and swallowed hard. Trust Mike.

The dogs set off a racket in the yard and the back of her neck tingled with a primitive warning.

Cara grabbed her arm. Her small fingers dug in with fearful strength. "What's that noise?"

Chapter Thirty-Four

Kings Mountain, 1:21:55 a.m.

The Rottweilers galloped toward his car, barking their fucking heads off. Morrison opened the window, shouted, "Platz!" over the ruckus and the stupid mutts sank on their haunches, whining.

He stepped out of the car with his laptop in one hand. In the quiet, Morrison heard a helicopter circling above the mountain. He swallowed his rage and hissed a vicious curse. How had they found him?

The copter crested the ridge, and he hurried toward the house. The pack trotted up the long hill after him.

The bedrooms were dark, but the big lug had left lights on in the kitchen and living room. Damn. Good as a fucking neon sign for the cops.

To avoid a patch of weeds, he stepped sideways, and his foot slipped on gravel. His knee cranked, but he caught himself and slowed to a limp. He had to get in and out fast if he wanted to stay alive. He'd learned self-preservation the hard way, on the streets. The only way he'd survive was to destroy the loose ends, all the loose ends. And Les had become a huge liability.

But first, he needed the dogs contained. He led them to the kennel and snapped the gate shut. He knelt gingerly on the porch steps and winced. Setting down his laptop, he flicked on his miniature flashlight and examined the gas meter beside the front door. Reaching underneath the pipe, he felt for the package. Everything was in order. Good old Sid set it up right. Too bad about good old Sid.

He checked the timer. Four minutes should give him time to reach his car after he triggered the device.

He listened. The copter must have landed. Make it three.

Suliman should be here any minute, but no telling how soon the fucking cavalry would arrive. He stood and dusted off his hands, slipping the remote into his back pocket. He'd make sure there wouldn't be much left to rescue.

****

1:23:25 a.m.

Mike loosened his fists, one finger at a time, checked his equipment and jumped out of the chopper. Adrenaline spiked, sharpening his focus.

Marino dropped to the ground and followed.

Night vision helmets in place, they loped through the rows of grapevines. At the base of a dry, exposed slope, Mike eyed the scrubby manzanita and toyon, threaded with wild berry canes.

Resisting the urge to crash through the brush and forge the shortest route to his family, he waved his arm and led the way, detouring around the thickest growth. A narrow path he hadn't spotted from the air trailed through the underbrush beneath the trees.

"Deer track," Marino huffed.

Redwoods replaced madrone and oak as he topped the hill with Marino a few paces behind. Jogging across a seasonal stream, the smell of dampness and growing things reminded him of their cabin sixty miles south.

And his family. He had to get to his girls in time. Fighting for air, he pressed harder.

Marino tripped over a gnarled root and landed with a thud. He scrambled to his knees and wiped the dirt from his face.

"Take it easy." Mike extended a hand. "Gotta get there in one piece."

"Yeah, thanks."

Mike checked the GPS reading and pointed. "The house should be on the right, about another quarter mile."

Marino nodded.

Sucking in another breath, he charged down a steep embankment and through a clearing near the road.

A small wooded area fronted the twelve-foot rock wall surrounding their target. Mike searched for the most likely spot to scale it unnoticed. "You circle around to the rear."

"Roger."

"I'll make my way through the trees inside and take the front." A twig snapped unexpectedly, and he caught a whiff of polecat.

"No sign of the captain's squad car," Marino hissed.

Mike hissed into his radio. "Kapulani?"

"We're close. Road's a bitch."

****

Kings Mountain, 1:32:58 a.m.

The drone's signal beeped out of control as Nate braked in front of tall iron gates set into a massive rock wall. He heaved a sigh of relief.

"Found the right place." Alyssa peered into the darkness.

"Excellent job."

The communicator buzzed. "Kapulani."

"Captain? Lopez here. We're rolling about two minutes behind Flynn and the FBI SWAT team. Their ETA—ten minutes."

"Any report on the bomb disposal at G-Tech?"

"Team's on it. They located the explosives."

"How'd Morrison manage to rig it right under Bausch's nose?"

"A couple pallets of liquid explosives disguised as water bottles. Shrouded 'em in six layers of plastic and trucked 'em in a couple weeks ago as earthquake supplies."

"Roger." Nate signed off and checked his weapon. He wouldn't wait for the SWAT team. Couldn't risk having the FBI turn this into another cluster fuck.

Alyssa was bent over, tinkering with the miniature drone.

"What're you doing?"

"Recalibrating, using the standard explosives screen. We don't need to track the boss's perfume any further."

"Okay. You stay put. I'm going in."

She flipped a toggle and the drone erupted with frantic, earsplitting beeps.

Alyssa looked at the readout and the color bleached from her face. Eyes wide, she turned to him. "There's a bomb!"

Chapter Thirty-Five

Kings Mountain, 1:34:03 a.m.

Liv's heart kicked inside her chest. Crouching at the top of the stairs, she peered over the railing into the dimly lit living room. Rage had turned Tom Morrison into a wild-eyed, fire-breathing lunatic.

She closed her eyes and leaned against the wall. She'd always been able to charm him. If she batted her lashes and flattered him, would the smooth operator reappear? Doubtful, but what choice did she have?

Tom Morrison waved her memory stick in Les's face. "Those rag heads will be here any second. If we can't get this open and show them the goods, they'll kill us. Get that fucking bitch and her brat down here this minute."

She winced and her fingers clutched the railing. Could she calm him enough?

"I got the code." Les sat up slowly and dug in his shirt pocket. "Give me a minute, Boss. I feel like shit."

"Stop stalling. I need it now," Tom ranted in a high-pitched, hysterical tone.

Shivering, she took a step forward. She had to intervene before he hurt someone.

"Fine. I'll get 'em." Les swung his legs over the edge of the sofa, cradling his injured arm.

"We'll see how long she holds out while her

daughter screams." Tom voice edged toward a maniacal gloat.

Frigid prickles scraped her battered nerves, and goose bumps covered her legs and arms.

"No need to hurt the kid, Boss. Her mama will tell you." Les winced as he rose from the couch.

"You moron. What the fuck have you been doing?"

"Watching the kid." Les straightened and loomed over Tom. "Exactly like you told me when you stranded me in this dump."

"No, you betrayed me to the feds." Tom's whole face twisted into an ugly scowl. "Fucking traitor!"

Les lowered his head, and his expression shifted from fear to fury. "You're the traitor!" When he charged, Tom sidestepped, drew a gun from his pocket, and fired two rounds.

Screaming, Les crumpled to the floor, holding his knee.

Her ears rang from the blast, and she huddled against the wall.

Tom aimed the gun at Les. "I'm gonna blow your head off."

Her stomach revolted, and she swallowed to keep from retching. Tom was frothing at the mouth, but she had to face him now. She had to protect Cara. Had to help the poor wounded man.

She straightened her shoulders, cleared her throat, and stepped into view. "I see you're a man of hidden talents, Tom."

He scowled. "Give me the access code or your kid'll be next."

"No need to involve Cara. The code's simple." She moved down the stairs holding her chin high. Her clammy hands squeaked along the banister, but she couldn't let go or her shaky legs would collapse.

"Show me." His eyes glittered malevolently in his flame-red face. One cheek twitched above his rigid jaw.

She met his gaze and forced her lips into a smile. "No problem. I'll show you. Then you can let us go."

Les moaned, and she ached to help him. Maybe he'd have a chance if she drew Tom's attention.

Tom jerked the barrel of his gun toward the laptop. "Take that into the kitchen and boot it. Then we'll test your code."

Her heart jumped painfully inside her ribs. She reached for the computer.

"Leave her alone," Les shouted and lunged for Tom's ankle. But Tom howled, pivoted, and fired.

Staring wide-eyed, she froze. Beyond fear, beyond panic, beyond horror.

Blood spread on the big man's shirt, oozed through his fingers. His face washed pale, and his mouth opened, gasping for air.

Tom's hand snaked out and seized her. He ground the hot gun barrel against her head. Her hair singed, and the acrid stink brought tears to her eyes.

"Move," he snarled and dragged her toward the kitchen.

Behind them, Les gurgled and went still.

A chill grabbed the base of her skull and shook hard.

The gun dug into her scorched temple and Tom's punishing grip bruised her arm. She whimpered, smelling his madness through the reek of her own terror. Her brain reconnected, and she shot out, "I said I'd help."

"Shut up, bitch." Plastered against her side, Tom shouldered open the door to the darkened kitchen.

Her heart skipped a beat. Mike. She bit her lip to keep from shouting his name.

He hid in the shadows, weapon drawn and aimed at her captor, but blood stained his clothes. Her heart skipped another beat.

"Thought you were long gone, Tomasini." Mike stepped forward. "You have something of mine. Release Liv."

Tom's free arm squeezed around her neck and choked her.

She felt his pulse pound through him. His muscles jumped with each hard, rapid throb, boosting her courage.

He screeched, "I'll kill her, I swear. Drop the gun, Gordon."

She bucked against him, tore at his arm with her nails, but Tom yanked her tighter.

"No. I made that mistake before and my partner took the bullet," Mike said, his voice deep. Slow. Arctic. "You need the access code. She'll give it to you, and I'll let you escape. Again."

Mike focused on her face and blinked once, raising his weapon almost imperceptibly.

He stilled for a fraction of a second that felt like six eons, then blinked again.

What was he doing? Signaling her? Her vision faded at the edges from the pressure on her windpipe. She gasped in a harsh breath. What did Mike want?

He blinked a third time, and it clicked. The hostage demonstration!

She knew. She knew what came next. Enveloped in

a sudden calm, she waited.

Blink.

She planted her heel in Tom's instep, snapped her arm up, knocked the laptop against his gun, dropped, and rolled.

Weapons exploded, and Tom fell in the doorway.

Thrown against the far wall, Mike collapsed with a gaping hole in his shirt.

The room fuzzed, thick and gray like winter fog. Terrible silence pierced her near deafness. Despair clawed at her heart and mind and soul.

She fought through it, lurched forward on her hands and knees. "Mike!"

Groaning, he struggled to sit. "Thanks for trusting me, Livy."

Her heart restarted with a jolt. She framed his face with her hands. "My God, Mike."

Wiping a tear from her cheek, Mike smiled weakly, tapping his chest. "Wore my body armor, but I'll have a hell of a bruise."

He glanced over her shoulder, and Liv followed his gaze. Blood puddled on the floor under Tom's head. Her stomach twisted. She looked away, but shudders ripped through her body, and her teeth chattered uncontrollably.

Mike crawled over, confiscated the gun, and checked for a pulse.

Nate burst through the door shouting, "There's a bomb. Everybody outside!"

"Where's Cara?" Mike demanded.

"I'll get her." Liv stepped over the corpse and rushed toward the stairs. She glanced at Les's still body, sobbing in a breath. His pale blue eyes were frozen, wide and unseeing, forever.

Jackson Marino materialized at the top of the stairs. "Found a back window, Mrs. G."

Behind him, Cara peeked out the bathroom door.

"Get Cara!" Liv pointed. "Morrison triggered a bomb!"

Jackson jerked, but turned and grabbed Cara.

"They're dead. Don't let her see."

Holding Cara against his chest, Jackson shielded the child's face and raced down the steps three at a time.

They burst into the kitchen as Nate pulled Mike to his feet.

"Leave the slimeball," Nate ordered. "Run!"

Mike grabbed Cara from Jackson and crashed through the door.

Alyssa knelt on the porch, inspecting the gas meter. Next to her, the drone unit screamed.

"I told you to stay in the car," Nate yelled. "Move it."

"Dragonfly found the bomb." Alyssa squinted at the readout. "Twenty seconds? Shit!"

"Run!" Nate half-carried her down the steps and broke into a gallop. Two hundred yards out he shouted, "Drop and cover!"

Liv and Mike sheltered Cara. With a deafening roar, the house erupted, raining debris.

Brilliant flames climbed high into the night sky, sucking the breath from her lungs.

Mike stood first, gazing behind them. He scooped up Cara and reached for Liv's hand. "Thank God."

Liv reached her arm around his waist, settling her head into the hollow of his shoulder. "What a horror!"

The intense, blue-white blaze consumed the structure in moments. Flashing lights from the arriving SWAT van and squad cars created an eerie backlight.

Alyssa stood and brushed the dried grass from her clothes.

"Great job." Liv hugged her, laughing with only a touch of hysteria in her voice. "I think I owe you another stock option grant."

Sam Blackthorn emerged from the cruiser. "Liv Gordon, you're under arrest for treason. Surrender those specs immediately."

Liv smiled innocently. "What specs?"

Epilogue

Monterey, Saturday, May 8, 7:20 p.m.

Mike leaned back against the windbreak with his knees bent and his arms around Liv. Sitting cross-legged, she nestled close with a blanket draped over her.

He let out a long breath and tunneled his toes into the warm sand. The quiet, the lapping waves, the pelicans fishing just offshore lent his mind the peace he needed.

But with Liv in his arms, with her scent filling his nose, his body ached with anticipation. Too many hours had passed since dawn.

A few feet away, a small blaze crackled inside a stone fire pit. Smoke curled down the beach. The fog bank hovered a hundred yards from shore and a breeze had kicked up, but the summer sunset lit the horseshoe beach in soft shades of yellow and red.

Where the surf lapped the sand, Cara tossed a squeaky blue ball in the air and Sevi, their new chocolate lab puppy, splashed into the shallows after it. Dripping with seawater, Sevi shook. Cara screamed in mock horror, and then hugged the pup.

Laughing, Liv snuggled closer.

He took a deep breath of the salt-tinged air and released it with a contented sigh. It felt so good to have her in his arms and to see both his girls happy.

"I'm glad you got her Sevi," Liv said.

"First time I suggested it, you weren't so sure."

"No. But you were right, and Dr. Holden agreed. We don't want Cara afraid of dogs."

"I'm proud of her. She came through fine, even figured out how to pop that lock in the cabin."

"Mommy! Daddy!" Cara ran toward the fire, shouting, "The sun's going down. Are we ready?"

He kissed Liv and offered her his hand. At her nod, he grinned at Cara. "Yep. Almost bedtime."

Liv pulled the file of legal documents from the picnic basket. His stomach kicked briefly at the sight of the papers in her fist. He'd come too close to losing everything.

"Let me, please," Cara begged, prancing with excitement.

Mike tugged Liv to her feet, keeping his arm around her waist.

They stood behind their daughter while she fed their divorce papers to the flames. Sparks whirled in the soft evening wind, winked into the air in a flurry of light. Crowing, Cara spun in a happy dance and darted across the sand, puppy at her heels.

Liv chuckled and combed her hand over her short, sexy hair.

Heat thrummed through his veins, and Mike pressed his lips on her nape. She turned and kissed him back, rubbing against his already stirred body. Tightening his grip, he cupped a hand behind her head and deepened the kiss.

When he broke away, her eyes were wide, her pupils huge. She coiled both hands around his neck and purred, "Good thing our room is just up the street?"

He nuzzled her, pressing his arousal against her softness and groaned, "Yeah, but we have to get there, first."

She sighed and pulled back a fraction, a question in her provocative brown eyes.

Easing his hold, he touched her cheek.

"Tell me," she insisted. "Bausch must have finished his report by now."

Mike blew out a breath. Think about the report. The paperwork. The red tape. Think about anything but burying himself deep inside her hot, velvet slickness. "Uh, Bausch brought the report in personally."

Her brows rose.

"He hobbled into the station on crutches yesterday, still complaining that Jana was cleared of all charges. Still grumbling because the keystroke tracker proved you copied a useless file."

"And because Ahmed's still in my class?"

Mike laughed. "That did come up."

"Dragonfly found all the explosives. Even the Orlando suicide bombers." She shuddered.

Mike looped his arms around her and grinned. "We pulled it off despite the feds." But a shiver ripped through him. He kissed her lightly on the nose. "Want to know the best part?"

"Sure."

"Guess who Bausch got transferred to a one-agent bureau in the frozen north?"

She slanted him a quizzical look.

"Sam Blackthorn."

"There is justice in this world." Liv looked out at the ocean for a long moment and then smiled back at him. "Let's get Cara and Sevi dried off and tucked in. I have plans for you." She reached up and tongued the cleft in his chin.

****

9:45 p.m.

The chilly ocean breeze blew in through the open windows of their gabled room on the top floor of the Victorian B & B. The sheer curtains rustled and the rush of waves breaking forty feet away filtered in with the faint scent of saltwater. From her position sprawled atop Mike's chest, Liv saw a star twinkle through a break in the fog bank.

The spasms of her orgasm gradually subsided into gentle twinges. She gave him a long, open-mouthed kiss. Using his shoulders for balance, she sat up and arched her back.

Her breath hissed in through her clenched teeth at the feel of his thick, rigid length still lodged inside her.

He held her hips, rocking against her, and another wave of pleasure speared through her.

"Mmm." She threw back her head and closed her eyes.

He ran his hands up her sides and cupped her breasts, outlining the tips with his fingers. The areolas puckered, and her nipples ached.

He rolled them gently until they tightened into hard, furled peaks.

She looked down into his smoky blue eyes and pressed her naked breasts harder against his hands.

"Like that?" He pinched and plucked, his big, warm hands kneading her pale breasts.

"Yes," she murmured. "More."

"Kiss me." He pushed his hardness into her again,

sending up more delicious sensations. She leaned over and kissed him slowly.

His tongue shaped her lips, filled her mouth, while his fingers worked her nipples.

His hands left her breasts and traced a slow path down her back. He cupped her bottom, holding her still with a firm hand on the small of her back.

Her legs were spread wide across his abdomen. Her sensitive core, pressed against his pubic bone, pulsed with each heartbeat. She twitched and the pressure coiled higher again, but she couldn't move enough to relieve the ache, and he didn't thrust.

She wound her fingers through the short, curly hairs at the nape of his neck and kissed his chin. She licked along the rigid cord of his neck to his ear, nipped the lobe, and sucked it into her mouth. Drew her nails across his shoulders and over the hard muscles of his upper arms.

Grinning, Mike shivered and held her tight, but he still didn't thrust.

"Please," she whimpered, her whole body begging for what she needed. "I love you."

He grasped her more tightly, throbbing inside her. The head of him was so deep, his hard penis stretched her. Her nipples were sensitive points, rubbed by the coarse hair on his chest.

She pushed against him and tried to squirm, but couldn't escape. Couldn't entice him to take his own release and give her hers. Teetering on the verge of pleasure, she felt any minute she would shatter.

She squeezed her inner muscles around him and twitched. A tiny orgasm burst fireworks into her veins, released some of her ache. But it wasn't enough. She moaned his name.

"We're not through yet, love. Just enjoy." He slipped out and shifted her onto her belly. He pressed open-mouthed kisses all over her neck and shoulders. His hands skimmed the curves of her hips and back.

She closed her eyes and savored the gentle, arousing touch of his warm hands.

"Your skin drives me crazy. So soft, so golden."

She turned her head toward him and moaned, "That feels incredible, but I want you inside me again."

"Me too." He raised her up onto her knees and nudged them apart with his leg, partially supporting her with one strong arm around her waist. He traced the cleft of her bottom with the other hand and delved between her delicate folds.

His fingers danced around the sensitive bundle of nerve endings, spreading her moisture, relentlessly building the tension. "Open your legs wider for me," he said, his voice low and deep.

She could sense his hot gaze on her naked flesh as he caressed her. In this position, she felt exposed and submissive.

Primitive.

She looked over her shoulder and started to object, but her protest stuck in her throat.

He froze, gazing at her intently with aching hunger written on his face. In a flash, she read his need to claim her. To possess her.

She blinked. She was his, only his, and she could trust him with her pleasure. Trust him with her body. Trust him with her life.

Her expression must have softened, because his eyes darkened, matching his slow, utterly male smile.

Not triumph, exactly, but clear, unmistakable, visceral pleasure at learning she wouldn't say no.

Letting out a ragged breath, she dropped her chest and arched her buttocks, giving him control, exquisitely vulnerable and wanton and completely open to him.

"I love you, Livy." Mike grabbed his pillow, bunching it beneath her for support. His hands smoothed her back, framing his lips as he kissed and licked a trail along her spine, awakening a cascade of hot shivers. Caressing the twin globes of her bottom, he reached beneath her and tenderly stroked her swollen, too-sensitive nub.

A jagged twinge pulsed, and she bit her lip to restrain a whimper. The featherlight, gliding pressure intensified with each brush of his fingers, sending delicious, liquid heat shimmering through her again in a magical flow.

She moaned, low and deep.

He rubbed his erection between her legs. The tip of him skated back and forth over her slickness, but he wasn't close enough, wasn't filling her damp, empty ache.

She pressed backwards and twisted, trying to coax more from him, tempting him inside her again. "I need you now, Mike. Please."

"Soon." He flicked and stroked, sliding back and forth, setting off electric spears of sensation, but he left her empty and straining for him. Grazing her nub with a fingernail, he squeezed softly and pushed her, trembling, over a higher peak.

She bucked and arched, screaming his name as every nerve ending fired. She couldn't draw enough air.

Before her explosive orgasm stopped, he seized her

hips and entered her with one hard, fast stroke, hard against the entrance to her womb. Electric jolts pulsed through her and her inner muscles clenched around him. Her whole body shuddered with pleasure.

Finally, he was where she wanted him. How she wanted him. Stiff, solid, and buried deep. Warmth filled her heart. He was hers. But there was more of him, and she wanted his entire length inside, needed him to give everything to this joining until they were locked together, soul deep.

Liv arched back, opening herself further, determined to take in all of him.

"Yes," Mike rumbled. Gripping her hips, he thrust slowly, leaving and then reentering her, slick, throbbing, inch by inch.

Gradually, he moved faster and harder with every stroke. Building speed. Intensity.

He pounded into her and touched impossibly deep hollows with his intense and powerful strokes and she writhed against him.

A long, low groan exploded from his lips. He bowed and thrust hard, pumped into her in a pulsing rush.

Violent pleasure erupted, and she roared over another dizzying crest with an ecstatic cry. Acute spasms of pleasure wracked her. Her vision blurred and her world spun.

Oblivion, safe in Mike's arms.

A word about the author...

Along with teaching, Joy began her writing career by publishing children's historical fiction. She later found writing romantic suspense fulfilled her need for travel and romance.

She lives with her husband and two dogs near Silicon Valley and the mythical town of Sereno.

http://www.ejbrighton.com